MAY 17

CH

*And Then
There Was Me*

ALSO BY SADEQA JOHNSON

Love in a Carry-On Bag

Second House from the Corner

And Then There Was Me

Sadeqa Johnson

Thomas Dunne Books
St. Martin's Press ♒ New York

THOMAS DUNNE BOOKS.
An imprint of St. Martin's Press.

AND THEN THERE WAS ME. Copyright © 2017 by Sadeqa Johnson. All rights reserved. Printed in the United States of America. For information, address St. Martin's Press, 175 Fifth Avenue, New York, N.Y. 10010.

www.thomasdunnebooks.com
www.stmartins.com

The Library of Congress Cataloging-in-Publication Data is available upon request.

ISBN 978-1-250-07416-4 (hardcover)
ISBN 978-1-4668-8582-0 (e-book)

Our books may be purchased in bulk for promotional, educational, or business use. Please contact your local bookseller or the Macmillan Corporate and Premium Sales Department at 1-800-221-7945, extension 5442, or by e-mail at MacmillanSpecialMarkets@macmillan.com.

First Edition: April 2017

10 9 8 7 6 5 4 3 2 1

To my beloved, Glenn, for always seeing more, and to my sibling loves, Tauja, Nadiyah, and Talib Murray, the power of us four

Acknowledgments

I would like to thank God for aligning, inspiring, and guiding my ideas into a third novel. Ashay! My heart is lifted in praise to the most High.

My extreme gratitude to you for picking up this book and giving me a chance.

To a wonderful and supportive family: my mother, Nancy Murray, for always being there with your love, humor, and advice. Tyrone Murray and Francine Cross Murray for your constant love and support. My grandmother, Yvonne Clair, and Aunt Mary Davis, the matriarchs of our family. To my sibs, Tauja, Nadiyah, and Talib Murray, for being my cheerleaders and friends. Twin nephews, Qualee and Quasaan, nothing can stop you. My in-laws: Paula Johnson, Glenn Johnson Sr., Pacita Perera, Marise Johnson, David Johnson, and Luqman Abram. Philadelphia, I love you.

To my mighty team: Cherise Fisher, the midwife and doula of all of my words, I am so glad I don't have to do this without you. Wendy Sherman, you are insightful and amazing, thanks for handling business. Laurie Chittenden, for your dedication to this book and my career. I promise you there is so much more to come. Sulay Hernandez, thanks for giving it the magic touch. Jessica Preeg, Karen Masnica, Annie Hulkower, and the amazing staff at Thomas Dunne Books/St. Martin's Press for believing. Sincere thanks to Ella D. Curry, Yolanda Gore, Mary Brown, Troy Johnson, Angela Wilson Lee, Deniecea David, and Kristi Tuck Austin for pushing my dreams forward.

To Ruth Bridges, Sharon Lucas, Lisa Renee Johnson, and the numerous book clubs who have supported me, fed me, and shared my novel. It is because of you that word is spreading across the country, and I thank you. A special note of gratitude to Curtis Bunn, for reaching back for me. To the James River Writers, for adopting me from day one. This book would not be what it is without the courageous people who have blogged about living with eating disorders, and I applaude you. A huge heartfelt thank you to Kelly Rivard, for walking me through your personal journey. Your honesty brought Bea's story to life.

To my amazing children: Miles, the apple of my eye; Zora, my middle diva with passion and purpose; and Lena, for your quirky humor and for never taking no for an answer. You three are my greatest creations. Thank you for choosing me. To my favorite person on the planet, top dog, partner, and husband, Glenn, your love wakes me up in the morning and tucks me in at night. It's because of your belief that I'm able.

PART 1

*It is not a lack of love, but a lack of friendship
that makes unhappy marriages.*

—FRIEDRICH NIETZSCHE

ONE

Playing Chicken

MEMORIAL DAY WEEKEND

Bea hated the beach. The sun didn't rev up her brain's endorphins the way it did for most people. In fact, it had the opposite effect on her. She never enjoyed peeling down to her bathing suit. Always feeling hideous in whatever she wore. Most of her time at the shore was spent feeling envious of the pretty girls in the teeny, triangle-topped bikinis, with lotus tattoos on the hollows of their backs. Bea would watch them slip and slide in the sand spiking a volleyball, feeling round where they were flat, ugly where they were cute. It was even worse when she was pregnant.

The other half of her time was spent playing "find the shade." Bea wasn't a woman who wanted a suntan, preferring her vitamin D in tablet form only. All day she had constantly moved her chair in search of relief.

"What're you doing?" Awilda, her best friend, looked over the edge of her cat-eye glasses.

"Trying to stay cool."

"Why in the hell you come to the beach to do all that is beyond me."

Awilda was right. The effort it took to keep the sun's rays from darkening her skin was draining: slathered sunscreen, dark umbrella, floppy hat, wide sunglasses, zinc oxide strip on her nose, and her feet tucked under a dry towel. Even with the prep, Bea still worried the ultraviolet rays were coming through the umbrella, roasting her skin by the millisecond.

"The beach was Lonnie's idea. Not mine."

"Well next year you need to speak up."

She had; he just didn't listen. Bea preferred renting a house on a lake with a wraparound porch, where she could hide under an awning and maxi dress. It was her husband, Lonnie, who insisted on the beach. Spring Lake to be exact. With two miles of white, pristine sand, bordered by the longest noncommercial boardwalk in the state of New Jersey, Spring Lake was a magnet for families of all ages. But the price of the homes made it inaccessible to everyone, and therefore the perfect getaway as far as Lonnie was concerned. It was sanitized and quiet except for the corner Awilda occupied.

Awilda was the contrary to Bea, lounging without the protection of an umbrella in a bright orange, high-waisted bikini. Her hair was big and bushy, and every tune that crooned from her iPhone was her finger-snapping, sing-along-to-the-beat song.

Bea turned her seven-month baby-belly in Awilda's direction in time to catch her shoving a handful of cool ranch potato chips into her candy-pink-painted mouth.

"You know there's no eating on the beach, Wilde," Bea chided.

Awilda knew this. There were signs posted along the boardwalk reminding folks to eat in the pavilion areas only. In fact, coolers were forbidden and instead left on the boardwalk.

"What're they going to do? Arrest me?" She smacked her lips.

"Might kick you off the beach."

"I'd like to see that." She shoved down two more chips. "We should be in DR instead of this snobby beach anyway. Your mama still have family down there?"

"Mami left Santo Domingo fifty years ago and has never looked back. I keep in touch with my cousins."

"We need to take a girls' trip down there and reconnect with your roots. After you drop that load. No kids, no husbands." Awilda tilted the bag of chips to her mouth and swallowed the crumbs.

Bea sucked her teeth. "You could at least eat under the umbrella."

"What's got you so uptight?"

Bea didn't want to give voice to what had been nagging at her, so she camouflaged with a lighthearted smile. "Probably just hormones."

"Well, unwrap that towel from your feet, girlfriend, and have a little fun."

"I am," Bea said. Though fun had become foreign. Since they moved back to New Jersey a year ago, her life had become so tied to keeping up with her husband and two children; there was no space for anything remotely connected to fun. Though she did daydream, and carrying a healthy baby brought her some peace.

"Hold up, wait a minute. This is my song." Awilda turned up her iPhone even louder than before.

Bea glanced at the older couple reading hardcover books, parked to their right. They were covered in as much stuff as Bea was. The wife looked up at Bea at the same time but didn't smile.

"Pass it to me."

"No."

"It's too loud."

"I can barely hear it."

Beyoncé seemed to take front and center on their little sliver of beach. *Yoncé on her knees.*

"There are children around, Wilde."

"It's the clean version."

"Do you always have to go against the grain?"

"You've known me twentysomething years. Don't act new."

"This place is conservative, I know, but . . ."

"Beasley, please with that mess." Awilda laughed out loud. "You remember how we use to go to the skating rink on Route 22 and dance until we couldn't breathe?"

Bea's shoulders relaxed. "Girl, we had to catch two buses. Your mother would have had a cow if she knew we weren't listening to music in my room."

"But we went and it was the highlight of our week."

"Except for you having every girl in Union wanting to fight us."

"Not true."

"Sis, please! When you started dropping it like it was hot, every boy in there wanted your number."

"Well, that's because I do what I feel. Nothing matters if things don't feel good. Take lessons, Bea." Awilda pulled up her shades and caught Bea's eye. "I'm worried about you."

Bea reached up and repinned her bun. "I'm cool. It's just growing pains. Staying home in the suburbs . . . it's not who I am."

"Sounds pretty cushy to me. I'd give up teaching those bad-ass kids in a minute to be a kept woman."

"Stop." She blushed in shame.

"Don't deny it." Awilda squirted on another layer of suntan lotion.

"You might as well be slathering yourself with cooking oil." Bea was grateful to be able to change the subject. "Why do you keep putting that crap on anyway? Haven't you heard of skin cancer?"

"When I get to work on Tuesday, people need to know that I've been somewhere."

"And you're worried about me?"

A mother with a toddler bent over to pick up a seashell in front of them. Bea reached inside her beach bag and tossed her earbuds to Awilda. She caught them in the air and flung them right back.

"Stop tripping, Bease, or you'll have a nervous breakdown. But don't fret. I'll be there making sure you get your food through a tube."

Bea crinkled her nose. "So funny."

Awilda pulled her sunglasses back down over her eyes. "You like my bikini?"

"Yeah. It's cuter than mine. I feel like a tub."

"Got it online. I wasn't sure it would fit. You know they don't make bottoms for a real booty like mine." Awilda rose from her seat and showed Bea the panties.

"Looks good on you. Glad to see your cheeks contained."

"I know how to tone it down for a family beach. But when we get to DR, I'm going to let it all hang out." She laughed.

"Help me up, crazy."

Awilda pulled Bea from her beach chair. Then she scooted her things farther into the shaded corner and pulled out her sunblock. The saleswoman at Sephora had talked her into spending extra on the European brand because it contained Indian gooseberry extracts, an ingredient that was supposed to prevent tanning. Bea's father's African-American blood was enough tint to her skin.

Awilda played a pop song that Bea liked as she gazed down the beach in the direction of her children: Alana, age five, and ten-year-old Chico playing paddleball. The kids were in a rare tender moment, with Chico holding Alana's hand and showing her how to hit the ball. It warmed her heart and she looked over to her husband to see if he was watching. Lonnie lifted his chin and winked at Bea. Warmth spread between her toes and she winked back. She liked it when Lonnie made her feel like she was the only woman in his world.

Her husband was one of those men who didn't have to work hard at being gorgeous. God had given him all of the ingredients: amber eyes, buttered skin, and swimmer's hair, the silky kind that dried straight from the water, no blow-drying necessary. It was Lonnie who took it to the next level by living in the gym and wearing clothes that looked tailored to fit. Bea always felt that people were surprised when she introduced him as her husband. In the looks department, she was as plain as nonfat yogurt, a little short and too pear-shaped for her own liking, with nostrils that flared too wide, especially during pregnancy. Bea knew that her saving grace was her hair. When it wasn't pinned up it hung heavily, well below her shoulders, in tight ringlets that curled around each other, creating a thick bundle that was full of sheen and body.

Bea was still admiring the kids when Lonnie puckered his lips and blew her a kiss. "That man." She looked over at Awilda. "You know the fool wanted me to have sex in the kitchen over a sink filled with dirty dishes?"

Awilda removed her glasses and pointed them at Bea. "Your ass is stupid. I would do it inside the sink of dishes."

"That's nasty."

"It's sexy." Awilda pressed her knees together.

"Still a horn dog."

She fanned. "It's been too long. Derrick better come correct tonight. It's our anniversary. Amare's staying with you. I don't even want to talk. Just ram it in me."

"A hot mess."

"It's been so off between us lately. I really need this anniversary to make things better. I'm tired, Bease."

Awilda slipped into her rampage of what was wrong with Derrick but Bea didn't have to listen. She had heard it all before. How Derrick's sex drive had plummeted since he was diagnosed with MS. The problems they had living in his mother's house.

"No matter how much I spend on healthy food, the man is still reaching for the crap that activates his MS."

Bea nodded her head like she was with Awilda but at that moment it was hard for her to concentrate on anything but the hunger that seemed to swish down on her. It had been like that through the whole pregnancy. One second she was full and the next she was so hungry she could eat a seashell filled with sand. Her mind started imagining how good a fish sandwich with extra hot sauce and mustard would be. She could taste the grease tinged with the red spicy sauce on her tongue, making her whole mouth feel alive.

"You know what I mean?" finished Awilda.

"Yeah." Bea replied, head in her beach bag. Alana's goldfish stared at her. Bea wanted to sneak a few in her mouth but Awilda would enjoy it too much. She pushed herself to stand. Adjusted her hat and told Awilda to keep an eye on the kids.

"I'm in the middle of telling you something."

"Sis, I've got to pee. The baby. Be right back."

In every direction, the beach was packed with people: skinny teens in too-small jean shorts, children wearing arm floaties, moms hiding under wide brims, and dads napping beneath headphones. It was hard waddling over the sand in her condition and Bea felt self-conscious, like everyone was looking at her. When she reached the boardwalk, she rested against the railing and looked out at the water to catch her breath. She could hear the call of the seagulls mixed with the ebb and flow of the waves lapping the shoreline. The vast blueness of the ocean seemed endless. The scent of the salty water made her craving for seafood more intense. She pulled down her beach hat and made her way to the snack shop in the South End Pavilion.

The lunch rush was over and Bea easily found a single seat at the counter. Two stools down from her sat an older man in a tank top watching the baseball game on the television hanging from the ceiling. Country music sounded from the speakers. The waitress nodded her head in Bea's direction as she wiped the Formica countertop down with a stained towel. It seemed that her hand moved more out of nervous energy than actually trying to get the top cleaned. Bea inhaled the smell of grease.

"What can I get you?"

"Fish sandwich."

."Out of fish today. Sorry."

Bea dropped her hand over her belly to soothe the baby who was kicking on her right.

"Got any shrimp?"

"Out of those too. We didn't get our shipment this morning and it was a busy lunch. We have hot dogs, burgers, pizza, chicken tenders . . ."

"I'll have two hot dogs with ketchup and relish and a large ice water."

The waitress took a pen from behind her ear. "It comes with potato chips."

"Hold the chips, please."

"You can have fries instead."

She hesitated for only a second and then nodded her head. She would only eat a few fries, she reasoned. Maybe wrap half up for Alana's snack. Bea glanced up at the game. The Mets were playing the Braves. Baseball was never her sport and she was glad to see the waitress return with the food.

"Thank you."

Ketchup went on everything. As she chewed, she looked out over the gorgeous Victorian homes and their manicured lawns that ran along the street side. Now that she was eating hot dogs, she would have to have two greens with her dinner to balance out her intake for the day. Her mind wandered over what she would make for dinner. Did they need to make a stop at the grocery store or were there enough cheese and buns left over for the burgers? What would they have for dessert? Alana was going to ask. They could go out for ice cream at Hoffman's. Maybe Lonnie would want to drive the kids to Point Pleasant for the amusement rides. Bea knew that she would be too pooped by nightfall to make the trip but would she want to send him alone? All of that time away from her would open up the opportunity for him to touch base. But she had no proof. Was she worrying herself to death for no reason or was Lonnie cheating on her again?

She wrapped her arms around herself and tried not to dwell on the latter. Kept reminding herself that things between them were fine now, and had been for a while, but the feeling gnawed at her. She ate the meal but could barely taste it as she searched for that click in her brain that brought her comfort. It didn't come. By the time she looked up, her plate was empty except for the remnants of ketchup. All of the fries. Gone. The regret was immediate. Bea belched in her napkin and breathed back the need to throw it all up. She fixed her eyes on the game, concentrating on the moves of the pitcher until the sensation ended.

Bea moved down the boardwalk past the swimming pool. The baby pressed down on her bladder and it reminded her that she needed to pee. Damn it. She should have peed before she ate. It was on her list of rules to avoid the bathroom after she ate. The bathroom had a toilet that could flush away her secrets and shame without anyone

being the wiser. But she would know. She had gotten better at keeping food down this time. After her last disastrous pregnancy, she
had promised herself to get through this one clean. This one was
her redemption and she had to make it.

The bathroom was tiny and full with mothers changing diapers
and teens checking out themselves in the mirror. A young woman
wearing a jean jumper insisted that Bea go before her.

"I wouldn't feel right making you wait in your condition."

Bea thanked her, went in and did her business without looking
in the toilet bowl, and came out clean.

"That was forever." Awilda flipped through *Cosmopolitan* magazine.
Pages were dog-eared and Bea knew that they showed pictures of
clothes Awilda wanted to make. She was a seamstress and designer,
in addition to being a sixth grade social studies teacher.

"The baby made me eat." Bea eased back down in her beach chair.
The trip had tired her out. The sun felt like it was right on her
shoulder and she reapplied more sunscreen.

"You know you're only supposed to apply that every two hours,
not every fifteen minutes."

Bea readjusted her hat.

Awilda held up the page. "Look at this miniskirt. I'm thinking
about giving it a try. I'm doing a street festival at Rutgers next
month and I need some short, sexy clothes that will appeal to college students. Something one size fits all. If I take this waist and add
a strip of Velcro, I think it will fit most. What do you think?"

Bea glanced at the picture and nodded her head.

"Yes, ma'am. I'm going to work my clothing line this summer."

"How's Derrick's job working out?"

"Well, he's had this assignment with Tishman for going on five months. That's stable in the construction business. Said it should carry him to Christmas so I'm not working summer school this year."

"Really?"

"It's been five years straight. I can't wait for the break."

Bea saw Alana running towards her and sat up. "What's wrong, butterbean?"

Alana flopped into her mother's arms crying, flinging sand all over Bea's neck and breasts.

"Sand. It's in my eyes. Get it out."

Bea reached for her towel and wiped at Alana's face. Sand was clumped in her hair, on her arms, and falling from her bathing suit top.

"Were you building a sand castle?"

"Yes."

Bea rubbed until Alana stood, satisfied.

"I'm hungry, Mama."

"Here, drink this." Bea handed her a warm juice box from her bag.

"I thought there was no eating on the beach."

"It's just juice not a whole bag of chips." Bea made her eyes big at Awilda.

"I want chips."

"Later, baby."

Lonnie and Derrick walked up. Lonnie was bare-chested and his shorts hung low on hips. Derrick wore a tank top over the bulge of his belly and yellow trunks.

"How cold was it?" Awilda looked from one man to the other.

"Pretty cold." Lonnie reached down and kissed Bea on the lips.

"Oh get a room, you two," Awilda scolded. "I wouldn't even put my toe in before the Fourth of July."

Derrick fell down into the seat next to her. "You just have to go right in. Don't even think about it."

Amare and Chico were still throwing the Nerf ball in the water.

Lonnie leaned back in his chair and tilted his face toward the sun. "It feels so good to just relax."

"Work been busy?" Awilda looked over.

"Yeah, crazy."

"This is actually the longest I've had my eyes on him in the past two weeks." Bea linked her fingers with Lonnie's. "Up before me, home after I've gone to bed."

"Still coaching Chico's baseball team?" asked Derrick.

"Yeah. I told them up front I wouldn't be there for everything. All the coaches look at the schedule and highlight the dates that might not work in advance. Most of the dads work in the city so we're all in the same boat."

"It's good that you do it, our sons need to see us on the front line doing battle for them." Derrick passed Lonnie a Coke.

"Yeah, it definitely feels good."

"I coached Amare's basketball team until he went over to AAU."

"And you still coach from the stands. Shouting out plays for him, embarrassing the hell out of our son at every game."

"That's my boy."

"I'm hungry, Mommy." Alana interrupted from her place in the sand.

Lonnie patted Bea's thigh. "Me too."

She batted her eyes at his dirty double meaning, hoping no one else caught it. "Then we should go fire up the grill for an early dinner. The kids can play out . . ." Bea's words stopped in her throat as Derrick took off toward the ocean. She looked and saw Chico bobbing and flailing his arms. The tide had started to come in and he'd gone out too far.

"Where's the lifeguard?" Bea stood.

Lonnie had taken off too, but before the men got to the ocean's edge, Amare had plucked Chico from the water and dragged him to where he could stand with the waves at his waist. Bea and Awilda made their way down to the shoreline.

"Baby, are you okay?" Bea reached for her son.

"I'm not a baby," coughed Chico, looking from Bea to Amare.

"Shh," Lonnie instructed and patted his son's back. "Let's get you back to the house."

"I'm fine." He coughed.

Lonnie put his arm around Chico's shoulders and steered him back to their things.

They had rented the same beach house for the past three Memorial Day weekends straight. It was a brick-red Dutch Colonial home with a backyard and swing set. It was walking distance from the beach so Awilda and Derrick had parked their car behind Lonnie's in the driveway.

"Thanks so much for letting Amare stay with you. Now I can dress up as the naughty nurse and be as loud as I want," Awilda whispered and then pinched Bea on her behind.

"Don't do anything I wouldn't do."

"Then I might as well stay right here," she teased. "Later, alligator."

"Babe, we need gas," Derrick reminded Awilda as she got into the car. Lonnie and Bea waved. Lonnie's arm was around Bea's waist.

"That was fun." He held the screen door open for Bea to pass through.

The living room had big windows, wide-planked hardwood floors, and a wood-burning fireplace that they had never used.

"It was."

He came up behind her in the kitchen and kissed her neck.

"I want you."

"Mmmm. You better fire up that grill before those boys come in here hungry as hostages."

"Just kiss me first."

Bea stopped and let Lonnie kiss her long and deep. "Now go," she said, pushing him toward the back patio. Maybe her instincts were all wrong and things were okay, she thought, moving around the country kitchen, pulling food to prep from the refrigerator.

"Mama, can you help me put on *Doc McStuffins*?" Alana dragged her dolls by the arm.

"Sure." Bea wiped her hands on a towel and then followed Alana into the television room and set up her show. The boys were on the side of the house throwing the ball. Even though Amare was a rising senior, he took great interest in Chico and treated him like a little brother. Bea liked that.

When she got back into the kitchen, the whiff of charcoal burning down delighted her. Barbeques always made it feel like summer. The ground beef was seasoned and Bea rolled the meat around between her hands and then pressed out patties. While she worked, she peeked at Lonnie on the patio. He sat in the Adirondack chair with his shirt unbuttoned, grinning at his phone in his hand. He read, typed, and smiled. Bea carried the burgers out to the deck.

"Who was that?" She set the food down.

"Something for work." Lonnie flashed that politician's charm that usually churned her into creamed butter, but it only revived her insecurity. Lonnie was good at tuning in to Bea, and held his arms out to her.

"Come here."

She sat down on his lap.

"Getting big, baby." He rubbed her belly.

"Almost time."

"I can't wait to have my wife back."

"I'm right here."

"You know what I mean." Lonnie leaned in and kissed her. Bea could taste the desire on his tongue.

"Babe, can you make me a mock-tail?"

"Anything for you."

Lonnie walked into the kitchen and pulled the screen door behind him. Bea reached for his phone and punched in the last passcode she'd lifted by looking over his shoulder. Locked. She tried it again. Locked. She tried another combination. Still locked. Bea knew that she could only try five times before the phone was disabled so she crossed her fingers and tried twice more, but neither gave her access. Bea placed the mobile where she had found it, slid the burgers onto the grill, and told herself to stop worrying. But she couldn't.

TWO

Operation Sneaky

Bea was one of those women who loved being pregnant. To experience life moving and growing inside of her was like no other feeling in the world. Not to mention that undeniable glow, extra sheen to her hair, and people falling over their feet to open doors for her like she was important. Even still, the third trimester was uncomfortable. She was up every two hours to pee and even when she was in bed, she tossed and moaned. Most mornings she gave up at around 6 A.M. and just went downstairs.

It was nice to be up early because it gave her at least an hour to herself before the mad morning rush. She pulled back the sliding-door blinds and cracked the window over the kitchen sink. The dewy, fresh air was like coffee to her brain and Bea sipped on it until she was buzzed and ready to start her tasks.

They lived in a two-story traditional home that had been remodeled from top to bottom before they purchased it a year ago. The downstairs had an open floor plan and the rooms were edged in white crown molding. The floors were oak with a ribbon trimming that

Bea liked. It reminded her of their previous home in D.C. That house she loved. This house Lonnie loved. It wasn't a stately home considering the money that they had spent, but Bea knew that what Lonnie treasured most was that it was in the village of Evergreen.

Last year, *Inside Jersey* magazine gave Evergreen a top-ten school district ranking, which meant that her taxes were high enough to send at least one of her kids to private school. The magazine bragged that Evergreen had virtually no crime and was one of the best places in the New York metropolitan area to raise a young family. A young white family maybe. Bea could walk through town for three days before she saw anyone with even a tint of brown in their skin. The suburb was short on diversity, and she often thought about the long-term effects of her children living in such a tiny, homogenous corner of the world.

Bea grew up straddling the fence. She'd lived in Elizabeth but went to an all-girls private high school in Scotch Plains. Code switching between her urban neighborhood and affluent school was necessary to survive, but her children only knew the grassier, fluffier, if-someone-hits-you-tell-the-teacher side, and it made her worry over them being prepared for life away from her protection.

Lonnie disagreed. He believed that outfitting them with the accoutrements of success early was the way to go, and at the top of his list was the neighborhood and school district. When they were looking for a home, he argued, "No one cares about the color of your skin anymore, baby. It's the bulge of your bank account." That was easy for him to say; he was lighter-skinned than Bea, Cuban and Italian, and had a bearing that she couldn't muster. In the end, Bea was never totally on board with the move to Evergreen, but as with most things in their marriage, she had conceded.

Lonnie's alarm went off and she heard him shuffle into the shower. Time was slipping away. Bea busied herself with packing the kids' lunches and snacks. She put on the coffee for Lonnie, the muffins into the toaster oven to warm, and went to wake the children.

"Good morning, Chico," she called, pulling open his curtains. "Time to get up, my love."

"Why do you have to do that?" He groaned, pulling the covers over his head.

"Do what?"

"Talk and sing."

This boy.

"How should I wake you up?"

"Rub me gently or something. The singing is annoying."

Bea sat on the edge of the bed and rubbed his head. "Time to get up, son."

"I know, Ma."

"Good, so do it," she retorted. "And don't come downstairs without making your bed."

Alana was already up when Bea went into her room, sitting at her table with two dolls.

"What are you doing, butterbean?"

"Having coffee with Juliette and Kacie."

"Can you get dressed and bring them downstairs for breakfast?"

"I don't want to wear that dress to school." She gestured to the pink one Bea had laid out the night before. Last month it had been her favorite. "I want to wear jeans."

"Okay." Bea pulled out a pair of jeans and held up two shirts. Alana selected the purple one.

"Get dressed. You have seven minutes."

Bea crossed the hallway into the master bedroom. Lonnie's cologne permeated the room. The scent was so heady she had to sit on the edge of the bed.

"You smell nice. Is that something new?" She fought the suspicion leaking into her voice.

"I've had it for a while. Just wasn't in the rotation." He smiled at her through the mirror.

Lonnie slipped his jacket over a stiffly starched shirt. The jacket was soft and thick in the shoulders but had been tapered perfectly at the waist courtesy of his personal tailor. Lonnie insisted on the perfect V-shaped silhouette. *A modern-day Don Draper,* Bea thought to herself. He noticed her studying him, walked to where she sat, and kissed her on the cheek. It made her skin burn.

"You make the coffee?"

"Don't I always?"

"How'd you sleep?"

"I slept okay. Don't forget about Chico's science fair today. We need to be there by three."

"I've arranged all of my meetings back-to-back this morning so that I can cut out early."

"Good." School events made her nervous. Lonnie was much better at chitchatting with the parents and blending in.

"Mama. Mamaaaaa." Alana's voice rang out.

Bea stood up.

"Mommy!"

She crossed the hall to Alana's room. "Didn't I tell you that if I don't answer you the first time to come find me instead of shouting my name?"

"Sorry."

"What is it?"

"Have you seen Kacie's shoes?"

"Alana, please go brush your teeth. You can find your doll's shoes after school."

"But . . ."

"No buts."

Chico's room was closest to the stairs, and when Bea passed by, she saw that not much had changed.

"Chico, I can't believe you. Up now."

"Dang, Mom."

"Dang nothing. Don't let me come back in here again."

"Why are you yelling?" He threw his legs over the side of the bed.

"Because when I talk in my normal voice nothing gets done."

Alana peeked her head out of the bathroom with her toothbrush in her mouth. "I'm doing what you said, Mama."

"Thank you."

Bea headed back down the stairs and plated the kids' breakfast. Lonnie came down.

"I'll drop the kids off on my way."

"Chico has baseball this week Thursday and Saturday. Make sure you put it on your calendar."

"I'm a coach, baby. It's on my calendar." Lonnie had his laptop open.

"Can you carry the suitcases upstairs for me before you go?"

"Sure." He answered with his head tilted toward the screen of his laptop. "And I'm running out of shirts."

"I'll drop them off."

Alana pulled her dolls up to the kitchen island with her. Bea put her muffin in front of her with a glass of milk.

"You forgot food for Kacie and Juliette."

"It's right next to you," Bea played along. "I made them blueberry."

Alana's face broke into a wide grin. Chico walked into the kitchen, picking out his hair.

"Babe, he needs a haircut."

"A shape up," Chico corrected.

"Son, it's going to be too hot for that hair soon."

"I'm fine, Mom."

"Before you leave I need you to put the trash out."

He sighed loudly. "Really?"

Bea raised her eyes at him in a way that she hoped suggested that he was on her last nerve, then turned her attention to shoving their lunch bags into their backpacks and dropping them at the back door.

Bea stood in the doorway and waved good-bye, feeling relieved that her first job was over. That morning rush always made her feel like she needed to take a nap afterward—so much to remember and remind. If she sat down and rested a minute, she risked not getting back up, so she put on a kettle of water for tea and then threw herself into cleaning the kitchen tornado that they had created. The coffeepot, turned off and emptied. White quartz countertop, wiped down. Morning dishes, washed up and dried. Floor, swept free of muffin crumbs. Done. Bea poured hot water over an English breakfast tea bag and then carried it upstairs. Along the way, she snatched up Lonnie's socks (he had a bad habit of just dropping them on the floor) and Alana's plastic princess shoes.

Once inside their bedroom, she placed her teacup on top of an old book and then pulled out the top drawer of her dresser. It was the drawer that held her undergarments, the kids' teeth, and credit cards that she didn't want in her wallet. She reached under the lace bras she hadn't worn in over a year for the white gloves. Growing up, her mother had worn white gloves when she checked on Bea's house chores. Bea wore the white gloves to check on her husband.

Bea had taken the closet down the hall because she had a quarter of what he owned. Her seasonal things were tucked away in the attic and all of her run-around clothes could be folded and put in a few drawers. The master closet was all Lonnie's. It had a hutch in the center with hanging poles on each side. Bea snapped on her gloves and started working from the front right. She hummed as she went through all of his suit jackets and pant pockets. She sniffed each one of his shirts for a whiff of anything other than him. Ran her gloves over the handkerchiefs looking for residue of makeup or perfume. She sorted what had to be dropped off at the cleaners and what needed washing. As she moved methodically through his closet, her mind flashed back to when she'd discovered his alias Instagram account.

He'd left his tablet open without closing the app. She wasn't really looking for anything. Had merely picked it up to check the next day's weather. That's when she saw Lonnie kissing a hussy and squeezing her ass in three different shots. The woman @DiscoDiva had posted the pictures and tagged Lonnie @Fortune5Alive.

How could Lonnie be that irresponsible? What if Chico had found the pictures? Bea tracked the woman down through Lonnie's mobile phone records. She was good at that. In college, Lonnie had referred to her as Carmen Santiago, the fictional 90s cartoon detective who never left any stone unturned. Bea went so far as to report the woman to her boss at the bank where she worked, complaining that she spent upward of forty minutes at a time on the phone with her husband. The woman called Bea at their house after she was fired. Pissed off, screaming. As Bea picked up Lonnie's dirty laundry, she felt ashamed of how low she'd sunk on the phone call. Getting caught up in the ping-pong of claiming a man.

I was sucking on him last night.

Yeah well, it was me you were tasting.

Ugh, even now remembering the conversation made her stomach turn. And then there was his Miami vice, but she wouldn't let herself spiral down that road. Being pregnant meant there was no Lexapro to catch her. She kept her focus on the job in front of her.

After going through his clothes, she went to his home computer in the corner of their bedroom. Even though Lonnie didn't like it when Bea went through his things, this password he knew better than to change.

She scrolled through his e-mail accounts, scanning through both personal and work. Next she read through their banking statements, checked activity on their mutual funds, stocks, and credit cards. The tea was stone cold when she was finished but she sipped it anyway.

Bea leaned back in the swivel chair feeling unsettled. Lonnie wasn't a careless cheat (the Instagram situation being an exception). She wouldn't find a condom foil in his front pocket, or a racy thong tucked into his trousers. An affair was something Lonnie could easily expense to his business account. He was more sophisticated with his affairs. But this knowledge didn't prevent her from putting on her white gloves at the beginning of every month and double-checking. The search was therapeutic. It made her feel in control.

The sun was hot on this side of the house. Before she knew it, it would be time to go to the science fair and she needed to knock off a few more chores before leaving. The easiest way for her to get the dry cleaning to the trunk of her car was in the laundry basket. When she picked up the basket, she saw a flash of glitter.

Something caught in Lonnie's shirtsleeve. Lonnie had a bad habit of unclasping the cuff link but not removing it from his shirt. Bea was always reminding that man to remove his links. She couldn't even count how many they had lost to the dry cleaner. Expensive links that she had combed through antique stores to find. When she reached for it, she realized it wasn't a cuff link at all. It was an earring. A gold square with diamond cuts. The sight of it forced her down on the bed, winded.

She wrung her hands and then rubbed her belly in an attempt to calm down. How many times had she caught her husband cheating? She'd lost count. And each time it opened up old wounds and leaked fresh pain. The fact that she stayed with him made her feel stupid. She was foolish and she knew it. Bea slung the basket in her arms and started toward the stairs. Why am I still here? She wanted to shout at the walls. But as she traveled down the hall, the answer was in the family photos she passed. Alana's first step, reaching for Daddy. Chico's baseball photo with Lonnie as the head coach. Family cruises and trips to Disney. The wall documented their lives together. Picture perfect.

She was at the bottom of the stairs peering at a snapshot she took. It was a selfie of the family at Liberty State Park before the Fourth of July fireworks. Everyone was squished together and Bea was toppling from the frame, caught between Chico's teeth and the back of Alana's head. She had affectionately named the photo, *And Then There Was Me.* That's how she felt. Blurred. An afterthought. Invisible.

Bea dumped the laundry basket by the back door and tucked the earring into the kitchen drawer beneath the aluminum foil. All of a sudden, it felt like a light bulb was shining in the corner of her mind and the chamber in charge of her self-control unlocked. It was what she referred to as the dark horse. That familiar, frenzied feeling that came over her, urging her to eat everything in sight. She considered making the twenty-minute drive to the closest McDonald's (there wasn't one in Evergreen) but realized she could not wait. Bea moved through the kitchen as a mental checklist of what was available started running through her head.

Just the feeling of her hands on the handle of the refrigerator brought her body to life with excitement. It was like being at Magic Kingdom and seeing the Cinderella castle for the first time. Bea swung both doors open and took visual stock. In the middle bin there was about a half-pound of gourmet salami and a good bit of provolone cheese. She could squeeze that between two thick slices of

French bread and slather on a ton of mayonnaise. The cold cuts and condiments filled her arms and she loved the weight of it against her chest. While she ate the sandwich, she would microwave that box of mozzarella sticks that was in the freezer. When she reached for the box and turned it over in her hand, it read four servings, but Bea would eat the whole ten ounces and all the dipping sauce. She closed the freezer and went back to the fridge. Was there any ham left over from last week's dinner? She ducked her head toward the bottom shelf but then changed her mind about the ham because she remembered the fresh bag of chocolate-chip cookies that she had purchased from Trader Joe's in the pantry. It was unopened. She would try to eat that bag slowly for dessert but she already knew that she would shove them into her mouth one after another, barely chewing them and definitely not tasting them. By then, she would be focused on going into the bathroom and throwing it all up.

A party-sized bag of mesquite barbeque chips would go so well right now, but she had stopped buying chips months ago. She pulled the cookies from her pantry, reasoning that they would do.

She gazed at her growing pile of food on the counter. She needed one more thing. She moved a few things around in her freezer. In the bottom drawer underneath the frozen mixed berries, she spied a Newman's Own thin and crispy, uncured pepperoni pizza. Normally she would split the box with the kids when Lonnie wasn't home. Today, she would enjoy the entire pie. The hot, dripping cheese coupled with the salty, chewy pepperoni would be the highlight of her meal. Bea could feel the saliva building in her mouth and the anticipation of her fix made her so heady she could barely breathe.

Dancing, Bea preheated the oven. She liked to have everything ready and spread out like a big feast so that she could go from one thing to the next without having to stop. The cold cuts were on the counter and she unwrapped the casing on the salami. The smell was overpowering and pungent. In her mind, she was already sucking on the chewy, marbled fat but she needed to slice it up first.

The best way Bea had found to cut the meat thin was with a sushi knife, and while she moved the other knives around in the drawer looking for hers, the telephone rang. She hesitated, but then reached for the cordless. It would have been more convenient to ignore it, but when she checked the caller ID, she knew there was no choice but to answer it.

"Hello."

"Oh my God, Bea, where have you been? I've been texting you all morning," Mena asked, panicked.

"I'm home. What's wrong?"

"Nothing. I just wanted to know how the baby was doing. And you. I'm just . . ."

"She's fine. I'm fine." Bea looked at the pile of food on her counter. Her joy deflated and disgust for herself dropped down into its place. Mena was the intended mother of the baby Bea was carrying and she had almost blown it. Binging and purging while pregnant caused birth defects and Bea knew this firsthand. How could she even consider it? Mena talked but all Bea could hear was:

You are despicable.

A complete failure.

Utter waste of space.

Unworthy. Unlovable.

Of course your husband cheats, look at you.

"Are you there?"

Bea pressed the phone to her ear to drown out the noise. "Yes, Mena, I'm still here."

"I was just saying that I'm so grateful, Bea. I wake up every morning giving thanks for you and this beautiful gift you are giving us."

"Oh, Mena. It's my pleasure."

"It's overwhelming at times, knowing I'm about to be a mother and it's all because of you."

The kind words were distracting and Bea willed herself to believe her. Mena was Lonnie's first cousin on his father's side. A cancer diagnosis led to a hysterectomy in her twenties. Lucky for Mena, her doctor suggested that she freeze her eggs before starting chemo. When Bea heard Mena's story being passed around the Thanksgiving table, she knew she wanted to help her bring a healthy child into the world. Listening to Mena talk helped Bea change her focus and remember why she was carrying the baby in the first place.

Before they moved back to New Jersey, Bea worked as a NICU nurse at Georgetown University Hospital in Washington, D.C. Her experience in the NICU made her sensitive to how hard it was to bring a healthy baby into the world. It wasn't called the miracle of life for nothing. Bea remembered the parents' visible relief when their babies made it out of the danger zone. The light in the mother's eyes when she held her infant to her breast for that first time and the father's joy in packing up the baby and finally being able to carry their beloved home. It always made Bea feel like she was doing powerful work, being a part of their process, and she missed it.

When she offered to carry the baby for Mena, Lonnie was against it. Arguing that if Bea was going to carry another baby it should be his. It was one of the few times that Bea wouldn't back down and whenever she talked to Mena, she was glad that she hadn't caved.

The process didn't turn out to be simple. They went through months of medical testing and mounds of paperwork. Bea pushed herself to eat right, exercise, and not slip up, but it still took three rounds of IVF before the baby took. From the moment Bea conceived, she had prided herself on doing right by Mena and she couldn't believe that she'd almost stumbled.

"I didn't mean to worry you. I was upstairs organizing the closet." She gave a half-truth. "We have the ringers turned off at night so that phone calls won't wake the kids."

"I'll have to steal that idea."

"It's always worked for us."

Reassuring Mena on the health of the baby helped bring Bea back to her senses. With the phone cradled between her ear and neck, she put the meat, cheese, and mayonnaise back. The frozen pizza and mozzarella sticks fit in place inside the freezer. The cookies were returned to the pantry. She reached for a banana, poured herself a large glass of cold water, and took the call into the family room. Bea needed to put some distance between herself and the kitchen until the fire was completely smothered.

"So how is my girl?"

Bea pushed her shoulders into the cushions of the sofa. "Little miss has been quiet today. Probably because I've been moving nonstop. It's not until I'm still that she starts partying."

"Glad she's active. That's always a good sign. Did you get the flowers I sent?"

Bea felt like a heel. "Yes, thank you, Mena. That was so thoughtful of you to send Mother's Day flowers. I should have thought to send you something too. Things have been crazy around here with the school year winding down."

"I understand."

"How's the baby's room?"

"Clark finished over the weekend. It's so bright and beautiful. I spend all of my time in there. You'll have to come see it. I want to feel her kick in her room."

"Whatever you want. Perhaps after our appointment this week."

"I just really need to be close to the baby. It's weird. I mean, you being in your third trimester . . . I mean us, you know, it's just . . . I'm so grateful, Bea. You are a queen to carry this baby for us." Mena started crying.

Bea softened her voice the way she did when she talked to Alana. "I'm happy to help you. I truly am. You get some rest and I'll see you on Friday."

Bea hung up the phone and then wrapped her arms around her elbows. She had been so close to losing it. It could not happen again. Self-loathing bubbled in her belly and she got up and paced the room. Her serenity journal was in her purse and she rummaged through it until she found it. On the front page she had taped sentences to restore her in moments like this.

You are capable of living this new healthy life.
Don't torture yourself because you've made a mistake.
Forgive yourself. Love yourself.
You are enough.

Bea read the words over and over again and even though she didn't quite believe them, she knew that in order to get through the rest of the day she had to forgive herself. It was rule number one for recovery. She was human. She had almost slipped but she hadn't. Catching herself before she fell was worth something.

Native American flute music drifted through her open kitchen window. She made her way over to it and her eyes followed the melody to her neighbor's backyard. Joney was on her back patio with her purple yoga mat. Her blond hair, streaked with gray, looked brilliant against the sun. Standing with her arms raised above her head, Joney stretched and then folded into herself. Watching her afternoon yoga was the most nourishing part of Bea's day, and she tried to catch her as often as she could. Divine and graceful but with the heart of a warrior, she moved. Bea observed with vicarious peace, taking a little bit of Joney's serenity for herself.

THREE

Never Enough

Bea had been living inside of her lie for so long that it felt like the truth. Not even her husband knew about her destructive history with food. Being a registered nurse made it that much more shameful. How was it that she could help others but couldn't help herself? For years it had felt like she was digging her way out of an underground tunnel with no devices. She needed a torch. Awilda was out of the question. Her mother wouldn't understand. Dr. Flora Spellman became her guiding light.

Dr. Spellman was the only doctor of color on the ob-gyn rotation, and Bea made it her business to attend to her whenever possible. She admired the doctor's powerful energy. Straightaway she noticed that Dr. Spellman wasn't afraid to stand up for what she believed and wouldn't back down to her white male colleagues. Bea would offer to grab her lunch when she was too busy to leave her patients. Eventually, they became lunch pals and ate in the cafeteria together on occasion. Dr. Spellman took a liking to Bea and started to look after her too. One day they were having lunch, and Dr. Spellman removed her glasses and stared pointedly at Bea.

"I'm going to ask you a question and you can either answer it or tell me to mind my business."

Bea looked up from the salad she had been playing with.

"Are you bulimic?"

"What do you mean?"

"Don't take this the wrong way, but I've noticed an acidic smell on your breath. Your fingers have a discoloring and bite marks."

Bea reached for her bobby pins and repinned her bun.

"You get jumpy when we have lunch and often head to the bathroom the moment that last morsel hits your mouth."

The tears were there without Bea calling for them. No one had ever taken notice of her so closely. She had been living with Lonnie and he had no clue. She nodded her head. There was something strangely cathartic about that small motion; it felt life changing. Bea felt the warmth of light.

Dr. Spellman started counseling her in private. Even though eating disorders weren't her specialty, she herself had suffered with bulimic-like tendencies in college. She taught Bea how to own her disorder and gave her the tools to turn on the light and pull herself out of the dungeon. When Dr. Spellman left D.C. for a job at Overlook Hospital in Summit, New Jersey, they kept in touch through e-mail. And then when Lonnie told Bea that they were moving, Bea knew someone was watching over her. When she decided to carry Mena's baby, Dr. Spellman was one of the OB doctors in the rotation and key in helping her get through the pregnancy.

After Bea had watched Joney for about an hour, the dark horse had settled down enough for Bea to go to her computer and write Dr. Spellman an e-mail, giving her all the details of the almost-binge. Writing to her had always been cleansing. Bea's fingertips swept over the keyboard, connecting her thoughts, walking Dr. Spellman through her journey: where it started and how she caught herself. The e-mail served Bea better than an hour of talk therapy. She had tried that before but she'd just clam up. The therapist felt judgy. Writing to Dr. Spellman freed her in an anonymous way and when she hit send, she felt absolved of her sins. It was almost like going to confession at church, except instead of praying the rosary, Bea took a hot shower, scrubbing every inch of her body until she felt clean.

Time had gotten away from her and Bea hustled to get ready. Usually she styled her hair up but since she was going to the school with Lonnie she untangled her curls and brushed it down below her shoulders. Long and loose was the way he loved it and Bea worked with what she had to look good beside him. She was searching for her car keys when her phone dinged with a text message.

Sorry honey but you will have to go without me. Office is crazy today. Take pics and give Chico my love.

Bea blew out her breath, remembering the earring and wondering if his excuse was true. Anger rose in her throat but she swallowed it back. She never felt comfortable at school functions without her husband. Most of the people in Evergreen had grown their families together from infancy. Their children had all gone to the same preschools and met at the playground long before Bea's family had moved onto the scene. Often she felt like a little girl with her face pressed against the glass, always on the periphery, always begging to be let in to the mothers' social club.

She did her best to fit the mold by never venturing to the school in the crumpled sweats she found at the bottom of the bed, instead wearing the spandex that seemed to be the suburban mom's uniform. It was the look that suggested that you were either on your way to the gym or on your way back. Or if not that look, then blue jeans.

Chico's classroom was on the third floor and Bea had to rest at the top of each landing. Knee problems had been another plague of this pregnancy, and she stretched them a little before continuing down the hall to his classroom on the right. The baby was up, moving and stretching in her lower abdomen, and Bea kept her hand on her belly as she entered the classroom. Several parents were already walking around the room. She spotted Chico and winked at him.

"Hey, Ma."

"'Sup, son." She giggled, and to her surprise her son laughed too.

"How's your day going?"

"Good. My desk is over here."

More parents had entered and were drifting around the room, listening to the kids' presentations. As Chico explained the effect gravity has on plant growth, two moms Bea had never seen approached his desk to listen. Even though Bea had helped him with the project, she was proud of how in the end he had taken control.

"Very nice. It's Alonzo, right?" said the mom with the brown braid and green eyes.

"Yes, ma'am," replied Chico. Bea beamed at his manners.

"Awesome, great job," clapped the second mother, waving her diamond absently in the air. "When are you due?" She turned to Bea.

"First week of August."

"Alonzo, are you excited about your new sibling?"

"It's not our baby," he replied drily, then ran off to catch his buddy at the next table.

The two mothers looked at Bea.

"I'm a surrogate—"

"Ah," interrupted the green-eyed mother. "Well, this town is pricey. My property taxes went up again. It's a small fortune."

Bea's temples tingled. "I am helping my husband's cousin who can't carry. I believe that every woman should be a mother if she desires it."

The woman who'd made the comment started choking, like she had a fish bone stuck in her windpipe. "Excuse me." She coughed. "These allergies are killing me."

"You are just incredible to do something like that," said the mother who'd been waving her ring. "What a saint."

They walked away quickly, and Bea stared at Chico's project, trying to regain her composure. Perspiration broke out across her forehead. To suggest that she was selling her body to pay her taxes was the craziest, most inappropriate thing she had ever heard in her life. Everyone was usually on their best behavior at these functions. Pretending that they were all the same, avoiding topics that could possibly offend. How dare they? Bea stood having a two-sided conversation in her head of what she should have said. Damn Lonnie for not being by her side. All of a sudden the heaviness of her day made her drowsy. Her eyes darted across the room, looking for a chair to plop down into.

"Hey there."

Bea had just lowered herself onto a hard seat near the window. It was Tyler's mother, Camille. Tyler and Chico were on the same baseball team, so she and Camille often chatted in the stands. Also a transplant, Camille had moved to Evergreen from Delaware a year before Bea. She was one of the few mothers that Bea had connected with in Chico's grade. Bea was sure that she had been voted prom queen in high school. Camille gave off that vibe: pretty, bubbly, popular, and sweet.

"Hey, Camille."

"What's wrong? That little baby acting up in there?"

"She's been busy today." Bea's hand dropped to her belly, happy to change the channel.

"How's her mother doing?"

"Anxious and excited."

"It must be a blessing to have someone carry a baby for you. But I can see the anxiety too. She must worry you to death wanting to know your every move."

Bea wished that she could get up and make eye contact with Camille, but the magnitude of her day kept her glued to her spot.

"She called me today freaking out but I get it."

Camille tossed her ponytail. "I'm so glad the school year is coming to an end."

"Me too. Looking forward to no rules and no homework."

"What are you doing for camp?"

They chatted a bit more. Bea needed to get going or she would be late picking up Alana.

"Coming to the game tomorrow night?"

"Yeah, I'll be there." Bea waved to Camille and went looking for Chico. When she got to the parking lot, she raked her fingers through her hair, raveled it up, and pinned it into a bun. The diamond-waving mother walked up beside her.

"Don't mind my friend. She's a loudmouth from Brooklyn with no filter. It's amazing what you're doing? Honestly, I'd never have the heart."

Bea smiled curtly and dismissed the woman with a turn of her shoulder, ushering Chico into the backseat of the SUV. It was hard to figure out what bothered her most. The fact that the mother had said it, or her friend's acknowledgment that it was insulting. As soon as she was behind the wheel, she fished her phone out of her pocket and texted Lonnie.

Word on the street is that I'm carrying Mena's baby to help pay the taxes on our house.

Who said that???

She knew that would hit a nerve.

Two moms at Chico's science fair.

What?

Would have been nice if you had been there.

I know, sorry babe. Work is crazy. How's my boy?

Fine.

Love you.

Whatever.

Bea dropped her phone into her bag and didn't respond. The conversation would have been a lot different had he been by her side, she was sure of it.

She survived the after-school snack rush and Alana's meltdown over Bea erasing her spelling homework and making her do it over. Dinner was simple. Costco's breaded tilapia, boxed mashed potatoes, and frozen peas. When Alana cried about taking a bath, she left Chico to reason with her. Bea needed some sleep. That was the only thing that would completely hit the reset button and give her a clear head for a fresh start. When the kids went down, she covered Lonnie's food, put it in the microwave, and went to bed right behind them.

FOUR

Fresh Air

Lonnie came in long after Bea was in bed and was up and out of the house before she got up. She got the kids off to school and then fished around the refrigerator, throwing out some of the food she'd been tempted by a few days ago and noting what she needed to replenish. Her relationship with food had shifted back to neutral, and as she worked, she whispered her affirmation. "I am providing fuel and sustenance for my body so Mena's baby can grow." For breakfast, she boiled two eggs to go with a slice of dry wheat toast while jotting down her grocery list.

It was the second Wednesday of the month, the day she picked Awilda up from work during her lunch hour so they could go to the open-air market located a few blocks from the middle school where Awilda worked. The membership belonged to Bea but she insisted that Awilda come along to shop for healthy foods for Derrick. It also gave them guaranteed time together without the interruption of their families. Bea stuck her head out of the driver's side window of her minivan and waved as Awilda walked up.

"What kind of school are you teaching dressed like that?"

Awilda stopped with her hands on her hips. She had on a yellow fitted dress that hugged all of her curves. A wide, black patent belt and high wedges. "Look, I've got to keep the job interesting. You should see the ducks I work with."

"You look like a bumblebee."

"Correction. I look like the queen bee." Awilda opened the door.

"Get in the car."

Bea pulled away from the school. Her radio was off but Awilda turned it on as soon as she slid her butt into the seat.

"How can you drive around in silence?"

"Gives me time to think."

"That's your problem, Bea. You spend too much time in your head. Girl, just do it."

"What are you, a Nike commercial?"

Awilda let down her window. "It feels good to be outside. That school is so stifling."

"Where were you last night? I called."

"The gym. Trying to blow off steam before you see me on the news for murdering my husband."

"What happened?"

"He's a liar."

Bea's tires grumbled against the gravel as she pulled into the parking lot of the market. Awilda recounted the story of running into one of Derrick's work buddies at the gas station on their way home from Spring Lake.

"The guy was like, 'D, how are things working out? You managed to find something else? Crazy how they let you go over that bullshit.'"

"Let him go from work?"

Awilda looked at her as if to say, *can you believe it?* "Imagine my face. This fool has been pretending to go to work for the past three weeks. Ain't that some shit?"

Bea turned the car off and tilted her head toward Awilda. A man's pride was everything and this MS was testing Derrick's.

"Sis."

"Don't take up for him." She sucked her teeth. "Had me breaking my neck packing his lunch every day. I should have known something was up when I came home on my lunch break to use the bathroom and he was sitting on the couch. Talking about how they let him go early because his hands had been shaking."

They got out of the car and Bea looped her arm through Awilda's.

"Why lie?" Awilda asked.

"He didn't want to disappoint you. Everyone in New Jersey can see how badly you wanted off this summer. He didn't want to let you down. He probably thought he could find something to tie him over."

They walked into the market and each grabbed a handheld basket.

"Well, that didn't happen and now I am working summer school in the straight-up hood. Everything in the easier districts has been filled since February. I can kiss Devinee good-bye."

"What?"

"Divine. Spelled with three *e*'s. The name of my clothing line. Devinee, heaven-sent to make a woman feel like an angel." Awilda made wings with her hands and Bea burst out laughing.

"Okay. I'm still working on the jingle but you catch my drift."

"I get it." Bea stopped in front of a table filled with green vegetables. She could literally feel her heartbeat slow down at the sight of the goodness. She dropped bunches of asparagus, cucumbers, cilantro, and mixed peppers into her basket.

"I don't know why I keep shopping at this high ass co-op with you when Derrick's not getting any better. He doesn't even eat what I buy." Awilda held a bunch of mint to her nose.

"Cut the man some slack. This thing is tough on him."

"I'm trying, Bea, I really am. But if I find one more McDonald's wrapper in the garbage, I'm going to cut him. What grown man still eats that junk?"

Bea rubbed her stomach, suddenly craving a Quarter Pounder with Cheese. She hadn't had Mickey D's in months. Fast food was number one on her list to avoid. It made her feel gross and when she felt gross she wanted to throw up. But damn the thought was comforting. Salty fries. Plenty of ketchup . . .

"Amare's getting ready to go to my parents' house for a couple of weeks. I wish I could drop Derrick's ass off too. That would be a real break."

"Well at least it was a lie about work."

Awilda stopped.

"I found an earring in your boy's laundry."

"Shut up."

"I'd take MS over him fucking other women any day. At least what's going on with Derrick is not his fault."

"Whoa, Bea. I can't remember the last time I heard you cuss."

There was a bench near the fresh-squeezed-lemonade stand and Awilda pulled Bea over onto the seat.

"What can I do?"

"What else is there to do? I haven't even had a chance to confront him yet. He came in late and left early."

"Shit like this makes me wish I never introduced you." Awilda and Lonnie had gone to high school together. When Bea ended up at Rowan College a year after Lonnie, Awilda connected them to each other.

"Stop, Wilde."

"Bea, you're pregnant! This ain't right."

"I'm trying not to jump to conclusions before I talk to him."

"You want a lemonade?"

Bea nodded. Awilda bought two drinks and a soft pretzel. She broke off a piece of pretzel and handed it to Bea.

"So what are you going to do?"

Bea sipped and shrugged her shoulders. The sweetness of the agave and the tartness of the lemon went straight to her head. "My life is exhausting. Do you know yesterday at the science fair this mother basically assumed I was a surrogate to help pay the taxes on my damn house?"

"Don't know what to say out their damn mouth."

"The nerve, right?"

"Well, let me know if I need to come up to that school and beat a bitch down. You know I will for you."

"I know." Bea smiled.

"Do or die. Thick or thin. Awilda and Beasley to the very end," Awilda chanted and they high-fived.

"Help me up."

"Yeah, I better finish my shopping before I get back late. You know me and the assistant principal had words last week?"

"What happened?"

Awilda yapped on about what had happened at her job, then moved on to her plans to drive Amare down to her mother's house in North Plainfield for his summer AAU basketball camp. The good thing about being with Awilda was that Bea knew her inside and out. Most times she could even finish her sentences. Awilda talked so much about the same stuff that Bea could get away with half listening and not miss a beat.

Bea dropped Awilda off at school. She unpacked her groceries and prepped dinner: lemon pepper chicken, asparagus, tomato salad, and basmati rice. Needing a breather, she sat at the kitchen island and munched on a handful of blueberries. The berries were perfect and plump and she couldn't get enough. She always had to remind herself that even though fruit was healthy she couldn't get into the habit of overeating that either. Making herself stop at two handfuls, she grabbed the rest of the box and put it in the freezer for Alana's after-school snack. Alana loved frozen blueberries and having something that would make her daughter smile made Bea feel happy. She grinned, picturing the look that would cross Alana's cute face, while separating the bills from the junk mail. The last envelope was addressed to Lonnie with feminine, curvy handwriting.

His Miami vice. Bea knew the return address by heart because she was the one who signed and mailed the check to her every month. Bea slipped her finger under the envelope's seal and yanked it open.

Dear Alonzo,

There has been a string of terrible incidents of violence at the school and it is making it hard for Alonzo to learn and be successful. I'm writing because I need an increase in child support for private school for our son. We both know how important the proper education is for him. Here is the school's brochure. Please take a look and get back to me. I would like to move him by September.

Yours in parenting,

Connie

Yours in parenting, give me a break, Bea thought. A school photo of the little boy beaming, missing his two front teeth, slipped out of the envelope. Bea felt a tightening in her chest as she pulled the picture closer. He could be one of her children; he looked so much like her own son. On the back of the photo was scribbled:

Alonzo Perez-Colon age 6.

Six years had passed since she'd found out about the boy in Miami. Lonnie and Bea were living in D.C., settled into the house she loved. Six months pregnant with Alana, Bea had done well with controlling her bulimia. Dr. Spellman had made Bea confess the disorder to her attending doctor, who agreed not to bring up the disorder in front of her husband. Alana's room was almost ready for her arrival and Bea was in there sorting baby blankets and towels when the phone rang.

"Woman to woman I thought it best for you to know." She had an accent. Bea pictured her as an island pageant queen with long, black hair, eggplant-colored toenails, slim waist, and lots of cleavage. Lonnie usually slept with white women so this accented chick was a change in his repertoire.

"I don't believe you," Bea told her and hung up with shaky palms. She thought that would be the end of it but the next day a FedEx package arrived. It was the results of the DNA test that Miami vice had ordered. She had swabbed Lonnie's toothbrush on his last visit: 99.9 percent. The three-week-old baby was her husband's. Bea threw up her lunch all over the kitchen floor. And then she ate everything that she could get her hands on. Then threw up again. The rage. The injustice. The humiliation.

The proof of paternity changed Bea. The stress of it made it easy for the bulimia to take over her life. She couldn't control Lonnie but she could control what came in and out of her body. Bea wasn't focused at work, couldn't take care of Chico (thank God for day care), and she stopped washing her hair. Half the time when she dressed in her scrubs she couldn't remember if they were clean or dirty. During the day, she spent her entire time planning her next binge: where she would eat, how she would get rid of it without anyone knowing. Every afternoon, she slid through the McDonald's drive thru and ordered two or three Quarter Pounders. She'd wolf it down and then throw up in the bag the food came in. Disposing of her secret before she even left the parking lot.

Her double life became draining. The urge to purge controlled her. She couldn't make herself stop. Every morning she woke up promising herself that she wouldn't do it again but after breakfast she was in the bathroom running the water from the faucet to cover the sounds of her heaving it back up. It became the only thing that mattered in her life. She was helpless to the feeling of relief as the food left her belly. It was her drug, her secret affair. The need for her fix drove everything out, even the safety of the baby she was carrying.

They lived daily with Lonnie's flaws but Bea didn't want him to know her vulnerability. When her blood pressure shot up, her electrolytes dropped low, and she tested positive for gestational diabetes, Bea implored her doctor to keep her patient confidentiality intact. Lonnie was told that Bea was suffering from pregnancy complications when she was hospitalized five weeks before her due date and pumped with magnesium.

At thirty-six weeks, Alana was born a month prematurely with a low birth weight but no detectable birth defects. It was wait and see. For nearly three weeks, Alana lived in the same NICU where Bea worked. It devastated Bea when she became one of the mothers that she was used to caring for.

Dr. Spellman was the only person who could talk her into getting real help, convincing her that with two children to care for it was impossible to recover alone. Bea lied to Lonnie and told him that she was visiting Alana but was really attending an eating disorder support group five blocks from the hospital. She hated going, despised listening to women talk about their disease. It was like holding up a magnifying glass to Bea's life and she didn't enjoy the sifting and sorting. Eventually she came around and started believing in the techniques and using the methods that they gave her to heal. Dr. Spellman recommended a nutritionist who helped Bea plan her meals. Exercise was a key distraction so Bea bought a jogging stroller.

When Alana came home and they started settling back into their lives, Lonnie tried to restore order by being around more. He bought Bea expensive handbags, took paternity leave from work, and promised her all sorts of things but Bea only wanted one thing.

"If you want this to work, if you want my forgiveness, then I never want you to see the child or that woman again. They are not our family. I'll send a monthly check, but that's it." In her heart Bea knew this was wrong but she rationalized that she was doing it for her children's sake, for appearance's sake, for her own sake. No one knew that the boy existed. Not even her mother. Not even Awilda.

FIVE

Daddy's Home

When Lonnie unlocked the side door, it was like the skies parted and streamed sunshine right into their kitchen. He had been getting home so late and leaving so early that Bea wondered why he came home at all. The kids had not laid eyes on him since the morning he'd driven them to school. Bea only felt his hands on her at night. Alana took off running when she heard the door open, chanting his name in her made-up song.

"Daddy, Daddy, Daddy. What did you bring me?"

"A kiss." Lonnie bent over and pecked her face.

"That all?"

"A hug." He smothered her in his arms.

"A piece of candy?"

He reached into his pocket and pulled out a peppermint.

"Yes. Thank you." And then she was off, back to whatever she'd been doing before he entered. Chico was much cooler, or tried to be anyway.

"'Sup, Dad." He leaned in for a chest bump. Lonnie ruffled his hair. "Don't do that. You'll mess it up."

"It's already a mess," Bea interjected.

"You ready for your game today?"

"Yeah. I finished all of my homework. What time are we leaving? I want to get there early."

"Right after dinner."

"Can I go outside?"

"Sure." Bea sat at the kitchen table checking Chico's math homework. Lonnie leaned down to kiss her lips but Bea turned her cheek.

"Oh boy, what's wrong?"

"Nothing."

"Mena's baby okay?"

He always referred to the baby as Mena's baby. Bea wasn't sure if that was his way of maintaining distance or not. Instead of responding, she grabbed his hand so that he could help her stand and pressed the earring she found into his palm. Their eyes met. Bea made her way to the stairs.

"Mom, can I have a snack?"

"No."

"But I'm hungry."

"Dinner will be served in a few minutes. Go out onto the deck and get some air."

Bea was upstairs, searching her closet for something to wear. Lonnie walked in behind her.

"Bea." He turned his amber eyes on her in that way he used to say that he could explain.

Bea tugged on a stretchy pair of maternity pants.

"Honey."

She pulled a fitted top down over her belly just as the baby moved.

"I saw that." Lonnie half-grinned.

Bea rubbed her tummy, reminding herself to calm down. *Don't get mad. Don't pass your anger on to the baby,* she coached herself. *Breathe.*

"I'm not going to the game with you. Dinner is on the stove. Alana will have to sit on the sidelines. Take a snack for her. She'll be hungry by halftime. When you get back, tell Chico to shower. You can just put Alana to bed."

"Can we talk?"

"No, we can't. I don't want to hear anything you make up to say. I'm tired, Lonnie."

"I can explain."

"Can't you always?" She clenched her teeth, trying to control the emotions that threatened to surface. She didn't want to let loose. For the baby's sake and her own children downstairs. When she received that initial call from Miami vice, Lonnie had come home and found her in their bedroom. When she saw him, she didn't think about being six months pregnant. All she felt was wrath. Bea jumped off the bed and onto Lonnie. Her fingers looped around his neck and she tried to choke him. She wasn't sure where the strength had come from but she wrestled him to the bed and squeezed his throat until he started coughing and pushed her off. Chico was standing in their bedroom doorway crying, terrified. After that, she vowed never to argue with him when the kids were within earshot. She wanted them to feel secure.

Lonnie blocked the doorway.

"Move."

"Just hear me out, please." He put his hands up in surrender, like he was the good guy.

"Just let me go. It's for the best."

Lonnie sighed and then stepped aside. Bea brushed past him. He grabbed her hand but she quickly unthreaded her fingertips.

"Kids, I have to run out. Dad's going to serve dinner."

"You're not coming to my game?" Chico whined, which threw her off guard. These days his world seemed to revolve around Lonnie. Bea was just his laundry lady, personal driver, secretary, and cook.

"I have to do something for Nona."

"Can't you do it tomorrow?"

"I don't want you to go," Alana cried.

"Sure you can't stay?" Lonnie was in the kitchen now, beside the kids. Bea grabbed her purse and her keys and walked out the back door.

She hadn't initially intended to go see her mother today but she really had nothing better to do. When the car started moving in that direction, Bea realized that there was nothing that she wanted more than to fall into her mother's arms, let her feed her, fuss over her, and baby her a bit. The city of Elizabeth was about fifteen minutes from Evergreen and Bea maneuvered her car without giving it much thought.

Her mother's building was an old walk-up. She still lived on the third floor in the two-bedroom apartment that Bea spent her entire adolescent life in. The walls were stained from years of handprints, and the hall smelled like *locrio de pollo,* rice with chicken. Bea hoped the smell was coming from her mother's apartment. She could use some Dominican comfort food.

"Ah, Beatrice. *Mija, donde has estado?*" Her mother called to her tenderly with her meaty hands in the air when Bea pushed opened the front door. Bea stopped a few steps in and saw Awilda sitting at the table sipping on her mother's famous coconut drink that she made by the gallon. Disappointed they weren't alone, she forced the door closed with her foot. She didn't feel like sharing her mother's attention today.

"What're you doing here, Wilde?" Bea leaned down to kiss her mother's cheeks. "Hi, Mami."

"Hanging out," Awilda replied, a bit sloshed from the drink.

"Oh, so dark, baby. Too much time in that hot sun last weekend? I told you, apply lots of sunscreen, wide hat, and glasses. You can't get away with browning your skin like Wilde."

Bea sunk heavily into a kitchen chair.

"No matter how dark she gets, she always has that little extra thing about her. What do the French call it?"

"*Je ne sais quoi.*" Awilda grinned.

Bea chewed her nail, not needing to be reminded of how Awilda had that "it" factor and she didn't.

"Irma, she wore so much sunscreen that I could have fried chicken on her thigh."

"Well, I guess it could have been worse." Awilda and Irma touched arms and laughed. "Even as a baby Bea would turn golden just from being in the car. My mami, may she rest in peace, use to give me such a headache about it. Telling me she already had her daddy's *cocolo* blood in her. She didn't need the sun too."

"I was the only kid playing outside in the summer wearing a sun visor and long sleeves in ninety-degree weather."

"It was for the best. I worked hard to keep your value up and look how things turned out. You know our men prefer their women with light, creamy skin," Irma said matter-of-factly.

"Not where I'm from. My father always said the darker the berry the sweeter the juice," Awilda piped in.

"Back in Santo Domingo, when I was growing up, you didn't

even get the best meat from the butcher if you were too brown. Women in this building still mix together products to bleach their skin."

"Mami, that's ridiculous."

"But it's true."

"What do you have to eat?" Bea interrupted, not wanting to take on any of her mother's colorist crap. She had been plagued with it her whole life; now that she was an adult she didn't want to put it on. The ignorance of it reminded her of her own childhood torment. Growing up on a block that was mostly Puerto Rican and Dominican, the name-calling was relentless. They called her *cocolo* because everybody knew her father was black, and *puerca,* a female pig, because she was bigger than most. And even with all of Bea's flaws, there were still *chicas* lower on the hierarchy of Hispanic beauty. They were the bitter and bold. Darker-skinned girls with beady hair that had been dyed, fried, and relaxed with chemicals until it came out in clumps. Those were the girls who treated Bea the cruelest. The ones who had Bea looking over her shoulder, accusing her of thinking she was better because she had "good hair." They would chase her down the street with gardening shears, threatening to cut it off so she would look like a true *cocolo,* sending her back to her roots, but she didn't want to think about all of that. She came to her mother's house to be cheered up, not torn down.

"Wilde's been trying to get me to try new food. What the hell is this again?"

"It's called *doro wat.* It's a chicken dish from that Ethiopian restaurant on South Orange Avenue. Try it, Bea." Awilda opened the container. Bea didn't like the smell of it, and since when did her mother eat anything but Dominican food?

"Nah, I'm good."

"Where are the kids?" Irma spooned a bit into her mouth. "Bea, it really is good. Sure you don't want a little nibble?"

Bea shook her head. "Chico has a game."

"Lonnie's coaching?"

"Yeah." Bea crossed her ankles. She knew where this conversation was heading. She could say her mother's line with her and be spot on.

"That's a good man. A really good man. My Beatrice is lucky to have him."

Bea could feel Awilda's eyes on her but she busied herself with a loose thread on her shirt.

Irma continued. "Did you know that man bought me a brand new cell phone and has been paying the bill as a birthday gift? I tell you, he's a good man." Irma made the sign of the cross. "I thank God every night down on my stiff knees that he heads our family."

Bea should have gone to the bookstore instead. A historical romance would have cheered her up much better than this. Irma pressed her hands down on the table and swung her wide hips toward the bathroom down the hall. In her day, Irma had been shaped like an acoustic guitar. Now she was more like a tom-tom drum. Bea thought to herself, *if my father was still living, she would have never let herself go like that.*

"You going to tell your mom about finding the earring?"

"Did you call your mom about Derrick?"

"Well that's pretty ugly."

"Why're you here?"

"Is there a problem, Bea?" She arched her brows.

"You didn't mention dropping by when I saw you."

"Oh, now I need permission to see Irma? Since when?"

"Forget it." Bea waved her hand.

She knew that Awilda visited her mother. They were old friends. When Awilda became pregnant with Amare, her mother kicked her out and Irma stepped in to help her. The two were like girlfriends and more often than not it irked Bea. Tonight, she would have preferred to be with her mother alone.

"I never see you out this time of night. What's got you all riled up?"

"Just needed some air." Bea dropped her head into her hands.

"*Mija,* what's wrong?" her mother was back down the hall.

"Just tired from the pregnancy."

"All that work and you're just going to give my grandchild away like yesterday's trash."

"Ma, I told you the baby isn't mine. It's Mena's egg and Clark's sperm. I'm just carrying it."

"I've never heard of such foolishness. You, Wilde?" She took a sip from her coconut drink.

"Yeah. It's becoming pretty common these days."

"Modern medicine is something." Irma sipped.

Lonnie sent Bea a text message.

Come home baby, please. So we can talk.

"Is that Lonnie?" Her mother smiled broadly. Bea was sickened by her admiration.

"Yeah."

"You better be heading home then."

Bea sighed. "I still have to get the clothes ready for school tomorrow."

"Okay, my lucky girl." Her mother kissed her cheek.

"Text me when you get in." Awilda waved.

Bea closed the door behind her with her mother's voice ringing in her ear. *You are so lucky. You are so lucky to have Lonnie. He's a good man.* It's all Bea had heard since she said *I do.* Even if her mother knew all about his secret transgressions, Bea wasn't convinced it would change her position. Irma equated a good man with him bringing his paycheck to the table and taking care of things. The very first time Bea caught Lonnie banging his secretary up against his desk, Bea ran home to her mother and told her it was over. She wouldn't stay with a man who cheated.

Irma told her, "Baby, cheating is the least of your worries. As long as that man brings his paycheck home to you, that's what matters." Lonnie paid the bills but she paid the emotional cost.

Bea had been driving with no destination in mind. Her eyes tuned in to her surroundings. Up ahead she spied the golden arches. Her pulse quickened. The taste of McDonald's had been on her tongue for several days. Just the smell of it would give her the comfort that her mother had not. Fast food was on her avoid list but if she splurged, it had to be in controlled portions. Bea breathed in the smell of salt and grease as she shifted her car into park. What she wanted to order and what she needed were two different meals. Her fixed McDonald's meal plan was a cheeseburger, small fries, and if she drank water she could have half of an apple pie. Her favorite was a Quarter Pounder with Cheese, but like potato chips she couldn't eat just one. Two or three of those meals could easily fit into her belly.

"Can I take your order?" The voice sounded scratchy through the speaker system.

"May I have a . . ."

Bea didn't have to look over her right shoulder to know that the dark horse had entered the car. She could feel the hairs on the back of her neck pull away from her skin.

"What? Repeat that?"

Bea was tongue-tied. A Quarter Pounder with Cheese meal was a number three. She could try to eat just one.

The dark horse breathed on her. *Do it.*

"I can't hear nothin' you're saying," the attendant said, nastier this time. In this part of town patience was an unheard-of virtue.

"Just . . . give me a cheeseburger, small fries, and an orange soda."

"That all?"

No.

Beads of sweat were on her temple. "No." She looked at the menu again. The saliva in her mouth was thick with want. She swallowed her desperation.

"Give me an apple pie. Make sure it's warm."

"We only serve 'em warm. Drive up to the next window."

Bea took her foot off the gas and floated to the next window. Fumbling in her purse until she produced a twenty-dollar bill, she told herself the apple pie was for the kids. She would put it in their lunchboxes tomorrow.

"That'll be seven twenty-nine."

Bea handed over the twenty. When she was on a binge, she always needed thirty dollars. See the positive. It was nice to hand over the twenty and get back change.

"Next window."

Why did they have so many windows?

"Any ketchup with that?"

"Yes, and napkins." Bea took the drink and sipped it long and strong before placing it into the cup holder. Her hands shook as she reached for her food. The aroma caressed her nose and the bag was warm like home in her lap. She pulled into a space in the parking lot facing Route 1 and watched the cars lick the road. Her throat felt sore. Bea took her first bite out of the burger. The bun was so soft and buttery that she barely had to chew. The mix of meat, cheese, ketchup, and raw onion delighted her, but what she wanted to taste was that thick, sliced pickle.

She opened her mouth, wider this time and got a chunk between her jaws. The vinegary taste made her whole body feel heated and alive. She reached for a handful of fries and licked the salt from each one before cramming them all into her mouth at once. Then she took another bite of burger and let all of the flavors insult her tongue. Ketchup ran from the corner of her mouth as she sipped the sugary soda, glad that she hadn't settled for water. Each bite erased the self-doubt, numbed the insecurity, empowered her, and curbed the anger she had clung to.

Bea remembered when she loved Lonnie so hard she could barely breathe. Just the thought of him made her sweat. When he worked long hours, she would get the chills and needed to sleep in his clothes, on his side of the bed, until he returned. Now after the affairs and an illegitimate son, she groped around for happiness. Spent more time than she cared to admit fretting, wondering what he was up to. Bea had thought about having an affair of her own to even the score but she wasn't wired like that. Bea wouldn't even know where to go to meet a man. The bar scene hadn't been her thing since college.

A euphoric rush spread between her fingertips and she tilted the bag of fries and dumped the rest into her mouth. She wanted to slow down but she was too wrapped up. The apple pie box pressed open and Bea gobbled it down without really tasting it. When she looked up, there wasn't a crumb to be found. Her belly pressed against the steering wheel and she felt too full.

Disgust for herself bubbled up like indigestion. She shouldn't have eaten the pie. She shouldn't have come to McDonald's. The need to bring it all up pressed against her shoulders. Bea could pretend like this meal didn't happen at all. She still had the bag. No one would know. How many months had it been since her last purge? Bea had lost count. That was a good thing, she reasoned with herself. The perspiration was building on her skin. Her head started to spin and she felt dizzy. Before the pregnancy, she would pop a pill that would make the symptoms subside, but her gastroenterologist had told her to stop taking them until after the baby was born. She had recommended natural remedies such as ginger and chamomile tea but that stuff didn't work as well. Bea felt a tightening in her belly that bordered on pain. She rolled the window down and hung her head out over the side, breathing in the mixture of fast food and motor oil. She reached for the notebook she kept in her purse. Bea found the page and read to calm and steady herself.

1. See yourself as beautiful. Flowering and giving life to the earth. This baby can't do it without you. You are important.
2. Food is your fuel. You need it in your body. It's your sustenance.
3. When you feel overwhelmed go for a walk, write down your feelings, or play your favorite songs.

Bea was not about to stroll down Route 1, so she rummaged through her mobile phone for her favorite playlist. "Happy" by Pharrell came on followed by Celia Cruz's "Mi Bomba Sono." Her mother used to play Celia Cruz Saturday mornings while preparing for Bea's father's visit. Singing along with the music helped distract her and she felt well enough to start the car.

The traffic was easy and by the time she pulled into her driveway, "Oye Como Va" was on by Tito Puente. Her block was dark, quiet, and safe. When she walked into her house she felt well enough. The kids were in bed but the kitchen waited for her. She'd expected that. Lonnie came straight toward her, not waiting for an invitation to touch her. His arms went around her waist.

"I was just about to clean the kitchen but I had a work call that ran long."

It was a lie but she was supposed to be grateful that he had at least tried to make the effort.

"It's fine."

"Did you eat?"

"Yeah."

"Listen. The earring isn't what it looks like. I haven't been with anyone. I swear on my grandmother's grave."

That was a new one, Bea thought, sweeping crumbs from the kitchen island into her hand.

"I called Jenna and she said it was hers."

Jenna was his assistant.

"She actually said she had been looking all over for it. You know she's a newlywed and has been spacey since she returned from her honeymoon. It must have fallen and caught my shirt."

Bea looked into his eyes. In spite of having years of practice, she still couldn't tell when he was lying.

"Okay," she offered after a beat. "Make sure you give it back to her."

"I will." He was visibly relieved. It was almost comical. "Don't worry about the kitchen, I'll get it later." This wasn't true either but Bea played along. "Come sit on the sofa and relax."

Bea followed Lonnie into the family room. The television was on. Her favorite orange ginger candles were lit.

"I was going to draw you a bath but I didn't know if you could still get down in the tub."

"Funny," she replied.

Lonnie adjusted the pillows behind her on the sofa and placed her feet in his lap.

"You want to watch *Love Jones*?"

Bea looked at him with her mouth open. It was her absolute

favorite movie. The movie she could recite line by line but he never wanted to watch.

"Are you sure?"

"I can't think of anything I'd rather do." He found the movie on Netflix and played it. As Bea sank into the torrid romance of Darius Lovehall and Nina Mosley, Lonnie kneaded the insteps of her feet, pushing their troubles away.

SIX

Mother Suburb

One of the things that Bea liked about living in Evergreen was the full-day kindergarten at Alana's school. There was also valet service for pickup and drop-off so she didn't have to get out of the car.

"Hey, butterbean. Strap in."

"Did you bring a snack?" Alana leaned over the middle console.

"Hello to you too." Bea smiled at Alana through her rearview mirror.

"I'm so hungry."

Bea tossed a bag with cut-up apples over the seat to Alana.

"Apples? Really, Mom?"

"What were you expecting?"

"Something better."

Bea pulled away from the curb. "That's what's available unless you want to wait until you get home."

Alana pouted on the drive. Chico's school was around the corner and up the hill. Twice a week he had math enrichment and was released thirty minutes later than usual. When Bea pulled into the parking lot, she could see his bushy hair before his beautiful face. His Miami Heat T-shirt was too small but he insisted on wearing it at least once a week because Lonnie had bought it for him in Miami. The shirt made Bea cringe each time she saw him in it. She made a note to hide it after the next wash. At his old school in D.C. they wore uniforms—which Bea preferred—but that was a mostly minority school, where uniforms were the trend. For the life of her she couldn't understand why living in a lofty suburb meant that the children didn't have to worry about the social pressures and the distractions of the latest fad, but in the urban areas the children did.

Bea let Alana out of the car. Chico moved toward them, jumping and throwing a little ball with a redheaded boy. Bea smiled when her son was close enough to see her. Chico was always moving. It made her dizzy. He didn't acknowledge her as he blew past her with the friend, still playing. A woman with the same red hair approached the car. Bea had never seen her before.

"I'm Marianne."

"Beatrice."

"Nice to meet you. All Jack can talk about is Alonzo. I'd like to have him over for a playdate."

"That sounds good."

"You can drop him off at our house and I'll bring him home if that's easier for you." Bea looked the mother over. She fit the Evergreen mold pretty well: ponytail, sunglasses, smear of blush, faint pink on her lips, lululemon athletica yoga gear, and a cotton vest.

"How long have you lived in Evergreen?" asked Marianne.

"A few months now. This is our first school year."

"Where are you from?"

"Elizabeth."

"No, I meant before that?"

Bea got this question often, especially in Evergreen, and she loathed it. She despised diving into her ethnicity because it felt invasive. What the mom really wanted to know was why did Bea look the way she did, and why did her children.

"I'm Dominican."

"Both of your parents are Dominican?"

"My father was black and from here."

"Your husband must be something else, your daughter doesn't look anything like you."

"We come in all shades," Bea said in a tone meant to end the line of questioning.

"Well, the Dominican Republic is lovely. We went last year for a family vacation. Stayed at an all-inclusive with a kids' camp. Pure heaven."

Bea smiled politely.

"Here's my info." Marianne handed Bea a business card. It read: MARIANNE BRENNAN, MOTHER OF JACK AND JAMES, and listed her telephone number and e-mail address. Bea looked from the card to Marianne.

"It's more convenient this way. I've been doing cards since they were little."

Bea nodded. "Is this your cell? I'll text you my information."

When they got inside the car, Chico's brows were creased and his cheeks puffed out.

Bea buckled her seat belt. "What's wrong?"

"Why do you have to do that?"

"Do what?"

"Embarrass me."

She pulled out of her parking space and merged with the local traffic. "Huh? Embarrass you how?"

"By smiling at me."

"I embarrassed you by smiling?"

"Yes, don't smile at me in front of my friends. I'm not a baby like Alana."

"I'm not a baby," Alana piped in.

"Yes, you are."

She shoved him. He pushed back.

"Stop it. Now!"

The two settled into their own corners of the car.

"Still, Mom, don't, okay?"

Chico stared at Bea through the rearview mirror. He was the same dust color as Bea. Alana's creaminess was all Lonnie. She'd also inherited his easy-to-comb-through hair, what the girls she grew up with would call "dead hair," which meant it didn't need a lot of prodding and pulling to make it lay right.

"Chico, do you have everything you need for homework?"

He didn't respond.

"Do you?"

He blew his breath. "I keep telling you my name is not Chico. Please, call me Alonzo. It's on my birth certificate."

If she had talked to her mother like that when she was his age, she wouldn't have seen the backhand coming. Just tasted the blood in her mouth from where her upper lip crashed against her teeth from the force of her mother's smack. She and Lonnie parented the new way: much talking, time-outs, and loss of privileges. Most of the time it didn't work. When she turned onto Main Street, her phone chimed.

"Did you set up the get-together with Jack?"

"His mom will text me."

"Is that her now?"

Bea read the text at the red light. It was from Lonnie.

On the train. Be home for dinner.

Her heart swelled.

"I want a playdate too," cried Alana.

"You're too little."

"No, I'm not."

"Yes, you are, little baby."

"Moooom. Tell Chico I'm not a baby."

"My name is not Chico."

"Chico, Chico, Chico!" Alana screamed.

"Guys, enough."

They kept at it as Bea turned into her driveway, her mind going over her menu for dinner.

The kids completed their homework and had been getting along for five minutes over a game of Connect Four when Lonnie walked in through the back door. He had left that morning before Bea had gotten a chance to lay eyes on him, so when he walked in looking fresh and crisp in a gray woven suit and light blue shirt, it took her breath away.

"You look good."

"Thanks, babe." He leaned in and kissed her with his mouth and tongue. "I missed you."

She blushed. "Me too."

"What's for dinner?"

"Asparagus, skirt steak, and roasted rosemary potatoes."

"Sounds delicious. Will go perfect with these." He held up a bag from Magnolia Bakery, her favorite bakery in the West Village.

"Honey."

"Vanilla, your favorite."

"Thank you." She kissed him again. Alana ran into the kitchen. She hugged her father and followed him upstairs, chatting his ears off while he changed. Bea called to Chico to help her set the table.

Over dinner, everyone had a chance to discuss their day.

"Can we tell jokes?" asked Chico. "I have a good one. Your mama is so fat that when she walked by the TV, I missed three episodes."

Bea and Lonnie burst out laughing.

"Finally a good one," Bea told him.

"My turn. Your mama is so stupid she needs sunglasses to see in the rain."

"Okay." Bea laughed at Alana's joke.

"Dad, your turn."

"I don't have any jokes."

"Come on, Dad."

Lonnie put a chunk of steak into his mouth and pretended like he couldn't speak.

"I'll go," said Bea. "Fat and Skinny were in the bed. Fat made a fart and Skinny dropped dead."

The kids laughed so hard that Chico almost knocked over his juice.

"Okay, that's it for the jokes. Clean up after yourself and go get ready for bed if you want dessert. Dad bought me cupcakes and I don't mind sharing."

The kids got up from the table.

"Do I have to take a shower?" Alana asked.

"Yes, a quick one."

"Aw, man."

Bea pulled her over and whispered in her ear. "You can take one in our bathroom to make it faster."

The baby had started kicking and Bea rubbed her stomach to try to soothe her. Alana smiled and ran away.

Lonnie lingered at the table.

"We got a letter from Connie." She paused and watched his reaction. He looked at her, his eyes steady. "She wants to send him to private school because of the neighborhood. Asking you—us—to pay for it."

"What do you think?"

Bea had only been able to go to her private high school because her father had paid for it. Education was the least they could do.

"I'm fine with it. I took a look at the brochure and worked out the monthly numbers. It's doable."

"Whatever you think is best, babe. You're the boss there."

That's right, Bea thought as she stood and cleared off the table.

"What we need to be discussing are the details for your birthday party. It's coming up."

"I don't want a party in my condition. Too much hassle." She picked up their stacked dinner plates.

"I'll get this. Why don't you go relax?"

Bea smiled. "I better go check on Alana before she floods our bathroom."

Lonnie squeezed her behind as she walked by.

"Don't start nothing." She looked back at him.

"What time do the kids go to bed?"

"In an hour."

"Good, let's take a bath."

"Really?"

"You said you can get in the tub. I want to be close to you." His eyes kissed her skin.

"Okay." She blushed.

Bea got the kids into bed while Lonnie set up the bath. The feature that sold Bea on the house was the two-person Jacuzzi tub in the master bath. She didn't bathe often in it but she liked having the option when she wanted to soak.

"I'm going to need some help getting in," Bea said. Lonnie held her hand and helped her in. Bea sank into the sudsy water feeling her body sigh.

"I really should be doing this more, especially now at the end of the pregnancy."

Lonnie's phone was connected to the portable speakers and love songs from the 90s crooned.

"I used to love this song," Lonnie said. It was "Vision of Love" by Mariah Carey.

"Me too. What's happening with Mariah? Is she bouncing back from the divorce?"

"She was just in the news for canceling her concert at the last minute at Caesars in Vegas."

"Why?"

"Claimed to have bronchitis. Folks were pissed."

"Yeah, I would have been too. I know the tickets cost an arm and a leg."

"We should go out to Vegas once the baby is born. Leave the kids with your mom for a few days."

Bea sank deeper in the tub, letting the bubbles pool around her neck. "I'd be up for that. Long as the weather is warm. Last time we went we couldn't even use the outside pool."

"I hate that I have to leave you tomorrow for Chicago."

She brought her knees up out of the water. "You could give a little more notice."

"I just found out this morning. Been meaning to text you all day."

"For how long?"

"I think it's just overnight. What do you want to do this weekend?"

"I was thinking we could go to the Brooklyn Museum to see Kehinde Wiley's exhibit."

"Who's that?"

"You know, the artist that I like that used to have his work at the Studio Museum in Harlem. He does the pictures with the black folks in European portraiture."

"Oh, yeah, him," Lonnie said, and then he was on her.

Kissing her, caressing her, and sucking on her ear. The heat from his body and the warmth of the water enraptured Bea. She turned her brain off, quieted her worries, and allowed him to take her to that place where they connected. He was her husband.

SEVEN

TGIF

Lonnie gave Bea the sweetest kiss good-bye at the front door. A black sedan was at the curb waiting for him. His heavy cologne made Bea sneeze.

"You okay?"

"I might be allergic to you," she teased.

"I won't be gone long. I left some cash for you in my top drawer, rolled in my Jets sock. Have some fun, take the kids to dinner and a movie or something."

"I hate sleeping in this house alone."

"We live in one of the safest neighborhoods in the county. Just remember to do a safety check tonight and put the alarm on."

"We should get a dog."

"You said you didn't want another child." He patted her belly.

"I have an appointment today."

"Everything will be fine. Tell my favorite cousin hello." He squeezed her hand. "I better go, don't want to miss my flight."

"Miss your flight." She pulled on his tie. Bea didn't know why she was feeling so vulnerable. Lonnie traveled often for business and usually it felt like a vacation for her. Today, she really didn't want him to go. She stood in the doorway until his car turned the corner.

In the kitchen she nibbled on a bowl of granola and then filled her water bottle up before heading out to her car. She had about thirty minutes to get to her monthly doctor's appointment. Mena had already texted her three times that morning to remind her, as if she would forget.

They met in the lobby of Morristown Medical Center and hugged.

"Hey, chica." Mena held on tight. She was a beautiful woman with dark, black hair. When she let Bea go from their embrace, Bea noticed that she had added in hair extensions. Her makeup was also heavier.

"You look nice," Bea commented. She reminded Bea of one of those women on the Bravo show *The Real Housewives of New Jersey*.

"What's the occasion?"

"This." Mena smiled sheepishly.

"Well, you look fabulous, darling. No Clark today?"

"He had to be in court. But he wants me to take a few pictures of your belly if that's okay."

"Of course."

Bea checked in with the receptionist and then they took a seat in the lobby. *Live with Kelly* was on. The waiting room was nearly empty, with only one other expectant mother on her phone in the corner with her toddler playing with a rubber toy.

"How have you been feeling?" Mena dropped her hand onto Bea's belly.

"Good. Tired but good." Bea looked into Mena's eyes. "What's going on with you?"

"The cancer came back," Mena blurted.

Bea felt her heart stop and then restart. "Oh, Mena."

"It's under control and I should be fine. They've already started radiation. My doctor said I should be recovering fine by the time the baby is born. I just want my child. I just want to be a mother." Her eyes welled up.

"It's going to happen before you know it. Everything is going to be fine."

The medical assistant opened the door. "Beatrice Colon."

"That's us." Bea took Mena's hand.

"Room three."

Mena took a seat in the corner.

"Okay, step up on the scale."

"No," Bea replied tightly. Mena looked at her. "Please check my file."

"Oh, sorry."

The assistant checked Bea's blood pressure, pulse, and other vitals and then told her that the doctor would be with her shortly.

"How come you never want to know how much you weigh?"

"It's a mind thing. Did it with all of the pregnancies."

Mena opened her mouth to say more but the doctor knocked and then entered. "My buddy, Beatrice. How's it going?"

"Dr. Spellman, you cut your hair. It looks amazing."

"Thanks. Just trying to change things up a bit." She grinned. Her hair was chopped short on the sides with a curly, cherry-red 'fro on top. She was curvy under her white lab coat and wore peep-toe platform pumps.

"Well, you look young and hip."

"Thank you." She flipped open her chart. "Well, you're not doing so badly yourself. Your urine came back normal and your blood pressure looks fine. How have you been feeling?"

Bea felt like a seasoned pro at carrying babies. "Fine for the most part. This baby kicks all the time so I have a little trouble sleeping."

"Oh, Bea, I'm sorry she's keeping you up."

Bea smiled at Mena. "My knees have been bothering me."

"Have you been exercising?"

"Not nearly as much as I should."

"Get out and walk. Ten to twenty minutes a day. Nothing too strenuous. That should help. Let me look at you."

Dr. Spellman went through the examination, measuring Bea's uterus and listening to her chest and back. "You must be dying to hear your baby's heartbeat." She smiled at Mena.

"Yes, I am." Mena beamed. "Do you mind if I call my husband?"

"Of course, whatever you need."

Mena got Clark on the phone and the doctor put the Doppler device on Bea's belly, moving it around until she found the heartbeat.

"Hear it, babe?" Mena shouted to Clark.

"Yes, wow!" he replied.

"Everything looks good," said the doctor. "The baby is growing well. Heart rate is perfect. Keep doing what you're doing, Beatrice, and we will have a healthy baby in no time."

"Thanks, doc."

"Oh, Bea. I need five minutes with you to go over some quick paperwork. How about we meet in my office in ten minutes. You know where it is, right?"

"Yeah. Sure."

When the doctor left, Mena exhaled.

"Come here." Bea opened her arms to her. "Relax. Take care of yourself, get better, and I promise to deliver you a healthy baby girl. No more worrying."

"Okay, Bea. Thanks for everything."

"I'll stop by to see the nursery this weekend. I'll bring the kids."

"Yeah, that would be good. I need to be close to her. The treatment makes me so tired."

"I'll bring some food."

"Don't bother, Clark can fire up the grill."

"Okay. Oh, here, take your monthly pictures of my belly." Bea lifted her shirt. Mena snapped away.

"Thanks, Bea. I really don't know what I'd do without you. You're my angel."

Bea made her way into Dr. Spellman's office. She was waiting behind her cherry wood desk when she entered. Degrees from Johns Hopkins and the University of Pennsylvania hung on the wall along with a family portrait of her husband, daughter Cecily, and their dog.

"What's up?"

"How's the eating going?"

"Fine."

"Any new incidents I should know about? I got your e-mail."

Bea shifted in her seat. "No, I've been really good since then. I'm back on track."

"Have you been attending any of the support groups I suggested?"

"No, I've got it under control."

"Bea, we are at the home stretch. It's my job to give you as much support as possible. I really want you to attend a monthly meeting. It's only going to help." She put on her reading glasses and then scribbled on her notepad.

"This group meets at St. Barnabas the first Saturday of the month. If you go twice, the baby will be born." She slid the paper across the desk.

Bea pouted.

"You really are doing an amazing job. This group will just help you end well."

"Okay. Thanks, doc."

"My pleasure."

"How are the college applications going for Cecily?"

"Girl, that's a job in itself. Her dad wants her to go to an HBCU, either Hampton or Spelman. I'd like to see her at one of my alma maters. We will see where she ends up."

"I can't imagine applying for college. Just thinking about Chico going to high school in a few years freaks me out."

"It goes fast."

"So I hear." Bea pushed herself to stand. "Well, see you next month."

"Go to the meeting, Bea. Please," the doctor pleaded.

Bea held up the slip of paper and left the office. A support group was the last thing she wanted. They worked but they also depressed her, brought her disease to light when she was doing a good job of controlling it on her own. When she got to the parking lot, she let the paper go and watched it sail into the wind before falling to the ground.

EIGHT

Sleepover

The errand list for today was to stop at the grocery store to pick up some quick kid food—nuggets or something—since Lonnie wouldn't be home and to get his things from the dry cleaner. Usually the man who owned the business would help her carry her things to the car but it was only the wife behind the counter. So Bea had to make two trips. When she walked out with her last load, she bumped into her neighbor, Joney.

"Hey."

"Hi." Joney smiled and her whole face lit up. Joney was feminine and dainty but walked with purpose. When she spoke, it was like her whole body was shining from within. Bea could never put her finger on Joney's inner mystery but she desperately wanted her secret.

"How are the kids?"

"Fine. Winding down the school year. Thank goodness. I'm ready for the break in the schedule."

"I remember those days. Now, mine barely call."

Bea's expression dropped.

"They prefer FaceTime or Skype." Joney added, "I'm running to the electronics store now to pick up my laptop. My lovely dog spilled my tea on it. Keep your fingers crossed for me that it still works."

"It will."

Joney rubbed Bea's belly. "Ready to birth this angel?"

"Almost. Is it still okay for the kids to come over when I go into labor?"

"Yes, of course. They'll be fun. It's been so long since I've had little people to make cookies with."

"Thanks, Joney, it really means a lot to me. I've packed them a little bag so they can have a few basic things. I'll drop it off this week."

"If I'm not there just leave it on the porch. No one will bother it." Joney looked up at the sky and then smacked her hand against her forehead. "Did you hear about the home invasion that happened yesterday?"

"No."

"Oh my God. Only a few blocks from us. The man beat the woman up in front of her children and then robbed the place."

"In this town?"

"No one can believe it. Honestly, I don't like to keep negative energy going in my vibration but this one has been hard to shake."

"Thanks for telling me. I never have time to watch the news."

"I don't either. It's filled with such garbage. Every story is a horrific murder or child abuse, or a robbery gone wrong. It's terrible. How can people sleep at night with all of that fear that the media is pumping? I wouldn't even want to know this but since it happened so close, everywhere I go people are talking about it."

"I'm surprised Lonnie didn't hear about it. He's my news guy."

"Well, just be safe, but honestly, don't linger on it too long. I'm going to a special Yin yoga class tonight to clean up my energy. I need to put this past me; it's really interfering with my sleep." She waved to Bea and headed in the opposite direction.

The news was all Bea could think about. As soon as she got into her house, she locked the back door, which she never did, and scanned for the news on her tablet. She came across a video and watched it.

Breaking news: An intruder entered a home in Evergreen. Beat a woman with his bare hands in front of her children and then robbed the place. It was all caught on the nanny cam.

Bea found herself tightening as she watched, hoping that the man wasn't any shade of brown. The incident took place three blocks from her house. That could have been her. She always left a window open and sometimes the sliding glass door to the patio for the fresh air. The broadcast flashed a picture of the man. He was big and black. Bea grabbed her cell phone and dialed Awilda.

"I need you to come stay the night with me."

"Why, where's the hubby?"

Bea explained.

"Slumber party it is then. It will be my pleasure to spend a night away from that man. Wait until I tell you what the fool has done now."

Bea was too frazzled to cook and instead ordered pizza and a Greek salad. She put a movie on for Alana and let Chico play the Xbox, while Awilda helped herself to Lonnie's liquor cabinet.

"This is supposed to be the crème of the suburbs. I can't even afford to rent a damn apartment on this side of town. Don't make sense to pay all of that and not be safe."

"Girl, my nerves are wrecked. Safety and school district were Lonnie's biggest selling points." Bea sat down on the love seat. Awilda sat in the reclining chair. "Remember that time that someone broke into Mrs. Lobo's apartment down the hall from me?"

"We were shaking in our boots because your mom left us in the house by ourselves to get her hair done."

Bea laughed. "The hallway was crawling with cops. I was scared that they were going to knock on the door and ask us if we'd seen anything."

"They did knock, remember? We hid in your mother's closet and turned off the lights and the TV trying to pretend that no one was there."

"Oh, yeah. Then we crept to the window and tried to listen to what was happening on the fire escape."

"That was when my mother had a beeper. I remember beeping her and putting in nine-one-one."

"I used to beep my boyfriend sixty-nine."

"'Cause you're fresh." Bea made eyes at Awilda. "I beeped mine sixty-eight. I owe you one."

"You wasn't doing nothing, Bea, but pretending to be down."

"I was down enough."

"If I were more like you I wouldn't have ended up pregnant with Amare."

Bea pulled the throw over her. "Derrick was always a good guy. If it had to happen with anyone, better him than some of those other knuckleheads."

"Derrick and his mother went behind my back and applied for disability."

"What's wrong with that? My mother lives off hers."

"It means he can't legally work again. Period. He's in the system."

"I thought he was managing things?"

"Me too." Awilda sucked her teeth. "Bea, I'm not trying to have a grown-ass man sitting up in the house all day watching *Jerry Springer* and *Judge Judy*."

"Those shows still come on?"

"They didn't even consult me, just went behind my back and filed."

"Did Derrick say why?"

"Because his mother thought it was a good idea. How the hell did I end up with such a mama's boy? I swear before God, if I hadn't been pregnant . . ."

"Stop it, Wilde. Let me fix you another drink." Bea leaned forward to get up off the sofa but Awilda stopped her.

"Girl, sit, I got it. You want anything?"

"Bring me a bowl of popcorn and a little seltzer—"

"With ice, I know."

Awilda returned, put the bowl in front of Bea, and took the remote back to her seat. She had a mixed drink and a napkin filled with chocolate-chip cookies.

"Man, this is like old times." She plopped down. "Want me to comb out your messy hair?"

Bea felt her bun. "I might take you up on that later. But you can grab the polish and paint my toes."

"How come you haven't gone for a pedicure?"

"I haven't had the time. Please?"

"Only 'cause you're pregnant, heffa." Awilda went into the powder room and came back with Bea's bag of polishes.

"Oooh, this one." Bea picked out raging red. Awilda settled down on the floor in front of her and placed Bea's foot in her lap.

"I often think about our weekends together growing up. Your place was the highlight of my week. I couldn't wait to get out of North Plainfield and be free of my mother."

"I always liked your mother."

"That's 'cause you didn't live with her. Remember her announcing that we were vegans when I was like fifteen?"

"She used to send your food to my house and everything."

"And it went right in the garbage."

Bea sipped her seltzer. "We used to eat so much on those weekends."

"If my mother knew I was over there eating Ding Dongs and Pop-Tarts instead of brown rice and tofu she would have had a fit."

"Sure would have."

"You still spitting up?"

The seltzer went down the wrong pipe and Bea coughed. "Huh?"

Awilda reached up and patted Bea's back. "You remember how we use to eat a ton and then throw it all up? I don't have the stomach for that anymore but it was cool in high school. Kept the pounds off. You remember?"

Bea dropped her shoulders, relieved. "Oh, girl. I haven't done that since that time we were rolling around on my bathroom floor."

Awilda looked up at Bea.

"Wilde, we ate everything we could get our hands on and then washed it down with my mother's coconut concoction."

"That drink was always her specialty. She could really make some money off of it."

"I think she was for a while, selling it to people in the building and for parties. Little extra income after my father died to make ends meet."

Awilda placed Bea's right foot on the ground and then put the left one in her lap. "You mother was a godsend. If it wasn't for her, I wouldn't have had any place to go once I got knocked up with Amare."

"Well, you know Irma loves you."

"My mother cared more about what her congregation thought. That's her problem. Always putting on airs."

"She is the first lady."

"So what? I'm her daughter. She went to great lengths to keep up appearances. So ready to drop me off at your mom's so she could follow my father around."

"Well, you coming over got me out into the real world. I never liked being an only child."

Awilda blew on Bea's toes. "Still, I'd never do that to Amare."

"I love that boy. He's so good with Chico."

"Yeah, my boy is going to be somebody. Despite my mother trying to get me to abort him. Now she worships the ground he walks on. At every game."

"Okay, this conversation is going in the toilet. I thought you came over to make me feel good?"

Awilda admired her work. "I've painted your old crusty toes."

"Do they look good? You know I can't even see my lady flower anymore."

"How do you know it's clean?"

"I can wash it, fool, I just can't see it."

Awilda held onto the end table and pulled herself up to a stand. "They look good, just don't move until they dry because I'm not getting down on this floor again. Man, I'm getting old."

"You have the remote. What do you want to watch?"

"Something trifling." Awilda clicked on the television and the surround sound from the TV burst into the room. "Damn, that's a beautiful picture. When the hell did you get a new television?"

"Girl, it's Lonnie's pride and joy. I can barely work the thing. He bought it as a birthday gift to himself last month."

"I know where the next Super Bowl party will be. Can't have ya'll over now watching my floor-model tube."

"No way. I wouldn't miss Derrick's hot wings and those barbeque shrimp for anything in the world."

"We can certainly bring them over." Awilda chuckled. "This picture is everything."

They watched a reality show on VH1 that Bea would have never caught on her own but once they started it, she couldn't tear herself away.

"So, wait, who is her baby's father?"

Awilda pointed to the screen. "He is, but he's also married to her sister."

"What?"

"I told you. Ratchet."

They watched two more episodes of the show before Bea called it a night.

"So glad it's the weekend."

"Who you telling?"

"You might as well come up and sleep in the playroom."

"This is good right here." Awilda patted the leather chair. "Just throw me down a pillow."

Bea woke up to the smell of buttermilk pancakes and coffee. Her belly felt heavy as she pushed herself to look at the digital clock on her nightstand. Man. She hadn't remembered sleeping so late in weeks. Perhaps it was because she had the whole bed to herself, she thought, tying her robe around her.

Lonnie was home. She could hear him laughing with Awilda in the kitchen. Bea took her time brushing her teeth, combed her hair into a neat ponytail, and washed her face while humming a tune that was in her head. When she trudged down the stairs, Lonnie smiled.

"Good morning, sleepyhead." Lonnie reached for Bea and folded her into his arms. "I've missed you."

"You do see me standing here," Awilda cracked. She wore a long T-shirt and leggings. Her bushy hair was all over her head. A plate of pancakes, eggs, and a mug of coffee sat in front of her. Bea craved the coffee.

"Is this decaf?" She lifted Awilda's cup to her nose.

"No dear, the real thing."

Bea took a gulp. "So good. As soon as I drop this little girl I'm going to have coffee for a week."

"What did the doctor say?"

"Everything is fine with me but Mena had a relapse."

"With the cancer?"

Bea nodded her head. "She's a mess."

"We should go over there."

"Yeah, I told her we would. She said Clark would throw something on the grill."

"Speaking of grills. What's the plan for your birthday, Bea? We need a party to come to."

"We aren't having a barbeque this year. It's too much."

"You have it every year. Everyone looks forward to it. It's like a national holiday."

"Actually," said Lonnie, "I've come up with an idea that might work."

Bea threw him a look. The last thing she wanted was a bunch of people parading around her house and yard, leaving a mess that she would have to clean up.

"I'm hiring everything out. The food, the cleaning, everything. This year we will just mix, mingle, and not lift a finger."

"Ooh, big spender," Awilda teased. "I'm scared of you."

"Lonnie, I don't need all of that."

Awilda did her best impression of the old lady in the subway scene from the movie *Coming to America*, when Akeem was trying to get Lisa to marry him. "Go ahead, honey, take a chance."

Bea cracked up. It was one of their favorite movie scenes and always made them laugh.

"I feel like I'm being set up. I'll think about it."

"What's there to think about?" Awilda pushed.

"I'll take that for now," coaxed Lonnie.

"You still have to make a pot of chili for the chili dogs, Lonnie. Don't outsource that."

"I wouldn't dream of it. You know that's the North Plainfield tradition, baby." Lonnie high-fived Awilda.

"Woot-woot, Canuck."

"Two cornballs."

"You missed out on the fun, Bea, going to that all-girls Catholic school." Awilda made a face.

"Even if I went to your high school I wouldn't have hung out with either of you."

"Then you would have been bored because we were it."

"Only has-beens still talk about high school a million years later."

Awilda turned. "Lon, did you hear about Lolita Bravehardt?"

He shook his head.

Awilda filled him in on one of their old classmates and before she knew it, they were having a conversation all by themselves. Bea watched the ease with which they communicated.

Chico ran into the kitchen. "Ma, can I play the Xbox?"

"For one hour."

"You time him?" asked Awilda.

"I have to or that boy will be on the game like it's a part-time job."

"That's how Amare is too."

"Wilde told me about the home invasion. Why didn't you call me?" Lonnie suddenly remembered.

"It's not like you could come back. You were in the air when I found out and I didn't want to worry you."

"It's my job to worry about you."

"Well, that's why I'm here. You know I took karate." Awilda put her legs in the stance position and karate chopped the air.

Lonnie mimicked a karate move and the two went back and forth chopping each other.

"Children." Bea smiled.

"Okay, family, my work here is done. I've got a shitload of things to do today. Enjoy your Saturday."

Awilda left the kitchen and Bea could hear her calling out her farewells to the kids.

"I missed you." Lonnie caught Bea's eye. He wore an orange polo shirt that brought out the undertones of his skin.

"Honey."

"When's the last day of school?"

"Tuesday."

"We should go somewhere. Do we have plans for Fourth of July?"

"I can't get on a plane in my condition." She started removing the dishes from the island and stacking them in the sink.

"What if it's someplace we can drive to? Like D.C. You love D.C. I'll see if I can get tickets to the Nationals game. The kids would love that. We could ride through the old neighborhood."

Bea felt happy all over. When things were good between them, they were amazing. With all of her doubts about Lonnie, he was a family man at heart and that's all she had ever wanted in a husband. A man who was the opposite of her father: present and involved with his children. Her mother was right. Bea was lucky.

"Okay, if that's what you want." She started washing the dishes.

He was behind her at the sink with his face nestled in her ear. Bea thought of the last time they were in this position and how uptight she had been, worrying over the dirty dishes and the kids walking in. She pushed herself to relax in his arms.

Lonnie licked her lobe. "What I want is to throw you a birthday party."

"Babe."

"Please, Bea, it brings me joy to celebrate the woman of my life." His hands traveled up to her breasts and cupped them both while kissing her neck. She tried not to squirm.

"Please," he breathed.

"Okay. Just don't go overboard."

"When do I ever go overboard?"

She turned toward him and kissed his lips. "Don't. I mean it. Keep it simple."

NINE

Anything But

Bea woke on the morning of her birthday party. It was the official first day of summer and she felt sweaty and off-center. She couldn't put words to what she was feeling. Dread maybe, but that didn't sum it all up for her. Hungry for sure. On Wednesday, she and Mena had gone in for a doctor's visit. Dr. Spellman knew Bea well enough to read in her body language that she had not attended the support group.

"End of pregnancy is the hardest time and you need a lifeline, Bea," she implored.

"I've been doing great," Bea coaxed. "Things are going well."

When Dr. Spellman realized that she couldn't convince her, she switched tactics.

"At the very least download an app to track your calories."

That Bea could agree to. Two thousand, five hundred calories was her maximum per day, but it was her birthday party and she wanted a slice of her cake. Bea decided to give herself an extra three hundred calories just for the occasion. Big events made it hard to stay focused on her goal of not overeating, but she was determined to take it slow. She had been anticipating a good Cuban sandwich, Derrick's barbeque shrimp, and a scoop of Awilda's potato salad all week. She got out of bed, hoping Awilda had remembered to ask Derrick about the shrimp. Her mobile was on the nightstand so she sent her a quick text.

When she got downstairs and looked out into her yard, she could see that Lonnie had indeed gone over the top. Purple, white, and pink balloons swung high in the air. A bouncy house had been set up for the kids on one side of the yard, with seating in the middle and the food stations and grill to the left. Lonnie had also set up a game section for the kids with a real poker table and dealer, horseshoes, and a chessboard. As Bea watched Lonnie with his clipboard directing traffic, she wondered if the party was really for her or for him.

She made herself two boiled eggs (140 calories) and smeared an English muffin with a tablespoon of peanut butter (200 calories). She'd have to eat a salad for lunch with no dressing to stay on track. She wondered where the children were as she ate her breakfast in silence. After she straightened up the kitchen, she was antsy. If she went into the yard, she would get involved with the party preparations and that was the last thing she wanted so she decided to go for a walk instead. The exercise would help with the extra calories. Bea moved from the kitchen to the mudroom where she kept her sneakers. On the bench she slipped her sneakers on but she couldn't reach past her belly to tie them.

"Chico?" she called.

"Yes."

"Come here, son."

"Where are you?"

"In here."

He appeared in the doorway, moving his fingers over his phone.

"Can you tie my shoes?"

"Really, Mom?"

"Really, son."

He knelt down and tied them. "Where are you going?"

"For a walk."

"Can I come?"

Bea tried masking her surprise by keeping her eyes even. "Yeah, sure. What's Alana doing?"

"In the yard helping Daddy wipe down the chairs."

"Okay, let's sneak out."

It was rare that Bea got to spend time with Chico alone. He was always more interested in his electronics or following his father around. Baseball was winding down and swim practice had begun two weeks ago. Already he had a shade of a tan.

"Someone hasn't been applying the sunscreen before swimming." She tugged on his ears. He always needed a haircut.

"I do, sometimes," Chico confessed.

"Mmm. Did any of your classmates try out for the team?"

"Nope."

"Do you recognize any of the kids from school?"

"Like one boy, he sits at my lunch table. But that's all."

"Is it diverse?"

"There's another brown kid on the team. They call him KJ."

Bea treaded lightly. As a parent, she wanted to empower her son with a strong sense of self without burdening him with her experience of race and color. On the one hand, she understood that kids saw other kids as age mates, but on the other, she was protective and concerned about him being mistreated. She needed to make sure that he was okay as a minority in this new town, because sometimes she wasn't.

"How does that make you feel?"

"Weird sometimes." He jumped to catch an imaginary football, then used her back to do a spin move. "Like I just wish I was white. Like Daddy."

"Your dad is Cuban and Italian, son. You know that."

"He doesn't speak Spanish."

"That's because no one taught him, but that doesn't change his heritage."

"Still."

Bea's jaw tightened. "Go on."

"I don't know. Don't take this the wrong way, Mom, but it just seems easier."

They turned the corner and started moving toward the park. Bea's thoughts were racing. She took a breath and concentrated on saying the right words.

"Chico, you have a lot of wonderful blood mixed up inside of you—"

"We were watching *The Watsons Go to Birmingham* at school last week and everyone was looking at me," he interrupted.

"I like that movie, it's an important moment in the history of this country."

"It's all a bunch of fighting."

"Sometimes you have to fight, son. If you don't stand for something you will fall for anything. Do you know who said that?"

"Nope."

"Malcolm X, and he was a man about change."

"I've heard of him."

"I still have his autobiography, somewhere. I think I read it when I was in eighth grade. Maybe we can read it together."

"Can we swing by the basketball court so I can see if anyone is there?"

Bea knew that it was all he could handle in one conversation.

"Sure." She ruffled his hair.

The seed was there. She needed to keep talking to him. She needed to give him more history lessons and make her son proud of the shoulders he stood on, instead of ashamed.

The party was in full swing by the time Mena and Clark arrived. Mena looked great in her pink shift dress and hair extensions. When she spotted Bea lounging in her special chair, decorated with pink ribbons and two floating HAPPY BIRTHDAY balloons attached to it, she finger waved and then made her way over. Clark was in tow.

"How's my princess doing?" He dropped his hand over Bea's belly.

"She might be into trucks and balls." Mena teased him.

"Your baby is doing wonderfully. I can feel the kicks up here. I think the doctor will tell us on the next visit that she is almost in position and ready to join your family."

"Bea, you're making us so happy." Mena squeezed her hand.

Clark stood. "Where's my boy?"

"Probably somewhere either directing traffic or playing horse-shoes."

Clark headed off and Mena dropped her head onto Bea's stomach. She whispered to the baby. "Hello there, it's Mama. I can't wait to meet you and kiss all of your fingers and toes. Mama loves you." When she sat up, she had a shine to her face. "I can't wait to hold my baby, Bea. You have no idea."

"I know. It's going to be life changing. You ready?"

"I'm so ready."

"That's what we all say. We never really are, but that's the beauty of it."

Mena moved her seat closer to Bea. "I need to talk to you about something." Her eyes were serious.

"Okay."

"Bea, I want to compensate you for this."

"Mena there's no . . ."

"Hear me out. I was thinking it could stay between us. I want to give you a little something for a rainy day. Lonnie and Clark do not have to know."

"Mena, I can't take your money."

"Listen, I looked up the going rate for surrogates and the price is astounding. We talked about this in the beginning."

"And Lonnie and I both agreed that we didn't want your money."

"This isn't about what Lonnie wants," Mena said sternly.

Bea looked at her.

"Honey, I know you have done this out of the kindness of that big old heart of yours. But please, let me do something for you that will make me feel good. Please don't make me beg, Bea. It means a lot to me."

Bea tapped Mena's hand. "Okay, Mena, whatever you want."

"Thanks, Bea. Thanks for seeing things my way."

They sat back and watched the crowd. The music was Latin funk and three little girls stood in the middle of the grass and danced. Bea caught a glimpse of Awilda walking into the yard. As always, Awilda looked like it was her party. She was alone and moved with confidence in a baby doll dress that stopped three inches above her knee, with big, natural hair and a fiery lipstick. Bea would kill to look that good in this moment. Next to Awilda, she felt like Humpty Dumpty.

"Clark and I would like for you and Lonnie to serve as godparents."

"Really?"

"Yes. There is no better godmother than the one who has carried my child. If anything was to ever happen to me, Bea . . ." Mena's voice trailed.

"Hey, don't think like that, Mena. You have to stay positive. How are the treatments going?"

Mena shook her head and rubbed her nose with the back of her hand. Bea noticed Joney moving through the yard, sure-footed and stunning. Bea reached her hand up and waved. Joney smiled brightly and waved back, tumbling her hair behind her.

"You're right about being positive. I've been reading this daily affirmation book and it has helped."

"Good, it all adds up."

Mena stood, wiping her hands on her dress. "I'm gonna get a plate. You want anything?"

"Not yet, thanks." Bea fanned herself.

"Lonnie said he had the caterer make *ropa vieja*. I sure hope it tastes as good as Nana's. I've been craving comfort food."

"That will go nicely with the potato salad."

"Is it that pink one Irma made? What did she put in it, beets?"

Bea nodded her head. "That's the Dominican version. My girl-friend Awilda made it. Old-school Southern black style. You'll have to try it."

"Sounds good." Mena winked and then was off.

Joney stood in front of Bea. "You look ripe and beautiful, dar-ling."

"Like a watermelon?"

"Like a flower with the petals in full bloom."

"Aw, thanks, Joney. How's it going?"

"There are no worries worth complaining about."

"I hear that. How's the yoga?"

"It's been amazing. As soon as you have the baby I'm dragging you to class with me."

Bea made her eyes wide. "I might just take you up on that. Have you eaten?"

"That's what I've come over for. You can smell the food from Main Street." She headed toward the buffet.

Bea watched the party buzz around her, wedged up in everyone's glee. The children's laughter rang out and every appreciating nod told her that it was a good party. Awilda teetered over to Bea clutching a plastic cup. When she sat next to her, Bea could see the fruit floating around on top.

"Didn't your mother tell you that you never show up and outshine the birthday girl?"

"You look beautiful, Beasley. I like those earrings. And look at that hair. 'Bout time you let it down." Awilda leaned in and air-kissed her.

"Did Derrick make my barbeque shrimp?"

"Yes, he was up at the crack of dawn making his special sauce. No one knows the recipe but him."

"You make the potato salad?"

"Just the way you like it: a little extra mustard but light on the celery. Hungry heifer."

"I've been saving my calories all week for that." Bea looked at Awilda's drink. "All I need now is that glass of sangria you're holding."

"It's a mama juana. Here." Awilda thrust the glass in her direction. "You can have a little sip."

"Chile, please, Mena would kill me. She's nervous enough as it is."

"She doesn't have to know. I'll pour a little—"

"Sis, I was kidding. You better be careful, don't drink more than a shot or two. That mixture will sneak up on you and have you doing freaky things."

"Umph." Awilda sipped.

"They say it's an aphrodisiac. Where are your menfolk anyway? I didn't see Derrick walk in with you."

"He's holed up back at the house with a case of beer and the re-mote. Told you the disability shit wasn't a good idea. With Amare down at my mother's, and Derrick and I constantly alone, I've come to the realization that I can't stand that man." Her face grew dark.

"Stop that. He's going through a rough patch."

"Rough my ass."

"You took vows, in sickness and in health. And he's sick. He hasn't cheated on you, hasn't beat you. Have mercy."

Awilda pursed her lips and blew her breath.

"Your makeup looks pretty."

Bea warmed at the compliment. "I feel like my nose is ginor-mous."

"It's not." Awilda started moving Bea's hair around on her shoul-ders. "There, perfect picture."

Bea blushed.

"Let's take a selfie." Awilda held up her phone and took the pic-ture. "I need more alcohol. Want anything?"

"I'm going to make myself a plate in a minute. I really don't want to get up because that means I'm going to have to talk to people."

"When did you become antisocial?"

"I just can't, Wilde."

"Who are you and where is Bea?"

"I don't know." Bea giggled. "A pregnant woman who doesn't feel like being bothered."

Awilda's dress swished around her round tail as her platform heels gobbled up the grass. Bea caught one of Lonnie's married coworkers watching her walk.

Just then, Alana came over to her, crying because one of the cous-ins pulled her hair.

"Let Mommy fix it," she said, smoothing her daughter's hair and planting a warm kiss on her forehead. Bea went and made herself a plate. She opted for the pulled pork slider, a big scoop of potato salad, two servings of barbeque shrimp, and Cuban corn on the cob. If she was lucky she had about one hundred and fifty calories left for cake.

"Let me carry that for you." Clark intercepted her plate. "What do you want to drink?"

She wanted punch but she told him a bottle of water. She ate as slowly as she could. It helped being at a table and mingling with some of the guests. Most of them were Lonnie's friends. Bea could count on one hand the people who'd actually come to see her. As soon as she'd had her last bite, Lonnie came over with the cake and everyone sang "Happy Birthday."

"Thank you," she said and then asked Lonnie to cut her a small piece. He heaped a good-sized one onto her plate and instead of complaining she ate it down to the last crumb and then licked her spoon. She was sure she had exhausted her calories but since it was her party, she decided to take a break from beating herself up and try her best to enjoy the moment.

The sun sank, half the children scrambled inside to the family room to watch television, and the other half went up to the playroom for video games. It was adult hour. Cigarettes were out and the laughter got louder. Bea noticed her younger cousin Benny and his friend heading to the garage. Her mind flashed to the gun case that she kept in there but it was locked and the key was hidden. So there was no danger. She had allowed her twentysomething cousins to smoke marijuana in the garage at Easter. Apparently since she'd said yes once, they didn't even bother to ask. Lonnie had told her the first time she let them how shocked he was at her being so liberal. They all laughed about it now and called the garage the boom-boom room. When Bea looked over, Awilda was heading in there. That girl.

Lonnie pulled up a chair next to her. His eyes glistened. Bea could tell that he was juiced up and jolly.

"Having a good time?"

"Not as much as you."

"It's a beautiful night. Look at our beautiful people. Think everyone had a good time?"

That was always Lonnie's concern, that the people who entered their home had fun.

"I think so."

"Are you happy?"

"I'm not unhappy."

"It's not the same as being happy. What can I do to make you happy?"

Awilda was holding onto the arm of Bea's younger cousin and heading to the bar.

"I think you are going to have to drive Wilde home since Derrick isn't here. She's been going hard all night." Bea pointed as Awilda stumbled and Benny caught her.

"Only if you promise to be waiting for me in that sexy sheer number I like."

"As if that fits."

"Really, you can just wait for me in nothing at all. I'm not picky."

"You're talking like a drunk man. You sure you can drive her?"

"Is the grass green? Just remember what I said." He blew her a kiss and stood. He punched the air with his hand and the DJ faded the song he was playing and spun Bea's favorite song by Rihanna, "Don't Stop the Music."

"Dance with me." Lonnie held his hand out to her. Bea took it.

"You're always up to something."

"It's all for you."

Bea popped her head and snapped her fingers. Lonnie pretended like he couldn't get up on her because of her belly and they both laughed. Bea danced to three songs before the exhaustion kicked in.

On her way to find a seat, people doled out hugs, great birthday wishes, and their so longs.

Bea was on the sofa with her feet up on the ottoman. The crew was in the yard breaking everything down. Her children were in bed, dirty and dreaming about the fun they'd had. Lonnie sauntered in. Seeing him gave Bea a rush to her head. He was handsome in his crème linen shirt and shorts, hair combed away from his face.

"Wilde okay?"

"She was drunk as a skunk." He slipped out of his leather Bally shoes and moved toward the armchair barefooted. Bea always thought he had pretty feet. "What's going on with her and Derrick?"

Bea shook her head. "They're not doing well. Why? What did she say?"

"She went from happy to sad in like point-five seconds. Crying and babbling."

"Like tears?"

"Yes. I had to search in the glove compartment for tissue. Then she started up with how she needed to get out more, her life was so boring, and how she just wanted to have sex."

"She said that to you?" Bea sat up.

Lonnie chuckled. "Not with me, babe. You know we are like brother and sister. I guess she meant with her husband."

"Still. That girl can be so inappropriate. You'd never know she was a preacher's daughter."

"So what's happening with them?"

Bea told Lonnie about Derrick losing his job, the disability, beer, and TV.

"I'll call him or swing by and check on the brother this week." Lonnie slid into the seat next to Bea. "Kids asleep?"

"Knocked out. Didn't even brush their teeth."

Lonnie wrapped his arms around Bea and she could smell every drink he had consumed. It made her feel nauseous.

"You ready for our trip?" He nibbled on her ear.

"Not at all. It's still a week away."

"When do you want to tell the children?"

"Tomorrow sounds good."

He put his hand on her thigh but Bea couldn't even pretend to be in the mood. She pushed his hand away.

"I'm tired, sweetie."

Lonnie's eyes flashed. "Okay."

When they got upstairs, he reached for her under the covers, moving his hand down her thigh.

"Can you just hold me?" she pleaded, rolling away from him.

He nodded his head and buried his face in her hair, snoring before Bea was anywhere close to asleep.

TEN

The Low Down

The next few days found Bea putting her house back together in the aftermath of the party, changing the children's closets over from winter to summer clothes, and sorting what needed to be donated. They had both outgrown their summer things from the previous year, so she spent two straight days running between the Mall at Short Hills and Livingston, stocking up on shorts, sundresses, and T-shirts. Bea didn't like to shop online, she preferred to touch and feel the items she bought. Since her family was going away, she skipped the open-air market with Awilda on Wednesday and opted to cook and get rid of the items that were in her fridge so there wouldn't be any waste.

When Awilda's picture flashed on her cellular phone the day of their D.C. trip, she realized they hadn't actually spoken in a week.

"Every sister ain't a sister," she teased.

"Girl, you know my life is crazy. But I need a big favor."

"What do you need?"

"Can you come to the school and lend me a quick hand?"

"Can't. Getting ready to head down to D.C."

"Please, Beasley. I need help breaking down my classroom for the summer. It has to happen today."

"So you call the pregnant woman?"

"I'm not asking you to get on a ladder. Just come help me organize a few things."

Bea blew her breath. "Can't you get a coworker?"

"I don't trust none of these bitches in here with my stuff."

"Wilde," she complained.

"Pretty please with cherries on top. I wouldn't ask you if I didn't need you."

"Yes, you would."

"Come on, Bea."

"I can give you an hour. Not a minute more. I have things to do too."

Bea hung up the telephone. The list of road snacks that she needed to pick up was on the counter. She folded it in half and then shoved it into her shorts pocket. Awilda's school was practically a straight shot from Bea's house and it wasn't long before she was wheeling her car into an empty spot. She dabbed at the sweat on her brows while texting Awilda to come and get her. She could never find her way through the maze of the school to Awilda's classroom.

Awilda burst out of the door in a hot-pink blouse and gray pencil pusher pants. "Thank you so much." Awilda wrapped her arms around Bea.

"Don't thank me yet. I'm only staying an hour."

Awilda led Bea through the hallway past the seventh grade lockers and up the stairs.

"I hope that's not your outfit for the trip."

Bea had on a black shirt and a pair of faded jean shorts that she'd worn when she was pregnant with Chico.

"What's wrong with what I'm wearing? I'm going to be in the car for four hours. This is comfortable."

"Bea, you're going away with your man. You can do better. Put on that maxi dress you wore last time we went to the open-air market." Awilda turned into her classroom.

Bea rolled her eyes.

"And a little lip gloss and mascara. Look happy."

"I'm not happy to help you with this classroom mess." She looked around while repinning her bun. "Dag, it's hot. Don't you have AC?"

"It's out. Repair man is working on it now."

"What do you want me to do?"

"Start over here. Just sort this pile for me in alphabetical order."

Bea sat behind the desk. Awilda had all the windows open wide and her iTunes was open on her computer, playing a song by Miguel.

"You were out of control on the night of my party."

"Girl, I shouldn't have smoked that joint with your little cousin. I was out of my mind. I woke up and didn't even remember how I got home, let alone into the bed."

"Lonnie drove you and you . . ."

"Did I embarrass myself? Please don't say I embarrassed myself in front of your company." Awilda's eyes pleaded. Bea thought about telling her what she'd said to Lonnie but decided not to. Nearly a week had passed since the party and she didn't want to come off sounding insecure and whiny.

"You just don't want to be that messed up out in the street. Something could happen to you."

"I wasn't in the street. I was at my best friend's house and I knew you would take good care of me. Like always." She stood on a chair and started pulling things down from her bulletin board. "You know your home is the only house I can just show up to without calling? I can't even do that with my mother."

Bea stacked the first pile and moved onto the next. "What's up with Derrick?"

"Same."

"I'm going to swing by and see him. I never thanked him for the barbeque shrimp. They were his best ever."

"He'd like to see you. Been holed up in the house getting fat."

"Maybe you two should head down to the beach this weekend."

"With what money? He hasn't gotten his first"—she made quotation marks with her fingers—"'disability check' yet so everything has been falling on me."

Bea looked down at the papers she was sorting. She made it a rule not to offer Awilda money because it was so easy for her to get swept up in fixing her problems.

"Something's bound to change."

"From your lips to God's ears. Here, work on this too."

Bea's phone chimed. It was Lonnie, texting that he would be home early. That relaxed Bea enough to get swept up in Awilda's gossip on a budding romance between two teachers in the building.

"One of them is married. His wife comes bearing fresh-baked cookies to every holiday party."

The conversation made Bea stay longer than the intended hour. When she got to the store, she was behind schedule and even more so once she reached home.

"Hey, baby." Lonnie kissed her cheek and took the reusable bags from her hands. His leather duffle bag rested against the back door.

Bea's mind raced. "Where're the kids?"

"Upstairs playing the Xbox."

"Are they ready to go?" she snapped.

"I think so. What's wrong?"

"I just hate being off schedule."

"We're fine. It's not like we have to be there at a particular time."

"Can you pack the snacks for the car while I get the rest of my things together?"

"I was about to check in with the office."

"Forget it." The pressure of getting everyone out of the house and making sure they didn't forget anything was too much all of a sudden. Anxiety had hunkered down in the middle of her chest. When was the last time she had eaten?

Lonnie's eyes took her in. "What do I need to pack?"

She sat at the counter and peeled a banana. "Just make little baggies for them from the snacks that I just bought. Can you pour me a glass of milk?"

He placed the glass in front of her and she drank it down in a few gulps. After her banana, she went upstairs.

"Chico, turn that game off. We were supposed to leave an hour ago."

"But you weren't here."

"Did you pack your toothbrush?"

"Yes, Mom."

Bea went into her room. The carry-on that she had brought down from the attic was opened on her bed and she threw in a few outfits. Where was her toiletries bag? She stood in the middle of her bathroom going over her list in her head, hoping she didn't forget anything essential. She usually put so much energy into preparing everything for her family when they traveled that she always forgot something vital like panties or deodorant. That's when she caught a glimpse of herself in the mirror. Awilda was right. She looked a mess.

Alana opened the bathroom door.

"Hey, Mom, what are you doing?"

"Trying to make sure I have everything."

"I have everything."

"Good. Why don't you go down and help Dad pack the snacks?"

"Okay. Can I bring Juliette and Kacie?"

"Sure."

"Can we bring some cookies?"

"I don't care." She wasn't really listening, she was trying to decide if she needed her bathing suit or not, then opted to bring it and a change of earrings. When her stuff was ready, she called to Chico.

"Son, come carry my bag."

"Really, Mom?"

"Dude, I'm teaching you how to be a gentleman."

He huffed and then lugged her bag out of her bedroom, making way too much noise pulling it down the stairs. Bea went down the hall to her closet, grabbed the maxi dress, and changed. Lonnie loved her hair down so she unloosened her bun and let it dangle past her shoulders. She had washed and combed it through yesterday so it had a lot of bounce and body. Full makeup was out of the question but lipstick was quick. She found a purple shade that would give her a pop.

"Babe, you look hot." Lonnie kissed her cheek while running his fingers through her hair. The exchange between them lightened her mood.

"Ready?"

"Yup."

The kids' snacks were packed but Bea needed something for herself. She sighed. Not in the mood to count calories, she grabbed the two eggs she had previously boiled, an apple, and put a few slices of cheese in a ziplock to pair with some of the kids' crackers. That should hold her over until dinner.

"Everyone go to the bathroom one more time because we are not stopping anytime soon," she called out.

When they got into the car, she was surprised when Chico and Alana agreed to watch the same movie, *Spy Kids 4*. Bea relaxed with a book in her lap. Lonnie squeezed her knee and pulled out of the driveway. These were the moments that mattered, she thought, looking up at the trees.

ELEVEN

Road Trip

With all of the traffic on the New Jersey Turnpike and then on I-95 around Baltimore, they didn't arrive in D.C. until well after the dinner rush. Instead of venturing out, they ate in the hotel restaurant and then put the kids to bed with the television on.

"If I hear you, I'm going to turn that TV off." Bea stood in their bedroom doorway. They'd reserved a two-bedroom, two-bath suite with a living area and small kitchenette.

"'K, Mom."

"Gotcha."

Bea carried her tablet into the living room and lowered herself onto the sofa next to Lonnie. He was watching baseball highlights on SportsCenter.

"What's on the agenda for tomorrow?" He looked up.

"I'm trying to decide between the Museum of Natural History, the National Museum of African American History and Culture, the Smithsonian Latino Center, and the Air and Space. I also want to shoot by the Martin Luther King, Jr. Memorial."

"Why don't we do them all? We have a few days. We can do two a day. Relax. You look tired."

Bea curled up next to him. "You know Chico had the nerve to tell me that he wished he was white, like you."

"Really?"

"That boy doesn't know the difference between white and light-skinned? We need to pump him with some culture. I feel like he's living in a land of lilies, not knowing who he is."

"The kids are fine. They're just growing up in a more well-rounded world than we did."

"I wouldn't call it well-rounded at all."

"Oh, babe."

"We're going to spend time this summer getting educated. If you don't know where you come from, you have no idea where you're going."

"You worry too much."

"Humph." She crossed her arms. Lonnie didn't worry enough.

The next morning the kids were up and dressed before Bea had to get on them.

"Where to first?" Chico asked.

She had decided to start with something fun to lure the kids in and then stick them with what she wanted them to learn about their mixed heritage.

"To the National Museum of Natural History. They have a new documentary on the great white shark that I thought you'd like."

Chico's eyes got big.

"What about me?" Alana huffed.

"And they have a butterfly exhibit."

"Cool."

Lonnie called down to the lobby for their car to be brought around.

When they got inside, the museum was packed. Lonnie was a natural history buff and Bea enjoyed watching him explain the exhibits to the children, but after exploring the Artic and learning about Iceland, her knees started to bother her.

"When does the movie start?" Alana seemed as tired of walking as Bea. She tucked her daughter under her arm and let her rest against her.

"We are heading over there now to get on line," Lonnie responded with his map in his hand. He wore a twill newsboy cap and cable knit sweater. The sight of him so engaged in their outing made her breath stall. This was the Lonnie she loved.

She followed them to the line and after what felt like fifteen minutes of standing, the doors opened to the theater. Bea sunk her heavy body down into the velvet seat. As soon as the lights went down, she drifted off to sleep.

"That was amazing," said Chico, stretching and yawning.

"Cover your mouth, son."

He did. "What's next?"

"How about we head to the gift shop?" Lonnie made his eyes big.

"Yeah."

Chico got a log building set that he promised to share with Alana. She opted for a plush portable dinosaur house. Bea waited on the steps of the museum with Alana while Chico and Lonnie got the car. The sun had sunk behind a cloud and the lightness of the day felt good.

"Did you have fun?"

"Yes." Alana pushed one of her dinosaurs in Bea's face. "You?"

"Always fun hanging with you, butterbean." She kissed her lips.

They drove over to Old Ebbitt Grill on Fifteenth Street for lunch.

The restaurant was just steps away from the White House and a D.C. tradition since 1856. Bea could feel herself wanting to eat like crazy so she concentrated on the salad menu only. She didn't want to become overwhelmed with choices.

"I'll have the kale and salmon salad," she told the waitress and then slid the menu away from her.

Alana ordered the mac and cheese and Chico the beef tacos. Lonnie went for a steak, and Bea knew she would have to take a bite. After lunch, they drove to the Martin Luther King, Jr. Memorial. Lonnie circled around trying to find the best parking and then wound up parking on Ohio Drive.

It felt like a ten-minute walk to the memorial but when they arrived, Bea was too excited to complain.

"Wow, look, you can see the Lincoln and Jefferson memorials from here," Bea called but the kids were too busy chasing each other in the fresh open air to hear her. Lonnie squeezed her hand.

"Okay, let me take a picture." The kids finally came back and stood in front of the memorial. Bea snapped a few pictures and then she asked a passerby to take a family photo. When she looked at her phone, she was in the middle surrounded by her family and you could see her entire face. That made her smile. They walked the wall and she and Lonnie took turns reading Dr. King's famous quotes.

"You want me to go back and get the car?"

"No, I'll walk with you guys." She linked arms with her husband, enjoying his bulk against her. This was why she stayed. This was what it was all about.

"We should head back to the hotel and rest a bit, it's been a long day."

"Ooh, can we go to the pool? Please say we can go to the pool. Please, please, please!" Alana put her hands together in the beggar's position.

"Okay."

"Yippee." The kids high-fived each other and jumped up and down.

Once Bea lowered herself onto the couch, it was a wrap. She couldn't move. The kids were changed and ready to go down to the pool in less than five minutes.

"You okay?" Lonnie sat down beside her.

"Yeah, just tired. That was a lot of walking. If the baby comes tonight, it's your fault," she teased.

"Then I'd have my wife back."

She hated when he said that. "Lonnie, I'm right here."

"You know what I mean."

"Mama, where's your swimming suit?"

"Mama's tired, butterbean. You go with Daddy. I'm going to take a little nap."

"You sure you don't want to come and rest by the side of the pool?"

"Positive. You three go ahead."

When they were gone, Bea relaxed into the silence. She was about to call Awilda when she heard Lonnie's phone ringing from the bedroom. She pushed herself to stand and moved much faster than she thought possible to the telephone. She could not believe he had forgotten his phone. These days it seemed that he didn't go to the bathroom without it. A 305 area code flashed across the screen and Bea answered it.

"Hello."

"Oh, I must have the wrong number."

"Who are you looking for?"

"Alonzo."

Bea could feel the pressure build in the back of her throat. "Whom may I say is calling?"

"Connie."

"This is his wife, Connie. What can I do for you?"

She stumbled. "I . . . I was calling to see if he received the letter I sent about . . . the private school."

"Calling my husband whenever you feel like it was not part of the deal, now, was it?"

Silence.

"As you know if you need us you are to send a letter. If you are worried that we didn't receive the letter then you follow up with *me* via e-mail. I've spelled this out to you in our paternity agreement. Do I need to fax you down a copy?"

"No."

"Good. I got your letter and I am considering your request."

"Alonzo wants to meet his father." Her voice quivered.

Bea's throat dried.

"He deserves to know who his father is. He had nothing to do with what happened between us."

"You should have thought about that before you laid down with my husband and had a baby. This is on you."

"It's not right."

"You signed the contract."

"I shouldn't have."

Bea couldn't believe the nerve of this chick, calling for more when she had already given her enough. She didn't mind kicking in the extra bucks for school but she wasn't going to share her family. If their existence came out . . . the shame would be more than she could bear.

"I'll get back to you regarding your request."

"I'll take it to the judge. A boy needs a father."

"I have to go. Please don't call my husband again." Bea hung up the telephone. Her fingers were shaking and before she could even digest her conversation with Connie, she realized that the phone didn't lock back after the call. She was inside of his phone.

Her fingers trembled. She keyed through his e-mail accounts, stopping to read anything that caught her attention. It was mostly business stuff, nothing there. Then she went through his text messages: zilch. All of the social media sites. Zero. She was about to give up when she discovered an app icon she didn't recognize. It was called text free and it was hidden in with his banking apps. When she clicked on it, it seemed to be an instant message/text app that hid the correspondence. There were a handful of names in the contact list but he had interacted with chili101 that morning. Based on the time stamp, their interaction had occurred while she was in the shower. She felt a tiny earthquake rumble in her gut as she read through the exchanges:

When are you coming back?

Soon.

I want some more.

Daddy only gives out one lick at a time.

Well perhaps you could make an exception. You've got me like a fiend.

That's how I do.

Cocky.

Bea scrolled back and read a message from last week.

Damn daddy, you know how to make a girl forget.

It's my specialty.

Wednesday night? Restaurant in Chatham?

For sure. Take a nap it's going to be a long night.

I like the sound of that. Perhaps we just skip dinner.

No, I need to feed you first. You'll need all of your strength to ride me.

Giddy up.

Bea felt the blood rush to her head as she flashed back to the previous Wednesday night. Chico had had swim practice. Lonnie came home late. When he slipped into bed, she'd peeked at her bedside clock. One-eleven flashed. He whispered that it was a late night at the office and that he had caught the last train out of the city. Now she remembered thinking that he still smelled fresh after such a long day. Fucking liar.

Bea scrolled back some more. She was so into the messages that she didn't hear the door open and the kids bound in. Alana was up on her, hair dripping wet.

"How come you didn't put a towel around your head?" Bea slipped the phone into her pocket. "Come, you need to shower."

"What do you want to do for dinner?" Lonnie closed the door behind them and called out to her. Bea slipped the phone back on the nightstand and followed Alana into the bathroom, closing and locking the door behind them.

"Why do you look like that, Mama?"

"Like what?"

"Like you had a bad dream or something."

"I did."

"What was it about? Monsters? Ghosts? Did someone try to steal you?"

"Something like that. How was the pool?"

Her face went from concern to glee. "Soooo much fun."

"Good."

"You missed it. You should have come."

"Babe." Lonnie tried to open the bathroom door.

"We'll be out in a minute."

She dried Alana's hair with a towel and concentrated on pulling it into a quick bun.

"Go put on some dry clothes. You can shower later," she said, although she knew she should have stuck her in the tub and rinsed that chlorine out of her hair. Bea needed all of her strength to get past Lonnie and out of the hotel room.

"Dinner?" he asked, standing in the middle of the living area barefoot.

Bea grabbed her purse and slung it over her arm. "Why don't you order room service for you and the kids? I'm going to run down the street."

He stepped closer. "Why don't you let us get into some dry clothes and we can all go."

"No, I need to pick something up. Tums for my heartburn. I'll be right back."

"Babe, you're shaking like a leaf."

"I'm fine. Need some air. Just feed the kids."

"She had a bad dream while we were at the pool," Alana piped up from the sofa.

Bea pushed past Lonnie and was at the door when Chico emerged from the kids' bedroom.

"Mommy, you should have come. Dad did an epic cannonball."

"Nice."

"Where are you going?"

"I'll be right back." Bea slipped into her sandals and out of the hotel room. She took off in a half jog to the elevator and pressed the down button frantically, like someone might follow her. The tears stung the rims of her eyes but she willed them not to fall.

Foolish. Wretched. Pitiful.

The elevator opened. Two teenage girls were in the back corner talking about a music video. Bea stood in the front with her back to them. Outside, a taxicab waited steps from the hotel entrance.

"Where to?"

Before she could close the door behind her, the dark horse got in beside her. Bea needed to score.

"McDonald's."

"Which one?"

"Whichever one is closest and easy for me to hail a cab back."

"No problem, ma'am."

She looked out the window as he drove. Ill to her core, she couldn't believe that she was in this godforsaken position again. Again. A-fucking-gain.

The golden arches looked like angel's wings. When she exited the car she felt shifty. Her sunglasses were pressed against her face, her head was bowed low, and her purse was clasped tightly in the crease of her underarm. The dark horse opened the door for her and she stepped in.

The smell of the McDonald's reminded her of her mother's home. The restaurant was nearly empty as she navigated her way to the counter.

"Let me get two number threes," she murmured. Gone was the polished talk. Bea was in her gutter.

"What kind of drinks?"

"I only need one drink. Orange. Large, please. And an apple pie. Warm."

"Will that be all?"

The dark horse breathed on her neck. It made the thin hairs stand up. "Nope, add a six-piece nugget to that." Might as well go all the way.

"Okay."

Bea handed the cashier two twenty-dollar bills and opened her palm for her meager change. While she waited for her order she wished that she had driven for the food. The car would have provided private shelter, but she was here. Her foot tapped absently; she was trying not to think.

"Number forty-eight."

Bea didn't have to look at her ticket to know that the tray on the counter was all for her. She picked it up. The smell of the fries went straight up her nose. She tucked three between her teeth and tongue while scanning the room. A booth was in the corner. It was secluded enough that she could see what was going on in the street but the workers behind the counter couldn't see her. She sat with her back to them. Bea unwrapped all of the items and set them up in the middle of the tray. Tearing the plastic package with her teeth, she then slathered extra ketchup onto her burgers. Damn, extra pickles would have been good but she wasn't going to go back for them and risk anything getting cold.

The frenzy was on her and the first burger went into her mouth. She started out with small bites but then quickly slipped into devour mode, stuffing the food down as fast as it would fit between her jaws. She could always taste the food in the beginning of a binge. Everything was succulent, the perfect mix of salty, moist, and sweet. Eventually her desire got ahead of her. The taste stopped mattering. It was just the feeling of getting the food down into her belly.

She ate down Lonnie's lack of love for her. Demolished the disgust that she felt in being the naïve, trusting wife for the umpteenth time. Sucked on the sick feeling of being despicable, disgusting, just a used body taking up space. She didn't deserve to live. Why was she alive anyway? Her husband didn't even respect her. She wondered what was worse: him not loving her or him not respecting her. Bea had a hard time settling on the feeling that hurt the most before she had finished every lick of food. Her stomach stretched beyond full.

All she could think of was how to get rid of that meal without anyone knowing. She looked around. No one was watching her. Why would they be? The cashier was so busy toying with the boy manning the fry station that she didn't even notice that Bea was still there. She dumped her tray and then called out, "Can you let me into the bathroom?"

She buzzed the door without breaking a stride from her flirtation. Bea went into the bathroom; the door clicked and locked behind her. The smell of the stall was wretched enough. All fast-food bathrooms smelled like disinfectant swished around with piss. Bea leaned over the bowl, pushed her pointer finger to the back of her throat, reaching until she hit that magic spot. She gagged three times before the food started traveling up. She had learned over the years that the closer she was to the toilet the better for splash control so she pressed her face all the way into the foul bowl. The smell was revolting enough to help all of the food out. Droplets dripped down her face and she stayed with her head hanging over the commode until there was nothing left to give.

PART 2

The truth is, everyone is going to hurt you.
You just got to find the ones worth suffering for.

—BOB MARLEY

TWELVE

Food Porn

The baby kicked and stretched in her abdomen. Bea rubbed circles on her stomach, shivering under a blanket of shame. How could she go on a binge? Mena trusted her with her daughter's life and Bea had risked it all. The moment she found out about Lonnie, she should have dialed Dr. Spellman. Or used one of her coping techniques. But instead she had let her husband's infidelity screw with her sense of reason.

Bea thanked the doorman as she entered the lobby of the Park Hyatt hotel. She wanted to check on her children but she couldn't make herself get on the elevator. Regret was lodged in her throat, like a piece of rock candy that refused to liquefy. She dropped her hand over her belly and then lowered down into a lounge armchair adjacent to the floor-to-ceiling windows. The patrons' conversations went on around her, crowding together into a harmonious song, but Bea couldn't make out the lyrics. Some drank fancy pots from the Tea Cellar, others cocktails from the bar. Her mouth stank of her sins.

When she binged regularly, she'd kept toothpaste, brush, and a travel-sized bottle of Febreze on her, but she hadn't needed it in such a long time that she had stopped carrying it. It was a part of her recovery, but now something was required to rid her of the odor, and she fumbled around in her purse until she found Listerine tabs. Bea rubbed her nose with one hand and slid two tabs on her tongue, sucking on them until they had completely dissolved. The minty taste helped and after six potent strips she made herself stop.

Her emotions kept dragging her back into the McDonald's bathroom. She could feel the weight in her chest as she recalled bringing up the food with the baby pressing on her bladder. She needed to distract herself so she picked up the *Men's Health* magazine that was on the table next to her. She scanned the headlines. THE BEST WORKOUT YOU CAN CRAM INTO 10 MINUTES. IS IT SAFE TO EAT TUNA FISH EVERY DAY? Bea wanted to know about the tuna but didn't want to read about food. She flipped on.

A few more pages in, she spied a distinguished, nut-brown man with a nice smile and thick, shiny hair. It was an ad for Hennessy. The model in the picture reminded her of her father. Bea hadn't thought of him in a long time, and just like that she could smell the woodsy cologne that he wore. Bea gazed out the window, not really watching the cars or people on the street pass by. Instead, she was remembering.

As a girl, Bea could set her watch by her mother's Saturday morning routine in preparation of her father's arrival.

9 A.M.—Wet hair wrung with a white towel, then parted and sectioned into four rows with hair carefully soaked in setting lotion and rolled as flat as possible over pink plastic rollers. When all the hair was set she would sit under the dryer for an hour and a half while she watched *telenovelas*. Eyes darting back and forth between the drama

on the screen and the bottle of passion pink that she would paint on her nails and toes in two thick coats.

11 A.M.—Green guck slathered all over her face and then she would let it sit for twenty minutes before peeling it off.

12 P.M.—Pot of water on for the rice. Her mother singing along to the radio as she prepared *locrio de salami,* her father's favorite dish.

1 P.M.—Shower, then hurrying around the house to get ready. Rollers out, curling iron in, face dusted, skin oiled and perfumed.

If Chip Campbell had not arrived by 2 P.M. on the dot, her mother would be at the window waiting. He was never more than fifteen minutes off schedule. When she saw his car turn the corner of their block, she would whisper.

"*Mija,* he's here." They would watch together as his car slid into the parking space in front of the building. The space that seemed to wait patiently for him every weekend, like it had his name on it.

Chip drove a shiny black sports car and wore driving gloves with knuckle holes. When he stepped onto the street, it was unhurried and deliberate. He wore a leather motorcycle jacket, dark shades, and pecan alligator boots. His hair was a thick, fully picked-out Afro that glistened with Ultra Sheen hair pomade and his skin was the color of tanning hide. Chip moved through the world like a man who could afford to take care of more than one woman.

At that point, Irma would dash down the hall to her bedroom, calling over her shoulder, "Let him in. And don't you interrupt us for nothing."

"What if the building catches fire?"

"Stop that foolishness and be a good girl, would you, please?" She closed her bedroom door.

Bea would stand in the kitchen and pretend to wipe the counter off but it was clean. Her mother spent her Friday nights after work cleaning the house to a spit shine in preparation. He always tapped the door three times with the soft part of his fist. Bea never understood why he didn't ring the bell.

"Hi," she said, tugging on her T-shirt that all of a sudden seemed too small over the soft ripple of her stomach. She ran her fingers through her hair; it never laid smooth in her ponytail when she combed it herself.

"There she is," he'd say with one hand behind his back. Bea had already spied him pulling the McDonald's bag out of his car trunk but she would play along with the surprise.

"How's school?"

"Fine."

"Keeping up those grades?"

"Yes."

"That a girl." He kissed Bea's cheek.

"Bought something for you." From behind his back came the Holy Grail of food. No matter how great Irma's *locrio de salami* tasted, nothing in the world beat a bag from Mickey D's.

"Save some for your mama."

Bea would nod.

"Is she here?" he'd ask every week as if her mother would be anywhere but waiting on him.

"Yeah," Bea said and turned with the bag to the kitchen table, listening to his thick heels echo down the hall to her mother's room. Bea would pretend not to watch them but would peek.

"Papi." Her mother would coo. Her nightie was tight and the silky robe that she had slipped into barely hid her goodies. They'd kiss right away and he would run his hands over her curves and tell her how much he'd missed her. Bea watched, thinking it was all very sickening.

"Ran three red lights to get here," he'd say, closing the door behind them. The last thing Bea would hear was her mother's high-pitched giggle that she saved only for him. The music would come next, usually something circa the 1970s, often starting with "Me and Mrs. Jones."

Bea would look into the bag and the aroma would go right to her head, making her giddy. There was a cheeseburger Happy Meal, Quarter Pounder with Cheese, large fry, and an apple pie. He never bought a drink. Bea wished he'd brought her an orange soda. It was her favorite.

She pulled out her Happy Meal, closed up the bag, and carried them with a napkin into the living room even though her mother forbade her from eating anywhere but the kitchen table. Bea had her own schedule to keep up with. At ten years old, she was too hungry for the Happy Meal but she would snack on it while watching the end of *Tom and Jerry*. *The Flintstones* came on at two-thirty and during commercial breaks she would sneak into the kitchen and steal a few of her mother's fries. By the end of the show they were gone too. When she realized she'd eaten them all, she reasoned that her mother would not want to reheat soggy fries anyway and then she licked the salt from inside the fry box.

The Jetsons came on at three-thirty. Bea never ever intended to eat more than a bite of her mother's Quarter Pounder, but it was something about the sour pickles and melted cheese that made her keep sampling until that was gone too. It wasn't until she had to channel surf for something to watch at four that she realized that she hadn't saved her mother anything except the apple pie.

While playing with her dolls, she vowed not to go near the pie. On Saturdays she was extra hungry. Her mother was so busy getting ready for the visit that Bea never had a suitable breakfast—just a bowl of cold cereal. Plus, Bea was restless. She wasn't allowed to go outside and didn't really have friends in the building. Dolls were her only company. In between television programs, she dressed them, combed their hair, and then lined them up on the couch next to her so they could watch her shows with her. By the time *Family Feud* came on at six, Bea broke her promise. She heated the apple pie in the microwave and ate it with a tall glass of whole milk.

The first time she ate all of her mother's food, she thought Irma would smack her upside her head the way she did sometimes and call her greedy, but she was so happy after her father's visit that she never said a word. That's when finishing the bag became Bea's Saturday norm.

Once the sun was good and retired, Chip would stroll back into the living room, smelling like sweaty feet and strong cologne. At that point Bea was bored out of her mind and dipping into her mother's pots, careful to save the biggest pieces of meat for her father.

"*Mija,*" her mother would scold. "I'll make the plates. *Lavate las manos!*"

Bea would walk down the hall to the bathroom and wash her hands. Irma heaped huge helpings of food onto each of their plates and pulled down the acrylic glasses that she reserved for guests.

The three sat at the round table together, her mother as close as humanly possible to her father without being in his lap. Feeding him bites from her plate even though they had the same meal.

"School okay? Getting good grades?" Chip asked, again. Bea would tell him yes, again, and then her mother would launch into Bea making honor roll or being asked to be the ambassador at her school.

Being with her makeshift family was the one thing that could strip Bea of her appetite. "May I be excused?"

"You barely ate, *mija.*" Her mother would look her over. "You feeling okay?"

"I'll come back for it." Bea scuffed her chair against the linoleum and escaped into the living room where the television was on. She would watch it while listening to her parents' conversation.

Before her father left the apartment, he'd reach into his pocket and peel off a five-dollar bill.

"Don't spend it all in one place," he'd say.

"I won't."

Chip would pat her on the head, kiss her mother until it took her breath away, and then slip out of their lives, until the next Saturday when they would play house again.

The next morning, her mother would be up early, happily humming Dominican hymns, fluffing her hair for ten o'clock mass. After church, Bea would slip into the corner bodega and spend the five dollars on junk food that she would ration for herself. The week would drag out and Saturday would repeat itself for the next two years, mundane and uneventful until Awilda showed up.

Irma was the secretary at Grace Wilday Junior High School. Awilda's mother, Dr. Rose McKinley, was the principal. From what Bea could see, Rose was a stiff woman and it was obvious that she didn't trust a lot of people. Bea overheard her mother on the telephone and found out that the reason Awilda started staying with them on the weekends was because Awilda's father, the pastor of the church, started traveling to other churches and conferences and she didn't trust him to go alone.

"Can't ever be too sure with your man," Irma had gabbed while putting on a pot of water for beans. "Mmm hmm. There are a lot of hussies with the wrong intentions. Sad to hear that you can't outrun them, even in the house of the Lord." She made the sign of the cross.

Bea watched her mother. Bea could always tell the difference between her home mom and the woman she was with Dr. McKinley, her work persona. Most times her mother stroked Dr. McKinley's ego and told her what she wanted to hear to keep her happy.

After that conversation, Awilda started coming over Friday after school and her mother would return for her bright and early most Sunday mornings so that they could travel to church together. Bea could remember the first time Awilda and Rose came to their apartment. It was a warm day and her mother had all of the windows open. Spanish food and music drifted from the neighbors' homes and you could hear the kids playing outside in front of her building.

"The girls will stay inside?" Rose said, looking around the apartment. Taking everything in with little subtlety.

"You can come in, Rose. Can I call you Rose off campus?"

"Of course." Rose stepped farther into the apartment. Awilda made her way over to Bea, who was standing near the kitchen table.

"Where's your room?"

"Awilda, please remember that you are a McKinley."

Awilda raised her eyebrows so only Bea could see, then walked and kissed her mother's cheek.

"The girls will be fine," Irma coaxed, taking an envelope from Rose's gloved hand. They talked some more but Bea couldn't see or hear any more because Awilda shut the bedroom door behind them.

"That woman plucks my last nerve."

Bea stared.

"Got any gum? I'm fiending for some sugar." Awilda kicked off her brand-new, white-and-gray Air Jordans and threw herself across Bea's twin-sized canopy bed as if they had been hanging forever. Bea had been begging her mother to buy her those shoes since the start of school but she'd said she wasn't paying ninety dollars for sneakers. Bea went into her secret candy stash and tossed Awilda a fresh pack of Juicy Fruit.

"Nice room."

"Thanks," Bea mumbled, timid.

"You need a Michael Jackson poster up in here. Why is that *Saved by the Bell* crap hanging on the wall?"

Bea blushed, immediately embarrassed. She hadn't changed anything in her room since she was in the fifth grade. *Saved by the Bell* was her show but she wouldn't tell Awilda that.

"I'll hook you up. Next time I come."

"Bet." Bea sat next to Awilda.

"What do you want to do?"

Awilda sat up and dug into her bag. "Here, put this tape in."

Bea did as she was told and out cranked MC Lyte's "Paper Thin." Bea had never heard it but right away she started moving her shoulders. Awilda got up and danced.

"This is my jam." She threw her arms up in the air and started rhyming with the words. "'When you say you love me, it doesn't matter/it goes into my head as just chitchatter.'"

Then Awilda walked over and examined Bea's ponytail. "You have such pretty hair. Why do you have it in this sad-looking bun?"

"It's hard for me to comb."

"I'm gonna show you. I need a spray bottle and some conditioner. You got any pink moisturizer?"

"I think so."

They listened to Awilda's mix tape while Awilda pulled the tangles out of Bea's hair.

"Did you see his picture in the new *Ebony*?" Awilda waved the comb in the air when Big Daddy Kane came on. "Girl, he fine. Look." She rummaged through her overnight duffle and tossed a few copies of *Black Beat* magazine on the bed. Bea flipped through the pictures while Awilda did her hair. When Awilda was finished, she appraised her work.

"The hair looks good. Now we gotta work on your clothes. You just look sloppy."

Bea looked down at her oversized T-shirt and ratty stirrups, embarrassed.

"You need some clothes that fit. Just 'cause you a little chubby don't mean you got to wear your daddy's shirt." Awilda stood in front of Bea's closet, picking through her clothes. She pulled down a pair of jeans that Bea had to squeeze into and then gave her an off-the-shoulder, neon-green T-shirt from her bag.

"Try this."

Bea was shy to change in front of Awilda so she grabbed the clothes and headed down the hall to the bathroom. As she did, she saw the back of her father's head as he closed her mother's door behind him. It was 2 P.M. She changed. When she got back into her room, Awilda had changed into denim overalls and a white bodysuit. Her hair was out of the ponytail and she had put on eyeliner and purple lip gloss.

"You look phat." Bea said, trying to sound cool.

"Let's go."

"Where're we going?"

"For a walk." Awilda slung her white patent leather mini backpack over her shoulder.

"My mother doesn't let me go outside."

"We can sit on the stoop."

Bea hesitated and then agreed. Her mother wasn't coming out of her room any time soon. They'd be back way before her father left. When they passed the kitchen Awilda spied the McDonald's bag.

"You want some?"

"Yeah girl, I haven't had anything but that bird food my mama fed me. When she goes on a diet, that means I'm on a diet." Bea grabbed the bag and followed Awilda out onto the stoop. They sat smelling the dew of spring while dipping their hands in for fries, biting the burgers, and splitting the apple pie in half.

That day, it seemed like everyone was out. Bea wasn't used to being outside of her apartment and the neighborhood seemed more vibrant next to Awilda. The music, the smells, the cars zipping by brought a symphony of noises. A young mama pushed a baby carriage. Two kids dribbled and passed a basketball on their way to the court at the end of the block. Four little girls took turns jumping double-dutch. A group of old men sat at a square table slamming around dominos. It was almost as if there was a block party going on and Bea had finally been invited.

"Is it always like this?" Awilda looked across the street. Three teenage boys, Jose, Pop, and big Nate, were sitting on the wall with a beat box playing the Beastie Boys. Bea watched as Awilda got up and started to dance.

"This is my song." She stuck out her tongue, pushing her hips behind her.

Jose was the finest Puerto Rican in the neighborhood. Bea's mother once said that he reminded her of El DeBarge. Jose cocked his head at Awilda and waved for her to come across the street.

"You going?"

"Naw."

"Everybody likes him."

Awilda kept dancing, popping her fingers and laughing with her mouth open. Jose whispered something to Pop and made his way across the street. He led with his shoulder and sort of dragged his left foot.

In front of them he stuck his hands down in his Guess jeans pockets and leaned back. "What's up, mami?"

"Taxes."

"Oh, you one of those smart ones? What's your name?"

She sucked her teeth. "Awilda."

"How old are you?"

"Old enough to wine and dine but not waste my time."

"She must not be from around here," Jose said to Bea. It was the first time in her life that he had talked to her and the slight attention made her blush. Then he was back to Awilda.

"Where you been all my life?"

"North Plainfield."

"Oh, you one of them?"

"What's that supposed to mean?"

"Nothing. Chill, little mami." He pushed his dimple in their faces. "If I give you my number, you gonna call me?"

"I don't know." Awilda rolled her eyes like he was boring her.

Jose shook his head and pulled out a piece of paper and a pen, conveniently from his back pocket. Her scribbled something down and then handed the paper to Awilda.

"I'll be waiting." He jogged back across the street.

Awilda sat down on the step next to Bea.

"Dag."

"Take lessons, Bea. That's how you do it. You can't act all Joe. You got to play hardball. Come on, let's go back upstairs."

The girls were fast friends. They were both only children and were like two opposite magnets attracting each other. The start of their weekend together began with Awilda combing out and bumping Bea's hair. She brought over clothes to mix and match with what

Bea had. Awilda and Irma got along well, keeping a casual rhythm between them, like big cousin/little cousin. When Bea was in ninth grade and Awilda in tenth grade, she had finally convinced Irma to let them go to Skate 22 on the bus. Irma made Awilda promise to never tell her mother.

"Wilde, don't tell your mother or I will lose my job," she said, making the sign of the cross.

Bea admired Awilda's quick wit and the ease with which she moved in her skin. She even started imitating her accent so that she could pretend to be Awilda on the phone with the boys that they met at the rink and on their walks around downtown Elizabeth.

Needing a change of scenery, Awilda started setting up dates for herself at the Jersey Gardens mall. They caught the #40 bus out there to meet her latest guy, who always tagged along a friend for Bea. The girls would have lunch, ditch the boys, window shop, and then prowl for new dudes to exchange numbers with. Since Irma was so concerned with Bea's father on Saturdays, she was none the wiser. Awilda became a relief and a blessing to both of them.

THIRTEEN

Life After

Bea was in the eleventh grade when her mother knocked on her bedroom door with the news that would change her young life. She was hunched over her physics textbook, suffering through the chapters on the quantum world of superposition, like they were written in Greek instead of English.

"*Mija.*"

Bea looked up, bothered by the interruption until she noticed her mother's dishevelment. Irma's face was puffy and her lipstick smeared.

"What's wrong?"

"It's your papi. He . . . passed away."

"Like died?"

Irma nodded her head.

Bea didn't feel anything at first. The words just sat on her skin, like excess lotion that needed smearing.

"Oh, *mija.* What are we going to do?" Her mother sat on the edge of Bea's bed and crushed her to her breasts. She smelled like talcum powder and her coconut drink concoction. Bea didn't have any tears and instead soothed her mother by pulling her close and running her fingers through her soft hair. Bea often wondered why she had not inherited her mother's silky tresses that did what she wanted without much of a fight.

"I have to see him."

Bea released her. "Where is he?"

"Uncle Bobo is going to come by tonight and pick us up so that we can view the body at the funeral home. I have to say my good-byes."

Bobo was her father's longtime friend and the only person Bea had ever met connected to him. Once when her father had been sick with the flu, Bobo came by and dropped some money off to get them through the week. Bea only met him a few times and never called him by name; she didn't know why her mother was referring to him as uncle anything.

A few hours later, her mother was dressed in a navy dress cinched at the waist with a faux snakeskin belt. Her hair was pulled back in a high bun and she clutched the Coach bag that Chip had given her last Christmas Eve. He came on Christmas Eve, never Christmas Day.

Bea hadn't changed out of her faded jeans, worn T-shirt, and distressed cardigan sweater, and to her surprise her mother was so busy worrying about herself that she didn't notice.

"Navy blue was your father's favorite color." She clipped on a pair of gold earrings and then touched her lips with a bright red tube.

Bobo waited in the car in front of their building but got out when he saw them to open the door for her mother.

"Thanks, dear." Her mother slid with grace into the front seat.

The grown-ups made small talk on the way to the viewing but Bea stayed quiet. Nothing felt right. Breathing hurt.

When they arrived, Bobo parked and whispered something to her mother before getting out of the car. Bea opened the car door to follow him but her mother stopped her.

"Hang on, *mija*."

"Aren't we going in?" Bea's foot dangled over the concrete.

"He's just going to confirm that the coast is clear."

"Clear from what?"

"Say a prayer for your father, sweetie. May God rest his beautiful soul." She clutched her rosary and made the sign of the cross. Bea pulled herself back in and looked out of the window. Minutes later Bobo came back and ushered them from the car. Her mother walked with her shoulders back but her head slightly bent into the funeral home. Their shoes traveled softly over the beige carpet. Irma put her hand over her heart and had to stop once to gather herself. There were three rooms with viewings and her father's was on the left. When they finally reached the body, Bobo said, "I'll wait out here to give ya'll some privacy."

Irma trembled so badly that Bea kept her hand on her elbow to make sure she didn't topple over. They were standing over the body. It was her father.

"You look well, *mi amor*. Oh, my love, my sweetheart. How could you leave me?" Irma bent over the body and kissed his cheek and then stood, clutching the side of the coffin with tears collected on her face. Bea stood next to her but didn't cry. She didn't know how to feel, except knowing that she didn't want to be there. Didn't want this to be happening. Irma was too busy murmuring to the body in Spanish and touching his thick head of hair to notice Bea. Then a woman's voice slapped them like a gust of strong wind just outside the door.

"What do you mean I can't go in, Bobo? You mean to tell me you brought that hussy down here to see my husband?"

Bea's neck snapped in that direction. She couldn't hear what Bobo said back.

"She ought to be ashamed to show her face down here. Harlot!"

"Who's that?" Bea turned to her mother.

"We should go." Irma gathered herself. As she dabbed the tears away from her cheeks, in walked a woman, also dressed in navy.

"You have no right to be here. Haven't you done enough?" The woman was shorter and plumper than Irma. Pie-shaped face, wearing a wig that made her look older than she probably was.

"I meant no harm."

"You meant no harm." The woman mocked Irma's accent. "You've been creeping 'round with my husband for years and you meant no harm?"

Her mother stiffened and reached for Bea's hand. "It was Chip's decision."

The woman looked like she wanted to spit. "If I wasn't a Christian woman, I swear 'fore God I would—"

"Out of respect for Chip, we'll leave."

"Jezebel." The woman spat. "You ruined my life."

"Not my fault you couldn't keep your man at home." Irma cocked her head like it was a gun.

"Excuse me?"

Irma glared at the woman and then pulled Bea from the room. Bobo was at the door.

"Sorry, Irma, I tried."

"It's fine."

From the room they heard the woman cry, "Lord, why have you forsaken me? What have I done to deserve to be disgraced by my husband's mistress, even in death?"

Her voice pierced into Bea, setting a chill in a place that never seemed to warm properly again.

When they got home and her mother changed into her house clothes and removed her lashes, she informed Bea: "Your father was a good man. He left you an insurance policy."

Bea didn't care about the money.

"Was that woman his wife?"

"Enough to get you through high school and something toward college. You're a lucky girl. Your father was a good man."

"Ma, Dad had a wife?"

"Stay out of grown folks' affairs."

"I'm sixteen." She put her hands on her hips. "Tell me."

Her mother shook her head, looked without seeing anything. "I never wanted you to find out like this. I was going to tell you when the time was right."

"Tell me now." Bea took a step closer.

"You're just like him. You know that?" Her mother wiped the corner of her eye. "Let's sit down."

"Ma, please."

"Yes, Beatrice, that woman was your father's wife."

Bea chewed on the sleeve of her sweater where the threading had already come loose. She had always thought of herself as a love child since her parents were not married but now she felt like *bastard* was a better term. She was illegitimate. Unwanted. Did his family even know she existed?

"Do they have kids?"

"Three girls."

"I have sisters?" Bea said, shocked.

"Half-sisters."

"I can't believe you." She slapped her thighs. "How could you do this to me?"

"I'm sorry, *mija*."

"That's why he never took me anywhere? He was ashamed of me. He probably didn't want me to be born. Why didn't you just have an abortion?"

"Don't say that!" Her mother stood. "He wanted you."

"What married man wants a child with another woman?"

"Stop it."

"It's true."

"I can't take this from you. Not today. Sweet Jesus." She made the sign of the cross and then ran down the hall to her bedroom where she slammed her door.

Bea went into her own room and took down the one photo that she had of her father clipped to her vanity mirror.

"Asshole," she shouted at the picture and then let it drop to the floor.

The funeral was held the next day. When her mother came into her bedroom to select Bea's clothes, she picked the picture up off the floor and pinned it back between the mirror and wooden frame. Bea was in her bed, writing in her diary. She noticed her mother but said nothing.

"Start getting ready. Don't want to be late."

Bea waited for her mother to close the door behind her and then hid her diary in the back of her closet in between her school gym uniform and a hoody. The dress was navy with three buttons and a plaid skirt. It wasn't what Bea would have picked but she put it on to keep the peace. She kept thinking about what would happen when she arrived at the church. Her father's wife was scary. Bea didn't want to be anywhere near her. She did hope to be introduced to her sisters. How weird would that be? Did they know about her? Did their mother tell them about the run-in at the funeral home? She had so many scenarios playing in her head that it wasn't until she slipped into her wedged heels that she realized her mother wasn't dressed.

"You have every right to be there." Her mother sat at the table in her bathrobe.

"You're not going with me?" Alarm rose in Bea's throat.

"*Mija,* I can't go. It would cause too much commotion. You saw what happened at the funeral parlor. I can't do that to Chip's memory." She made the sign of the cross. "May he rest eternally in peace."

"Then I'm not going either."

"Yes, you are. He'd want you there."

"Did he tell you that?"

Her mother sighed.

"And by myself? Without you?" Her breathing grew shallow.

The doorbell rang and when her mother opened the door in walked Awilda. Dressed in all black with a yellow purse. Bea had never been more excited to see her in her life.

"Wilde! You're going with me?"

"Beasley." Awilda threw her arms around Bea. "I couldn't sleep last night after you told me what happened. Of course I'm going to support you."

"Thanks."

"Bea and Awilda to the end." They slapped hands and then went through their secret handshake that ended with two snaps.

"Take care of her, Wilde. Don't let my Bea out of your sight." Irma shoved some money for carfare into Bea's hand and went back to her bedroom.

Bea looked down the hall after her mother.

"Oh, here." Awilda reached into her bag and fished out an over-sized pair of sunglasses that she shoved onto Bea's face. "Let's rock."

They walked in silence to the bus stop. Bobo had slipped Bea the information for the service when he dropped them off the night before. Awilda knew how to get everywhere on public transportation, probably because she played hooky from school. They arrived ten minutes early so the family processional had not begun. The limo was parked at the curb but the family had not gotten out. Bea wondered if they could see her through the dark windows. Did they even know who she was? Awilda pulled Bea through the crowd of mourners, marched them in, and found a seat on the left, opposite the section marked off for immediate family.

The cathedral was grand, with stained-glass windows, wooden pews, and royal-blue carpet. Her father's casket was open. Wreaths and standing spray flowers crowded the pulpit. The organ played a slow tune. Everything was beautiful. She would report to her mother that his home-going was fitting.

"Are you going to go up to the family?"

"I don't know."

The organ began and the family proceeded in. Bea picked out the three daughters right away. Two were at their mother's elbow and the other led them down the aisle. The four seemed to be in synch, moving and grieving as one. Her father's wife walked with a netted veil over her face, but Bea could still see her. She was matronly; every thread, piece of jewelry, bulge of fat, was tucked into their proper place. She wore no makeup and on top of her head sat another unstylish wig. Between her fingers she clutched her Bible. The wife was nothing like her mother, who wouldn't greet her father without red lips, tight curls, and skin soaked in perfume.

After a selection from the choir, the microphone was open for those who wanted to say something about Chip Campbell. Bea listened to the people who knew him, amazed at the man he was away from her apartment. She didn't know that he liked to go fishing after church on Sunday and could clean a catfish in fifteen seconds, that he had been a Big Brother to two motherless boys from Camden for the past two decades and helped them through college. Chip was originally from Waycross, Georgia, loved to hunt, and worked for the city of Roselle for thirty-five years. He had been a deacon at his church, a master chess player, and a Mason. For Bea, he had been more her mother's man than her father. All that they'd shared was a pat on the head, McDonald's Happy Meals, and five-dollar bills. She had missed out on a real relationship with him.

Then the eldest daughter, who looked to be fresh out of college, went up to speak. Her two sisters—one was college-aged and the other high school—walked with her. They stood before the congregation. Bea could tell they were close to each other and close to him. The middle sister looked the most like Bea, same complexion and that nose. It was something about her body language that had Bea longing to know her better. Wanting to move in their sisterly circle. But there was no place in their lives for her. They had the same mother and same father. She was the unwanted.

"On behalf of the Campbell family we'd like to thank you all for coming out. My father was an amazing man. He was faithful to his family and his church and he had a sense of humor that often had my sisters and me rolling around on the carpet. We will miss him dearly." Her voice cracked and then she stepped away from the microphone. The preacher stepped in and began with his closing remarks.

While he spoke about coming home to Jesus, Bea read the obituary. She got to who Chip Campbell left behind: "Two brothers, a host of nieces and nephews, and too many cousins to count. A loving and faithful wife, Anita Campbell, and three daughters: Caroline, Corrine, and Catrina Campbell." Nothing about Beatrice Sardina. She was not surprised to see that she had not been mentioned. It hurt but she wasn't shocked. A few believers shouted, "Hallelujah."

That's when she got up and told Awilda they were leaving. They slipped out the side door.

"You don't want to go to the repast?"

"Hell no. But I'm hungry."

"Come on." There was a bus across the street and Awilda pulled Bea to hop on it.

"Where are we going?"

"We can stop and get some food and go to my house. My parents are at work so we can eat and chill."

Bea looked out of the window during the ride and Awilda didn't push her to talk. When they got off of the bus, Awilda asked, "McDonald's or Pizza Hut?"

"Mickey D's."

When they walked in, Awilda told her to order what she wanted. Bea ordered a Filet-O-Fish meal, a Quarter Pounder with Cheese meal, an apple pie, and cookies.

"Damn, you're hungry," Awilda teased.

Bea was embarrassed. "I didn't have breakfast."

They sipped their sodas on the walk. Awilda lived on a quiet, tree-lined street. The house was a corner split-level. The girls entered through the garage door.

"My mother thinks I went to school today, she doesn't know I skipped."

"What if she comes home?"

"Irma will call first. She knows where we are."

"You two worked this all out?"

Awilda nodded her head as she took a seat at the kitchen table. They listened to Snoop Doggy Dogg while they demolished the food.

"'Rolling down the street smokin' indo, sippin' on gin and juice.'" Awilda popped her neck.

"'Laid back,'" Bea sang. "'With my mind on my money and my money on my mind.'"

"I have ice cream too."

"I'm too full. I shouldn't have eaten that much."

"You did get down like you had the munchies."

Bea smiled.

"Come on, I know how to make you feel better."

She led Bea down the steps to the bottom level. Down there was the family room, Awilda's bedroom suite, and then a recreation area and a powder room. Even though Awilda's family's house was spacious, Bea always felt chilly inside. Awilda took Bea into her bathroom and closed the door.

"Watch me." She leaned her head over the toilet bowl, put her finger down her throat, and threw it all up.

"Ewe, that's disgusting."

"I feel so much better though." She wiped her mouth with the back of her hand. "Look, just put your finger here until you gag and then the food will come up. It's not rocket science."

Bea followed Awilda's instructions and after two tries found the magic spot that made her food come back up.

"You're right. It feels like my stomach can breathe."

"I wish we had a joint or something."

Bea didn't wish they had a joint. The few times she'd smoked with Awilda it made her too loopy. Bea liked being in control.

"Oh, shit." Awilda opened the bathroom door. "You won't believe what I found in the back of my father's closet. Wait here."

Bea sat on the wraparound sofa. Awilda returned with a VHS tape in her hand and a Kool-Aid smile on her face.

"What is that?"

"A porno. You want to watch?"

"Sure."

"Let's brush our teeth first. My mouth feels disgusting."

They did and rinsed with Listerine. Awilda put the video on. The scene opened with a man knocking on the door and a woman letting him in. The two on the screen undressed quickly and went straight to it. The girls watched for a while, then Awilda turned to her.

"Here, let me show you what it's supposed to feel like when a boy starts sucking your titties."

Bea's whole body was tingling from watching the video. "Huh?"

"You need to be prepared when it happens. You can't act all virginal. Like you don't know shit."

Bea kept her eyes on the television while she unbuttoned the top of her dress and then unsnapped her bra. The girl in the video had her knees up in the air with the man's head between her legs. Bea leaned back and Awilda whipped her tongue over her nipples. Then she stuck her hand under Bea's dress, and it made the world go fuzzy.

FOURTEEN

Accidents Happen

Bea tapped the magic spot and the large sausage pizza she'd had delivered from Mimmo's Kitchen and the chocolate cake she'd picked up from Delightful Cake Kreations in Springfield came rushing out. The powder room to the left of the kitchen smelled rancid. She had been rotating bathrooms, going between the one the kids shared and the one she was in. To hide her deed, she sprayed the surfaces down with all-purpose Green Works, but even after she left the windows open for hours, the stank of her offense was still there.

How many times had Bea thrown up? She had lost count. What she knew was that three weeks had passed since she'd read the exchange between Lonnie and his new whore, chili101, and Bea hadn't said a word to him about it. She knew what would come next. Lonnie would say sorry like it was a song on repeat, and she wasn't in the mood for his falsetto. Every time Bea hung her head over the toilet she promised Mena's baby that it would be the last time, but just like Lonnie couldn't keep his dick in his pants, she couldn't keep her finger out of her throat.

Bea stood at the sink in her master, rinsing her mouth with Listerine, when her cell phone rang. It was Awilda. Bea knew this because Awilda had programmed "Soul Sister" by Cree Summer as her ringtone and up flashed a picture of the two of them a few years back at Bea's birthday party. Bea liked the picture because she wasn't pregnant and with Awilda's help had looked damn good in her halter dress and pink lipstick.

I want you to feel good.

I want you to let it all go.

"Hey, sis."

"Bease. Can you meet me at the school? Something terrible has happened!" Awilda's voice was high pitched and screeching.

"What?"

"Just hurry."

Bea scribbled down the address of where Awilda taught summer school. Between the binge and Awilda's call, her belly felt woozy, like she was on a ship swishing around at sea. Awilda always had to play little dramatic mind games. She could have told her what the emergency was instead of having Bea worry the whole drive. When she pulled up to the high school, Awilda was standing out front wearing a tight blouse and pleated skirt.

"Un-freaking-believable." Awilda came to the passenger side window and stuck her head in.

"Would you tell me what the problem is, Ms. Drama?" Bea gripped the steering wheel. She had enough going on without Awilda getting her pressure up.

"The damn fools broke into my car. Snatched out my radio, busted in my back window. My laptop was in there and some fabric that I went all the way into the city to purchase for a dress I'm making. I just want to holler."

Bea took a deep breath, trying to get her own emotions in check.

"Two nights ago a pipe burst in the basement, flooding the whole laundry room, and now this. Who has the money to pay for all of this mess?"

"Your insurance should cover it," Bea said, working hard at being the voice of reason.

"Yeah, however long that takes." She opened the door and got in. "The tow truck took my car. Where are the kids? Can you take me home?"

"They're at playground camp until three-thirty."

Awilda fiddled with the radio station. "I don't know how much more I can handle."

Bea hadn't told Awilda what she'd found on Lonnie's phone in D.C. She couldn't take Awilda stirring in her two cents and making her feel even sourer.

"I'm hungry."

An expert at driving and doling out snacks, Bea reached into her bag and tossed Awilda a granola bar and a small bag of pretzels. "There's some bottled water in the trunk if you'd like me to pull over? I can polish your shoes too while I'm at it."

Awilda rubbed Bea's belly. "Always taking care of me, Bea."

Awilda's house was on the border of two neighborhoods, one considered seedy, the other posh and popular. She lived at the edge, on a dead end block that backed into a park. All of the houses were a bit different from each other. Her neighbors were a mix of eclectic and traditional and Bea loved to comb through their things when they hosted their annual spring yard sale.

"You coming in?"

"Yeah, I should say hello to Derrick. Is he home?"

"Where else could he be? He doesn't have a job, thanks to his mother."

"Wilde, stop. Mercy, remember?"

Awilda unlocked the door. The house was dark and smelled moldy or musky or both. Bea walked over to the living room window, pulled back the curtains, and turned back the blinds.

"Derrick," Awilda yelled. "Bea's here to see you." Awilda headed into the kitchen and pulled an ice-cold Pepsi from the fridge. "You want one?"

"Shouldn't have too much caffeine. Just a quarter of a glass." Bea sat down on the leather sofa thinking about the irony of worrying over caffeine when she couldn't keep her food down. The material snapped and crackled beneath her.

Derrick's footsteps were heavy on the steps and he trudged toward them. He was wearing a white T-shirt and jean shorts. He could use a haircut and his belly was rounder than it had been at the beach. Was that the last time that Bea saw him?

"Hey Bea." He leaned over and kissed her on the cheek. "Baby ready to come out?"

"Almost cooked. Thank goodness."

"Did you eat?" Awilda interrupted.

"Not really."

"I left some veggie pasta in the fridge for you." She sounded as if she was talking to Amare.

"I'll get to it." Derrick leaned against the banister.

"I'm going to check on the water in the basement. Have you been down there?"

"Early this morning. It seems fine."

Awilda headed to the back of the house and down the stairs.

"How have you been? You haven't been coming around."

"I've been so-so. Trying to keep busy. Started taking on small jobs in the neighborhood and helping my mom with some stuff."

"Anything I can do?"

"Yea, get your girl off my case. She thinks I'm one of her little schoolchildren."

Bea giggled. "Awilda thinks we are all her children. Remember that time she couldn't find me because I dropped my phone in the toilet?"

Derrick nodded.

"Man, you would have thought I ran away from home the way she was acting. Point is she loves you. Don't let that hard shell fool you. She's scared, this is new territory for her and you know Awilda does not like change."

"That's why she's still walking around with the iPhone 4—because she doesn't want the new charger."

Bea laughed but she could see from the expression in his weary eyes that he was broken. She knew the feeling. The look. The way depression started in the shoulders and made its way down to the fingertips.

"Look," she said, standing. "This is messed up, and it's okay for you to feel that. One of my favorite authors, Clarissa Pinkola Estés, said, 'I too have felt despair many times in my life, but I don't keep a chair for it; I will not entertain it. It's not allowed to eat from my plate.'"

"I hear you, Bea. Thanks." He helped her from the sofa and they hugged.

Bea was better at giving advice than listening to her own heart. "Anytime. Call me anytime. I actually have a project at the house I could use a hand with. Are you free tomorrow?"

"I could swing by."

"Okay, around nine."

Awilda came upstairs with a basket of laundry. Bea wasn't used to seeing her as a domestic and Awilda caught her smirk.

"Ya'll talking about me?"

"No, never."

"Whatever."

Bea gathered her purse and keys. "I've got to run. You two take care of one another."

Bea steered her SUV in the direction of Evergreen, wishing that she could take her own advice. She had lied to Derrick. Despair was eating off her plate. Had made room for itself at every meal and pushed her into the bathroom to release it back up. Even after that it clung to her sweat.

She had been here before with Lonnie but each time didn't make it easier. Instead, it marked her as a failure. Bea wasn't used to failing at anything. She had passed her driving test the first time. Scored higher than 85 percent of students taking the SATs. Was inducted into the National Honor Society. Finished first in her class in nursing school and even held study groups to help her peers. Motherhood was a challenge but it was in marriage that she scored her first F. Why wasn't she enough for her husband? She had lost count of the chances she had given Lonnie. Boy, had she tried. She should have run when they were living together in D.C. and he took her heart in his hand and crushed it that first time.

Bea recalled surprising him at work with his favorite beef-and-pork lasagna. It had taken her over two hours to prepare the meal. From chopping the onions, peppers, mushrooms, tomatoes, and garlic that gave the dish flavor to grating the cheese by hand—provolone, mozzarella, and Romano. Then kneading the meat with spices and browning it on the stovetop.

She had baked the lasagna in a tin pan and wrapped it in two layers of heavy-duty aluminum foil, then stuffed the pan into a nylon insulated food bag. When it touched his lips, she wanted the cheeses and meat to melt against his tongue like butter so that he would know how much she loved him. Bea didn't drink much but she had even put a chilled beer in the side pocket of the bag to wash his dinner down.

On the walk down the hall to his office, she kept picturing the surprised look on his face. They had both been putting in so many hours at work that they had not shared a meal in a few days. When she rounded the corner and opened his office door, he had his trousers down around his ankles. The front-desk receptionist, Heather, was bent over his desk while he grunted and plunged into her like a starved man.

Bea dropped the food bag. All of her hard work crashed to the floor. When Lonnie turned to see that it was her, he pushed Heather away.

"Bea, Christ." He fumbled for his clothes.

She ran. He tried to follow her but got caught up fixing his pants and Bea was fast. She took the stairs instead of the elevator. Straight from his office she drove her car to Union Station, parked it in the lot, and then caught the eight-thirty train back to her mother's house in New Jersey. Irma was alarmed when her daughter showed up so late but she had the decency to let her go to bed with the promise to discuss it in the morning.

Bea called in sick to work and moped around the house for a week, eating way too much fast food and ignoring her mother's reasons for why she should go back. Lonnie called four, five times a day but she wouldn't take the phone. He sent Godiva chocolate truffles and bouquets of ranunculus, orchids, and tulips. When none of his gifts worked, he showed up at her door in all ivory linen, hat in his hand, hair slicked and shining, smelling like he just stepped from the shower.

"*Mija,* men make mistakes," her mother said, pushing her out the door. "He's a good man and he loves you."

Bea wished she'd listened when Oprah told her viewers, "When people show you who they are, believe them the first time." Instead she stood there listening to Lonnie as he proposed marriage to her with a two-carat emerald-cut ring with pavé diamonds in the platinum band. All her mother's prayers had been answered. He wanted to make an honest woman out of her. She married Lonnie six months later on a beach in the Dominican Republic.

Now she was elbow deep in twelve years of stuff: a mortgage, two sprouting children, the suburbs, and no source of income of her own. What was she supposed to do? Let the floozies win? Take back all that she had sacrificed her adult life for? Single people were pitied. Divorced mothers were looked at as culprits, not the victims. Her children were growing up with privileges that most kids couldn't even dream of. Hell, she was too, even if she was miserable. How could she keep that up without Lonnie? He provided it all.

Bea had never intended to stay home. Work had been a constant part of her adult life and she was good at what she did. Lonnie had suggested that she take time off when Chico was born and she did, for six months, and then they hired a nanny. Once Alana was born, she decided on her own to double the time at home because of Alana's low birth weight and the worry over her cognitive development. The remorse of putting her daughter's life in jeopardy before she had even been born was heart-wrenching. As a mother and a nurse, Bea needed to watch Alana's every developmental milestone to make sure she hadn't damaged her with her illness. One year had quickly turned into two, and Bea didn't go back to work until Alana entered preschool at three, when she was certain that her daughter's brain functioned properly and that her fine motor skills were age-level appropriate.

By then Chico's sports schedule had increased and Alana's progress fared fine (though she needed speech therapy three days a week). Lonnie was busy climbing over people's shoulders at work so Bea dropped her hours to part time. When she became pregnant for Mena and they made the hasty move to New Jersey, she let the job go altogether. She missed her patients, her title, her colleagues, and her sense of importance outside of being a mother and wife. But the kids, as they got older, needed her more—to run errands, chauffer and chaperone, and control the constant chaos. Lonnie wanted her home too. It lightened his load and as he often told her, "I don't have to worry about the children because I know you're with them. That makes it easier for me to provide." His importance was tied to financing the family and Bea had become the unintentional housewife right before her eyes. The lifeline who kept everyone's world spinning on its axis while she stumbled.

The Evergreen town pool was tucked away off Main Street. After she left Awilda's house, Bea had about ten minutes before she had to get out of the car to sign her children out for the day. There was one banana left in her bag and she nibbled on it, feeling hot and anxious. Her due date was three weeks away and she honestly wished the baby would come now. That would make what she was going through less complicated. And she was doing a horrible job of taking care of Mena's baby. She didn't want the banana; she craved hot dogs with relish, cheese pizza, and a bag of chocolate-chip cookies. Bea sat on her hands and tried to breathe the sensation away.

Get your thoughts under control, she chided to herself. Her affirmation notebook wasn't in her purse so Bea opened the door and got out of the car. Walking helped. Another tool for fighting the urge was to focus on her children. When she made her way beyond the gates of the pool, Alana was in a group doing arts and crafts.

"Mommy." She dropped her markers and threw her arms around Bea's waist. Her hands couldn't touch.

"Hey, sweetie." She pushed Alana's hair out of her face, nodded to the teenage counselor, and helped Alana gather her things. They held hands on their stroll around the pool looking for Chico. He was on the diving board.

"Mom, watch," he shouted and then ran and dove into the pool. Bea was impressed. She could swim but never got up the nerve to dive.

"Guess what?" said Alana.

"What?"

"I stayed underwater for ten seconds."

"Nice."

"Hudson was scared. She wouldn't even put her head in. I told her it was easy. It was easy for me." She shrugged her shoulders. Alana wanted to be a big girl so badly that it was comical. Bea was constantly reminding her to enjoy being five but life was moving too slowly for Alana. She always wanted more, now, faster, higher. Bea hoped those qualities would make her a go-getter in the real world. She hoped that Alana wouldn't end up like her.

Chico dripped his water all over both of them.

"Man, son." Bea wiped her hand on her shorts.

He grinned. "Did you see that dive, Mama? I've been practicing it all day. Coach said that I am the fastest at freestyle on the team."

"Wonderful, dear. Let's go."

"Can we stay? Please, all my friends stay after camp."

Bea looked past Chico to the grassy area, noting that the beautiful mothers had already stripped down into their bikinis (Bea couldn't remember the last time she'd worn one of those) and instead of rushing home after camp to prepare dinner, they relaxed, tanned, flipped through magazines, and giggled to each other over God knows what was in those adult sip cups. Bea didn't see anyone she would want to giggle with even if she wasn't fat and pregnant. Standing in her black shorts and too-tight T-shirt, she suddenly felt like a whale on display for all to see.

"No, baby. We have to go."

"Why?" he pleaded. "It's too hot to go home."

"Maybe another day. Promise."

Chico stomped off in front of her. Bea thought about how the one time she had stomped her feet in her mother's house, her mother had grabbed her heels in the air and slapped the soles of her feet until Bea pleaded for mercy. In comparison, Chico got away with murder and Bea didn't have enough chutzpah to do more.

Three weeks of pregnancy dwindled to two and then Bea was down to one. She had decided to play the complacent wife until after the baby was born. The additional stress of confronting Lonnie was too much for her to deal with right now. In the back of her mind she knew that the longer she waited the easier it would be for him to make it go away but still she knew it was best to hold off. Bea would deal with the holes in her marriage after Mena's baby was born healthy and strong. Keeping her food down was hard enough. She had purged almost every single day since D.C., constantly fearing the effects that it would have on Mena's baby, but her addiction was out of control. If she could stop she would.

At their thirty-nine-week appointment, the radiation treatments had Mena feeling too weak to come with Bea.

"I'm pushing myself to just rest it out so that when the baby comes,

I'm ready," Mena told Bea over the telephone and so Clark came by himself. He was awkward without Mena. When the rotating doctor closed his clipboard and told Bea to expect the baby any day, Clark's face was wet and his eyes filled with emotion.

"The proud papa." The doctor patted him on the back.

"Yes."

"Well, your baby will be here soon enough. Please give Mena my best and tell her to get ready."

The doctor left and Clark tried to pull himself together.

"What is it?"

"Mena wanted so much to be able to go through this whole process with you. To feel connected, you know? Damn cancer. Why does it have to be her? She doesn't deserve this. Not now. All she wants in the world is to be a mother." He wept openly, and Bea slid to the edge of the examining table and put her arms around him, pushing him closer to his baby.

"Clark, it's going to be okay. Mena will be okay. You two are about to be parents and everything else will become a distant memory."

"I know."

"You have to believe it. If you believe it then Mena will too."

"Thanks, Bea. You're such a good person."

If he only knew.

Lonnie called just as she got into her car.

"Babe, I'm not going to make it to practice today."

"It's not practice, Lonnie. It's an away game in Kenilworth," she snapped.

"Can't do it."

Dread tinged with hatred swept through her. "You have to. You're the coach."

"I got called to do a presentation at the office in Tarrytown. I have to head up there now."

"Call the other coaches."

"I did. But they want you to come sit in the dugout. They don't have enough coaches today. Regulations."

"You've got to be kidding me."

"I'm sorry to ask."

"You should be."

"I know, baby."

"I'm not doing it."

"Come on, Bea."

"You're crazy. I'm a few seconds away from giving birth. I'm not sitting on a hard bench with a bunch of fifth grade boys. And risk getting hit by a ball? Are you even thinking about what you're asking?"

"What am I supposed to do?"

"Fucking figure it out."

"Whoa."

"Show up when you say you are and stop relying on me for everything." Bea hung up the phone. She turned the ringer off and dropped it in her purse.

Exhale, she reminded herself. *Don't get upset. What you feel the baby feels.* But she was pissed. The nerve. How could he not put Chico's needs first?

It wasn't until she reached home that she realized half of her outrage came from not knowing if he was telling the truth. She pulled a bowl of grapes from the refrigerator and used calling Awilda as a tactic to not overeat.

"Whatcha been up to?"

"Girl, working out, making clothes, anything to keep my mind off of my summer gig. Have I mentioned how much I hate it? Half the kids come to school in their pajamas and only a handful even remember to bring their books. Three days left and I am free. Last week of August is all mine before I head back to my own school. Never thought I'd say it but I've missed that place."

"That's good."

"What's wrong with you?"

"Nothing."

"Don't tell me nothing, I can hear it in your voice."

"Lonnie just called to say he couldn't make Chico's game. He's the freakin' coach."

Bea could hear Awilda slurping a soda. "What was his excuse?"

"Meeting in Tarrytown. He had the nerve to ask me to sit in the dugout for him. In my condition."

"That's a good idea." Awilda snickered.

"That's a terrible idea. I don't know the first thing about baseball and even if I did, I'm about to pop, Awilda. The baby is coming any minute."

"Okay, don't get your panties all in a bunch, I'm not the problem."

Bea pushed her palms against her eyes. "Plus, I'm not even sure if he's telling the truth." She hesitated and then let it drop. "I found something on his phone. Messages between him and a woman."

"Oh, Beasley. Are you serious?"

"He's never home. And why should he be? I'm fat, gross, and ugly. I'm so swollen that it's hard for me to get out of bed in the morning. What was I thinking, carrying this baby for Mena?"

"Oh, Bea, stop it. You're doing the right thing for Mena. You will get through all of this."

"Can you come over? I could use your energy."

Awilda burped.

"Yuck, Wilde."

"Excuse me. I can't, sweetie. Not tonight. I have a dress that I'm making and the woman is coming by tomorrow. I'm so behind on it."

"You can sew over here."

"Girl, it's too much to lug. I'll try to stop by tomorrow."

"Okay," Bea whined.

"Cheer up, sweetie. The baby needs you to be positive."

Bea hung up the phone, knowing that Awilda was right, but all she could think to do to distract herself was to eat. So she did.

FIFTEEN

Forced

Bea had birthed two children and never failed at pushing a baby out with ten fingers and toes and a steady heartbeat. With Alana, she was already in the hospital and was mostly drugged but she still got her out. Chico, she went completely natural with both a doula and a midwife. Now, Bea was on the kitchen floor doubled over in pain as a contraction ripped through her belly. In her hand was her cell phone. She dialed Lonnie's office. When his assistant picked up she tried to keep her voice even and pain free but her worlds came out constipated.

"Is . . . Alonzo . . . in?"

"No, ma'am. He asked me to clear his appointments. He's out for the whole day."

"Out where?"

"Um, let me check." She put Bea on hold. A contraction ran through her.

"I'm sorry, Mrs. Colon, I'm not really sure."

"Thanks." She hung up the phone, her mind wrapped around her husband being AWOL. Then another sharp pain ripped through her body. It felt like she was climbing up a mountain and then when she finally made it to the top, she slid down on her butt back to the rocky bottom. Once the pain subsided, she called Awilda. Voice mail. Bea would call her mother but Irma didn't drive, and 911 would mean she would be handled by strangers. The pain hit again. Climb the mountain, look out at the countryside, slide down on her butt again. She texted Lonnie. Her cell phone rang.

"Hell . . . hello."

"Bea, are you all right?"

It was Mena.

"I'm . . ." The pain hit her so hard she bit down on her tongue until she tasted salt.

"Are you in labor?"

"Yes."

"Are you alone?"

Breath. "Yes. Come. Get me."

"We're on our way. Stay on the phone with me."

Bea shrieked. "Kitchen floor. I'll unlock the back door. Just come in." Bea had gotten into the habit of locking her back door. The man who'd broken in and beaten her neighbor silly was still on the loose. They had a picture of him, had flashed it everywhere, but the only thing it did was instill more fear of black men in her community.

Mena lived ten minutes west, in an even more posh suburb than Evergreen. By the time she and Clark burst through Bea's back door, her water had broken and dripped down her leg and onto the floor.

"Why didn't you call nine-one-one?" Mena cried.

Bea breathed. She was in such a state that her teeth chattered. Talking required too much energy. Mena grabbed her favorite kitchen towel and started mopping Bea off.

"Bea, you're bleeding." Mena's eyes widened. "Is that normal?"

"Yes," Bea lied.

"Maybe we should call the ambulance?"

"Please, don't." The contraction ripped through her again. She doubled over until the pain passed. "I don't want to cause a scene with the neighbors."

"And I don't want to put my baby at risk," Mena shot back.

"And you think I do?" Bea replied, even though she had been purging for weeks.

Clark swooped in. Picked Bea up off the floor and started barking orders to Mena. "Bring some bottled water and grab a big bath towel that we can put under her in the car. Don't worry, Bea, we'll get you there."

Bea insisted on walking down the driveway, and Mena was there to help her into the car.

"You want to wear your seat belt?"

"No." Then Bea remembered. "My kids . . . someone needs to tell Joney."

"I have her number, remember? I'll call her. Don't worry, Bea," said Clark.

"Tell her to pick them up from the pool at three-thirty. Ask her to keep them until . . ." Her body started climbing the mountain again. It took her thoughts away.

"Bea, stop worrying. We've got it. You've gone over it a million times. Your kids will be safe. Let us get you to the hospital."

Mena was right. Bea had prearranged with Joney, sent Joney an e-mail, and copied Mena, Clark, Awilda, and Lonnie so that everyone would be on the same page. But still, she needed reassurance that her children were cared for before she left.

"Clark, please just go knock on Joney's door."

"Okay."

Mena had calmed a bit and did a good job of being brave. She had attended the birthing classes with Bea and did her part in the backseat to help Bea breathe through the discomfort.

Clark jumped behind the wheel. "Here, Joney told me to give you this. She said it would guide you through the birth."

It was a crystal of some sort. Bea clutched it with her right hand, then leaned over the side, opened the car door, and threw up.

The hospital was not far but the ride was a rough one for Bea. When they pulled up to the Emergency Room, the attendant put her in a wheelchair and Mena joined her as she was rushed up to labor and delivery. Within minutes, Clark had finished parking the car and was by their side. Bea looked at him. Clark was a thoughtful husband to Mena. She was the lucky one.

"Can you try Lonnie again?" Bea had never delivered a baby without her husband by her side and she was scared. As soon as she got to the hospital they gave her Demerol intravenously to ease her pain. She could talk now without her teeth chattering but she still felt terrible.

"I left him another message, Bea. I'm sure he'll be on his way soon."

Bea turned her face. She hoped the children didn't give Joney any problems. Had she remembered to tell Clark to lock her back door? Where was her husband?

"Hello there." It was a woman obstetrician from the rotation, Dr. Garrison. Bea had only met her once and she wasn't happy to see her.

"Where's Dr. Spellman?"

"Attending another birth. Today is a busy day."

"Can you call her?"

The doctor smiled at Bea. Then she pushed Bea's hair off of her forehead. It felt loving, like a mother's touch. Bea found herself relaxing instantly.

"Everything is going to be just fine, Beatrice," said Dr. Garrison. "Here, sit up a little." When Bea moved, she felt the baby slip down.

"Oh. Oh, I think it's time."

"Then let's go to work," said the doctor. She lifted the blanket around Bea's waist and put her feet in the stirrups. Bea could hear Mena praying her rosary and wondered if Clark was still in the room. She knew he was. He wouldn't leave Mena's side.

Bea assumed having Mena's baby would be easy since her body was open from having her own children. But with the Demerol wearing thin and her refusal of the epidural, the pain was prominent. She pushed for two hours and the baby only moved down an inch.

Where was Lonnie?

Bea was exhausted but the baby wouldn't descend. Then she felt hot. Very hot all over, and a tingling, burning sensation wrapped around her like she had stumbled into a pit of coals and fire. Then code colors were being shouted from voices she didn't recognize and doctors started to rush in. Bea felt herself drifting in a way that she couldn't control. Then her head was spinning and then it all stopped.

Later, when Bea felt her presence return to the room, she felt heavy and drugged. Something wasn't right with her body. Something had happened and Bea didn't know what it was, but she was sure that it was the consequence of her actions. No bad deed went unpunished. She had lost control. Purged more times than she could count. How could she do that to Mena? To the baby? This pregnancy was supposed to be her redemption and she'd failed. Slowly, she opened her eyes. A nurse was standing over her with a flashlight, looking into her pupils.

"You okay?"

"No."

"We had to do an emergency C-section. You had a mild placental abruption and we needed to get the baby out before she lost too much oxygen."

"Is she okay?"

"The baby appears to be fine."

Bea surprised herself by making the sign of the cross: touching her forehead, her heart, and crossing her chest the way her mother always did at the sign of any news.

"You'll be fine too. I just need to check your vitals."

"Where is my husband?"

The nurse looked startled. "There's a couple out by the nursery. I can send for them if you like."

Bea's nose started to run. The tears welled and fell. In her family there was pride in pushing a baby out. Lonnie knew that a C-section would have been the very last option but he wasn't there to ask questions. Bea had almost died and her husband was nowhere to be found.

"Let me give you something to make you more comfortable." The nurse adjusted Bea's IV and then Bea was out again. She dreamt of unsavory things.

SIXTEEN

Promises Kept

The first voice Bea heard was Lonnie's. He was speaking in that charming I-have-the-room-in-my-palm tone. It was one of the things that she'd liked about him when they first met but now got under her skin. How he controlled every situation and people just stepped aside so he could. She kept her head on her pillow with her eyes closed and just listened as he launched into one of his stories.

"It was our first trip with Chico. We took him out to Napa Valley. He was like two or three months old but Bea and I had it in our minds that we were going to make parenting en vogue."

Mena laughed.

"I thought I was helping Bea by packing the Pampers, wipes, and those little essentials so she could focus on him. When we got to the airport, don't you know I left the bag at home? I was rushing through the airport looking for diapers and almost missed the plane."

"Thank God for me," she croaked.

Everyone looked in her direction.

"Baby." He looked down at her with concern.

"I had six diapers in my bag. That's how we made the plane."

He rubbed her nose the way he did when they first met. "I was so worried about you. How are you feeling?"

Her voice was husky. "Okay."

Mena brought the baby over to the side of the bed and turned her around so that Bea could see her.

"Awwww," Bea moaned.

She was swaddled in a pink-and-white blanket and had a matching hat on her head. Her skin was so pale it was translucent.

"Bea, you did it. Isn't she beautiful?" Mena's voice cracked as she buried the baby back against her chest. Bea longed to feel her in her arms, smell her skin.

"We did it."

Awilda stood in the corner, her fingers moving over her phone. "I just checked in with Joney. The kids are being bad. Want me to go over there and beat them silly?" She smiled.

"Yeah, until you get tired."

"Girl, right now I'm wide awake."

Bea cracked a smile and flagged Awilda. "How long have you guys been standing over me?"

"It feels like I've been waiting for you to open your eyes forever," said Lonnie, clutching her hand in his. "I'm so proud of you."

He was lathering it on thick. Bea felt a pain in her abdomen and wasn't sure if it was physical or just disgust. She turned her face away from Lonnie and tried to get another peek of the baby.

"Bea, you must be starved. Do you want me to run out and get you some dinner?" Clark stood on the other side of her.

"What time is it?"

"Almost eight," replied Awilda. "You missed dinner, you need to eat something."

"Okay."

"What?"

"Maybe some soup. Iced tea or just something sweet."

"Coming right up."

Her recovery was slow. It was nothing like how she felt after giving birth vaginally. Her skin was itchy and every time she opened her eyes she was nauseous. The center of her body suffered from a tender mushiness, like a half-baked cake, and it hurt when she shifted her weight.

After her second night in the hospital, her nurse, Merry (*like Merry Christmas,* she told her in a cheery voice that annoyed Bea), removed the catheter and encouraged Bea to move around a bit. Bea didn't want to move but once she sipped that second cup of tea, she had to use the bathroom.

The next morning, she was up walking gingerly back to her bed when Mena wheeled the baby in.

"You're out of the bed. Still in pain?"

Bea lied. "No, I feel fine. How's little miss?"

"Doing well. Just waiting for the discharge papers so that we can take her home. This is just surreal, Bea. Thank you so much for doing this. You have changed our lives forever."

Bea sat on the edge of the bed. "Let me see her." Mena told her that they had named her Sophia, which meant wisdom. Bea peered at her little face and thought that the name fit. It was still astonishing to her that she'd brought this little person into the world for Mena and Clark. That she had no biological connection at all after carrying her for nine months. Sophia didn't look like her children. Why would she?

"She is the spitting image of my baby pictures," Mena boasted. To Bea, Sophia didn't look like any of them.

"Perfect little angel." Bea could sense that Mena wanted the baby back and so she handed her over. "I'm happy for you. Motherhood is an amazing journey. Just know that you can't get it right and you'll never get it all done. That will take some of the pressure off. And it goes fast. I can't believe Chico is already double digits."

"I haven't forgotten what we talked about." Mena stood up and closed the door with her free hand, clutching Sophia close to her breast with the other. Out of her purse she pulled a crème colored envelope and handed it over to Bea.

"Mena . . ."

"Shh, Bea. You promised. No one knows about this but me. And no one should know."

Bea opened the envelope and discovered three checks for nine thousand dollars each.

"Mena! Are you crazy? This is insane."

"The amount is not even close to enough." Mena kissed Bea on the forehead and then held Sophia to her heart. "I'll love you forever for this."

Bea didn't know what to say. Clark knocked and as he walked in Bea slid the envelope under the bedcovers.

"Hey Bea, you're looking good."

Bea knew she looked a mess. She hadn't combed her hair in the three days that she had been in the hospital.

"Our daughter is all checked out and ready to go home, sweetie."

"Finally. I better get her dressed."

"I'll go down to the car and grab her seat," said Clark. "Bea, you want anything from the cafeteria?"

"No, thank you." Clark left. "What are you taking the baby home in?"

Mena handed Bea the baby while she retrieved the carry-on bag from the corner. When she opened it she had enough baby clothes for a week.

"Are you going on vacation from here?"

"I just didn't want to leave anything at home."

"Darling, you have enough stuff in that suitcase to dress every baby in the nursery."

Mena held up a pink sleeper with a matching hat.

"Precious."

Mena reached for Sophia and sat on the edge of Bea's bed. The baby stirred, opening her mouth into a little yawn. "Awwwww, precious love," Mena said and then started coughing.

"You been feeling okay?"

"Just tired from my meds. And the baby hasn't even made it home yet." Mena wore her hair extensions and Bea could see that she had taken time to powder the sickness from her face.

"If you need my help, I'll come by in a few days."

"You've done enough, Bea. This next step is on me."

Bea knew Mena was right but that didn't stop the pinch of sadness from coming over her when she had to say good-bye to the new family. The one she had helped create.

Dr. Spellman came by to check on her shortly after Mena left and insisted that Bea remain in the hospital a fourth day for observation. Secretly, she was happy to stay. She enjoyed the meds that the nurses gave her and when given a choice, insisted on the strongest dose available. The television was on and she watched in a fog, not thinking much of anything. Time passed without her keeping track. It was the most rest she'd had in months.

On the morning she was to be discharged, Lonnie took the day off from work to bring her home.

"Hey, baby." He leaned down for a kiss. He had a bouquet of flowers and they made her smile.

"They're beautiful. Thank you." She brushed her hair. "Where're the kids?"

"Your mother has them. She insisted on them staying with her until you got home."

He'd had three nights to run the streets.

"Ready?"

"I guess." Bea didn't want to leave her hospital room. Once she did, she would have to deal with her real life, and being here had made it easy to pretend.

"Can I get you anything?"

"No, nothing."

SEVENTEEN

Naked and Afraid

Bea had only been home recuperating for three days when Lonnie left for a five-day business trip.

"Really? You have to go with me in this condition? School starts in a week and I haven't gotten anything done."

"Babe, this is how I pay the bills. They need me."

"I need you."

"I don't want to leave you. Trust me, I don't." He looked deeply into her eyes, forcing her to look away. "Irma is downstairs cooking up a storm. She promised me that she'd take good care of you until you got better."

"I'm not sick, Lonnie. I had a baby. They cut me open." *I almost died in that hospital and you weren't there.* She reached for her painkillers.

"Would you get me some water?"

Lonnie was bent over wiping a smudge from his brown loafers, the casual ones that he wore when he traveled. "Of course, baby."

He had been sugary sweet since he'd announced that he had to leave.

"Here." Lonnie returned with a big cup of ice water.

"I didn't ask for ice."

Lonnie went into the bathroom, dumped the ice out, and brought the water back.

"Why do you have to go?"

"Bea, we've been through this. Please don't make this harder than it has to be."

"Why weren't you at the hospital when Sophia was born?"

"We've been through this too. I was in a meeting that ran long. I'm sorry. You know I wanted to be there for you."

Bea rolled over and stared at the wall. How did she know anything when it concerned him?

"When I get back, we'll do something special. Get yourself better so I can take you out and show you a good time." He kissed her cheek. Then she heard his luggage clunking down the stairs. Bea fell asleep. When her eyes opened she wasn't sure how much time had passed but she could smell her mother's special soup, *asopao de pollo,* wafting from the kitchen. Her mother thought that the thick meaty soup with yucca and vegetables was the cure-all for everything. After her father's funeral, she made the soup. The time Bea showed up at her house after catching Lonnie with his assistant, they ate the soup. After Chico was born, her mother brought the soup down on Amtrak to D.C.

"To heal your female parts, *mija,*" she had said then.

"You're up." Irma paused in the doorway. It seemed to Bea that her mother's hips were getting wider every time she saw her. She had urged Irma to go to the community center where they had workout classes for seniors but she never went. When Bea's father died, it was like he took her mother's beauty with him. She just stopped caring. Instead she sat with dinner on a tray in front of *telenovelas.* The only place Irma walked was to the bus stop, which was a half block from her apartment. Most times she didn't do that. She had a medical plan that allowed her to call for ride shares and that van picked her up right in front of her house.

"I'm not hungry."

"You need to eat. The kids are asking for you. They are worried. Said you've been spending all of your time in your bed. I told them you were just recovering and would be down soon. Will you be down soon?"

Bea pulled the covers over her head. "Just leave it there. I'm tired."

"Do you want to talk?"

"No."

"Okay. I bought you a magazine."

Irma left it on the edge of Bea's bed and then backed out and closed the door. Bea's breasts were leaking. She had asked Lonnie to bring her a head of cabbage so that she could dry up the milk and he had bought lettuce.

In the days that followed, Bea had not gotten out of bed for more than it took to go to the bathroom. If she remembered, she brushed her teeth. It had become difficult to rouse herself to be bothered with anything. The kids talked without her remembering the conversation. They asked for things and she just said yes.

"I think you are suffering from that postpartum depression, honey." Irma put her hand on Bea's forehead like she would know with one touch. "Not good. Should I call the doctor?"

"I'm fine, Ma."

"I don't know. I saw it on *Dr. Oz*. Women who have babies and then can't get out of bed. They have thoughts of suicide. You feel depressed?"

"No. I'm just tired."

"You've been in bed for three days. You can't let Lonnie come back and see you like this."

Fuck Lonnie, Bea thought and rolled away from her mother's gaze.

Irma stood with her hands on her hips and took the tone she'd used on Bea during her difficult adolescent years. "You're going to eat dinner tonight if I have to spoon-feed you myself." She turned and left.

Bea waited until she was sure her mother was in the kitchen and pulled her feet from the bed. It hurt. She moved to the rocking chair that she kept by the window in time to see Joney raise her hands to the sky and then fold over on her yoga mat. Bea watched Joney move through the air with ease and surety. Bea felt an emotional pendulum fight for space in her chest. She went from happy at seeing Joney to crying breathlessly. It was as if a switch had been turned in her head and she went from light to dark and then had crashed into sad. Images of her father lying in the coffin at the funeral home came to her. Then the sound of his wife's voice pierced into her ears. Bea remembered how desperate she'd sounded when she screamed, "Oh Lord, why have you forsaken me?"

Bea could relate to her weeping. She felt left out in the desert, alone to die with no one or nothing to comfort her. If only she could open up her chest and stop the pain. The nightgown she wore was irritating her skin and she took it off. She went into her bathroom and started a bath. When the tub was filled with hot water, Bea couldn't stop picturing herself getting into the tub and holding her head under the water until she was no more.

What the hell was happening to her? She knew the baby was Mena's and not once during her pregnancy had she thought of the child as her own, but now she felt lost without the kicks of the baby. She was no longer important. Didn't have a job to do. With the distraction of the pregnancy out of the way, now she had to deal with her life. It felt unbearable so Bea climbed back into bed.

She had listened all day to the rhythms of the house. Dinnertime. Bath time. Bedtime. Her mother cleaning the dishes and prepping for the next day. The digital clock on her nightstand flashed 1:53 A.M. The dark horse had climbed into bed with her and urged her to get up. Bea didn't want to, it still hurt a bit to walk up and down the steps. She was supposed to be up and walking from the moment she got home so that her body would adjust but she had been in bed.

When Bea walked into her kitchen it was spotless. It smelled like Pine-Sol and white vinegar. The room was cleaner than when the cleaning lady came every other week. Her mother was like that. You could eat off the floor. Saliva gathered on her tongue as the dark horse pushed her to open the French doors of the refrigerator. It was well stocked. Lonnie must have taken Irma shopping before he left. She didn't stop to think. She pulled out everything that she could get her hands on: containers of rice, beans, and *puerco asado*, the pork. She warmed the soup in the microwave and found bags of chips, pretzels, Wheat Thins, and peanuts from the pantry and made herself a party mix.

Bea lined up all of her treats on the kitchen counter and then went from item to item like she was being timed. Full, she burped. Inside the downstairs powder room she locked the door, ran the faucet, and then made it all come back up.

EIGHTEEN

Sniffing for Happy

Bea watched television in the family room on Lonnie's supersized television with the surround sound turned low. She had flipped through the channels until she landed on QVC. The discovery of this channel had both delighted and mesmerized her. The host, David Venable, convinced her to order Bobby Chez's famous jumbo lump crab cakes, Kansas City filet mignons, and gadgets for pizza night. In the next hour, Jayne Brown sold her backpacks and water bottles for the children's return to school, and a stainless steel bracelet that read FAITH. Bea had never ordered anything on television before and for a brief inkling she experienced the same high she felt when she binged.

It was that time between the middle of the night and morning when she went back upstairs to her bedroom. She was again restless. Her eyes darted around for something to do. She went into Lonnie's closet and without even putting on her white gloves went through all of his clothes, pulling them down one by one until more than half of what he owned was in a big pile on the floor. Bea curled up in the pile and went to sleep.

She hadn't heard her mother come in until she was standing over her.

"*Dios mio!* Beatrice, what's the matter with you?"

Bea looked at her but said nothing.

Bea was still there an hour later when the door opened again. This time Bea was butt-naked on the hardwood floor with the clothes piled on top of her.

"Bea."

Awilda walked into the closet and got down on the floor next to her. "I brought your favorite." She held up a bag of Chewy Chips Ahoy.

Bea swallowed her saliva, searching for her voice.

"What's wrong?"

"I don't know."

"You miss the baby?"

"I don't know."

"Lonnie?"

"Not really."

"So what is it?"

"I don't want to be here. I'm just taking up space. Wilde, I can't even stand to hear my kids' voices. Can't do this family thing anymore. I just want out."

"All right."

"All right, what?"

"We'll leave. Get dressed and we'll go."

Bea let Awilda help her up from the floor. Bea was already naked so it wasn't hard to get her into the shower. At first Bea just stood there and let the hot water crash over her.

"Use some soap," Awilda commanded.

Bea did what she was told. Awilda handed her a clean towel.

"These are like hotel towels. Where'd you get them?"

"Nordstrom's in Short Hills. Lonnie only likes white Turkish cotton towels, like he gets at a hotel."

"Next time grab me two. I'll pay for them."

Bea nodded.

"Come, let me wash your hair." Awilda made Bea get onto her knees and lean over the bathtub while she washed and conditioned her hair. The lavender smell from the shampoo relaxed Bea. With a towel wrapped around her head, Awilda led her to the rocking chair and she combed her hair piece by piece. When it was combed out, she gave Bea two French braids.

"Good as new."

When Bea looked out the window, the sun had checked out for the night. "What time is it?"

"TV time. Come." Awilda crawled onto Bea's bed and flicked on the television.

"Here, have a cookie."

They stayed in Bea's bed, eating the whole package of cookies until Bea drifted off to sleep.

The next morning when Bea woke up, she heard the shower running. She couldn't remember Lonnie coming home. Then Awilda came out wrapped in one of her plush towels, hair piled on top of her head.

"I need these towels. Don't forget, Bea."

"I gotcha."

"I need to borrow something to wear."

"My clothes are down the hall in the playroom closet."

Awilda left and returned with two sets of yoga pants and long shirts, one for each of them.

"Get dressed, we're going out."

Bea did as she was told.

"Where are we going?" Standing in her driveway, the fresh air felt good on her skin. It was a cool day with just the right amount of sunshine.

"For a drive."

Awilda drove a two-door Nissan Altima. It was always a treat to be in her car, without granola bars, tangerine peelings, and french fries crusted into the seats.

"Here, put some lip gloss on." Awilda handed her a tube. She snaked the car through three neighborhoods before she reached an office building. It was one that Bea had been to before. It was Dr. Spellman's office.

"Why are we here?"

"You had an appointment, remember?"

"No. I thought we were going someplace fun."

"We are, after you check in with Dr. Spellman. It's going to be quick. I promise."

Bea got out of the car. She did not want to see Dr. Spellman. She wanted to go someplace fun but they were here, and knowing Awilda the way she did, they were staying until she saw the doctor.

"Fine." Bea stomped over to the office and signed in.

They waited only five minutes before a medical assistant called her back.

Dr. Spellman walked in with that award-winning smile that put Bea at ease, then it made her tear up.

"What's wrong with my favorite patient?"

"I don't know. I'm just sad."

"Do you miss the baby?"

"I don't know what it is. It feels like I used to be full and now I'm empty."

"How's your diet?"

"I haven't been eating." She could tell from the flash in Dr. Spellman's eyes that she knew that she was lying.

"I went on a binge and now I'm worried about the baby." She put her hands up to her head.

Dr. Spellman put her hand on her shoulder. "Don't cry, Bea, just tell me what happened."

Bea recounted the first binge at McDonald's and how she'd tried to get it under control but the dark horse just kept breathing down her neck every day, urging her to do it.

"How often?"

"At least once a day for the past few weeks. Since July."

"I haven't checked the baby's paperwork but I will."

"Don't say anything, please."

"Beatrice. I want to help you feel better. Tell me how else you feel."

"I'm just tired. I feel trapped and I think . . . about bad things."

She typed on her laptop. "Like what?"

Bea whispered. "Like I want to cut myself open and jump out of my skin."

"Go on."

"I hate myself. I'm worthless. Everyone just uses me and would be better off if I was gone. I don't want to see my children. I just want to be in bed. Even the sound of the crickets makes me miserable. I just wish they would shut up."

She typed some more and then turned her attention toward Bea. "Beatrice, have you heard of postpartum depression?"

"I studied it in nursing school but that was so long ago now." She looked away.

"Okay, good, so you know a little. Postpartum is caused by a hormonal shift that occurs after childbirth. When you were pregnant, your estrogen and progesterone levels were very high. When the baby was born they dropped back to normal. This swift change in hormones is what has you feeling out of whack. It's causing the despair."

"Well, can you fix me?"

"I think a low level antidepressant will help. You should feel some changes in a week or two and be back to normal in six to eight weeks."

"How long will I have to take the pills?"

"Let's meet in two weeks and we'll see how it's going. The important thing is for you to start feeling better."

"Okay."

"Great, same pharmacy?"

"Yes."

"I'll send the prescription right over. In the meantime, find a hobby that you like, take walks, anything to keep your mind occupied until the pills kick in."

"Thanks, doc."

Awilda drove her to the pharmacy so they could pick up the pills. Bea swallowed her first Paxil in the car.

"I hope this works."

"Give it time, it will. I know a few teachers at work that take Paxil and they seem fine."

"I hate that I need drugs to feel normal."

"Get over it. I just want you to feel better."

"Where are we going?"

"It's Wednesday, I was thinking we could have lunch at the open-air market."

Bea smiled. "You always know what to say, Wilde."

Awilda turned on the radio to music that thumped and steered her car toward what Bea usually felt like was her piece of heaven. Being around fresh flowers, smelling the just-baked bread, touching the organic leafy vegetables, and drinking the tart, fresh-squeezed lemonade always made her feel better.

Lonnie had called to say that he needed to extend his trip by a day and would be home on Friday. It was the start of the weekend. Irma made homemade pizza and what the kids referred to as back-in-the-day popcorn because she made it on the stovetop and not in the microwave. Bea had been glad the kids were busy with her mother in the kitchen because it took the focus off of her. When they were around all they wanted to do was touch her and that irritated her skin. While they cooked and listened to Celia Cruz, she sat on the back patio and read *Outlander* by Diana Gabaldon. Dr. Spellman had recommended that Bea do things to take her mind off of how she was feeling and there was nothing Bea loved more than historical fiction. Books were her favorite escape and she was lost between the pages when Lonnie appeared, looking like he just walked out of a fashion magazine, not weathered in the least from his flight. He swept her up into his arms and kissed her like a man would kiss a woman at the end of a romantic movie. She actually smiled.

"You missed me?"

"I did."

"Let's go to Basilico for dinner. Your mom has everything covered here."

She had on the one maxi dress that didn't make her look pregnant and her mother had forced her into her good bra and a pair of

Spanx to pull the baby fat together two hours before Lonnie was supposed to arrive.

"Okay."

Basilico, an upscale Italian restaurant on Main Street, was known for being a trendy BYOB with dependably good food, a New York restaurant atmosphere, and a well-trained waitstaff. Bea had read about the spot in the paper but had never dined there. She was looking forward to having a good meal that she would force herself to keep down. Lonnie pulled a bottle of red wine from the trunk of his car and ushered Bea toward the restaurant.

"Reservation?" asked the blond hostess. Her eyes were black rimmed and her breasts spilled forward. She looked at Lonnie but not Bea.

"Colon, for two."

"Right this way, Mr. Colon."

At the table Bea asked, "What, am I invisible?"

Lonnie patted her hand. "What would you like to start off with?"

"Have you been here before?"

"No, sweetie."

"Maybe we should go to your special restaurant in Chatham." Bea touched her lips, unable to control the flow of words. "I know all about chili101 so don't come home trying to play the loving husband."

The disbelief played around his eyes. She could tell by the way he swallowed his saliva that he was searching for a bucket of water to quench the fire.

"Bea."

"Don't *Bea* me. Open your phone," she demanded. The waiter interrupted.

"Would you like to hear the specials?"

"Not now."

Lonnie ordered the *carpaccio di manzo* and the burrata to start, in a voice that apologized for his wife. "Honey, do you want to try the skirt steak?"

"Sure."

"I'll have the salmon."

The waiter collected the menus. Lonnie passed Bea his phone. She glared at him and then moved her fingers over the screen, searching through his apps for the one that she'd found in D.C. Wine was poured into her glass but she didn't look up. It felt like the temperature in the restaurant was rising. The red velvet walls seem to close in. Nearby table conversations were too noisy. The app was gone.

"You're such a liar." She slammed the phone down onto the table. The water goblet shook but nothing tipped over.

"Baby, calm down. I know you haven't been feeling like yourself lately. I'm doing my best to support you."

"Do you really think I'm that stupid?"

"You are the smartest woman that I know."

Bea picked up the glass and gulped the wine. It was smoky and sweet, one of her favorite combinations. She took another sip.

"I spoke to Clark, he said Mena and the baby were doing fine. We should probably go for a visit." Lonnie drummed his fingers on the tabletop, a bad habit he had when he was displeased.

The food was beautifully arranged when it arrived. Bea wanted to wolf it down. After confronting Lonnie it would be nearly impossible to keep it down. She glanced to the back of the restaurant.

"Excuse me." She placed her napkin next to her plate. Lonnie rose to help her with her chair.

Bea found the ladies' room and it was just as she'd thought. Communal stalls. Not a good situation for a purge, especially with the place being so crowded on a Friday night. She washed her hands and returned to the table.

"Everything okay?"

The wine was smooth as silk as it coated her throat. Bea wondered why she didn't drink more. The lightness felt heady.

Lonnie sliced a piece of steak off of Bea's plate. "Are you going to eat?"

She didn't respond.

"I don't know why you just can't be happy. You have everything a woman could possibly ask for. A beautiful home in the best suburb."

"Your choice. Not mine."

"You have . . ."

"Everything but you."

Lonnie gripped his napkin. "I'm here for Christ's sake."

Bea finished the glass of wine. "Not all of you."

"This is ridiculous."

"From that first time at your office . . . to that bitch in Miami . . . Ms. Instagram . . . and now the new one that you've erased from your phone like I'm some stupid little schoolgirl."

The waiter appeared and refreshed their wine. Bea watched him walk away.

"Why did you marry me in the first place if I wasn't enough? You begged me."

"Because I love you. Stop this, will you?"

Bea couldn't control the emotions that welled up in her face.

"I'll get the food to go."

"I just had your cousin's baby."

"Your choice. Not mine."

"So this new chick is my punishment?"

"There is no new anything."

"I would respect you more if you had the decency to be honest." Bea snatched the keys off the table and walked out of the restaurant. When she got into the car, she wanted so badly to leave him. Make a big scene like she had often seen on television. But the two glasses of wine that she'd guzzled down had her feeing too loopy to drive.

Lonnie climbed into the driver's seat and placed the to-go bag behind him. He said nothing to her as he pulled away from the curb. She looked out the window at the high-end specialty shops, and then at the mature array of trees, and the colonial, Tudor, and craftsman homes that were tucked safely away from the street. Everything about this life was buttoned-up and sterile. Except for the emotional roller coaster that Bea constantly rode. This was not how Bea had pictured her life. She was unhappy more than happy, an in-home spy inflicting self-harm, and now on prescription medication. She was disgraceful. That's why he cheated. He probably felt sorry for her. The last thing Bea wanted was pity. She grabbed the to-go bag out of the backseat and headed toward the garage.

"Don't follow me," she hissed.

"I won't."

And he didn't.

Fright

Awilda had handmade Chico's and Alana's Halloween costumes every year since the children were born. They were always more creative than anything you could get at the store, lasting way past Halloween and then worn for dress-up until too small. Bea still had a few in the attic, saving them for God knows who because her tribe was finished. Perhaps she just hung onto them sentimentally since Awilda had made them. This year Alana wanted to be a spy from the movie *Spy Kids* and Chico a teen wolf. Bea wasn't clear if it was *Teen Wolf* the television show, or *Teen Wolf* the movie with Michael J. Fox, but she was sure Awilda would figure it out and nail them both.

Lonnie usually took the children trick-or-treating while Bea stayed at the house and gave away the candy. Before they went to bed, they were allowed three pieces of their choosing. Having the sweets in the house was dangerous and Bea would have to throw it away after a week or so because she wouldn't be able to stop eating it. Bea hadn't heard from Awilda in over a week so she sat at the kitchen island and called.

"Sis, where have you been?" she said in her mama voice.

"Huh?"

"I haven't heard from you."

"You didn't get my text?"

"That was two days ago."

"I know. Sorry. We're giving a new test at school in the spring. It's going to be the first one the kids take on the computer so everyone has been freakin' out. I've been working late and dealing with these crazy-ass parents."

"I confronted your boy about the new heffa."

"What he say?"

"He's such a liar. He deleted the app, so when he let me look in his phone, the conversation I read was gone."

"Aw, Bea."

"Right? I'm not stupid. I'd be able to handle this better if he were honest."

"So what are you going to do?"

"I'm tired, sis. Right now I'm trying not to think about it. The kids are so busy. The school quarter is ending. What's up with the Halloween costumes?"

"Huh?"

"For Chico and Alana. It's right around the corner."

"Oh, shit."

"What does that mean?"

"Bea, I totally forgot."

"The kids sent you e-mails with what they wanted."

"I know. Hon, it's been crazy. I don't think I'll be able to do them this year."

Bea was silent.

"I know, I know. I suck. I'm so sorry. I'll pay for the costumes if you want."

Bea would never take Awilda's money, especially with Derrick out of work. "They're going to be so disappointed."

"I'll make it up to them. I promise. When you get the costumes take a picture of them and perhaps I can add a little flare."

"Whatever."

"Seriously. I can't take it when you pout, Beasely."

"Well, I'm pouting."

Awilda sighed. "How have you been feeling otherwise?"

"More like myself."

"The pills are working?"

"Yeah. I'm thinking I may not need them much longer, I've been feeling pretty good."

"Talk to Dr. Spellman first, Bea. Don't just do your own self-diagnosis."

"I know. I will."

"I need to drop by for dinner one night soon."

"Sophia's christening is the Sunday after Halloween. I'm thinking about having a little dinner party for them the following Saturday. Invite my neighbor Joney over as a thank-you for keeping the kids when I was in the hospital. I never did anything for her."

"That date works for me."

Bea sucked her teeth. "I'm totally pissed about the costumes, Wilde."

"I know, Bea."

"Now I'm going to be at Party City last minute with the rest of the fools this week picking through plastic."

"My bad, really. I'll drop by in a day or two and you can make me lunch."

"Sounds like a plan."

Only Alana was upset about Awilda not making the costumes. Chico didn't seem fazed.

"I'm too old for costumes anyway. I just want a mask and some teeth. Oh, and some fake blood."

"How are we supposed to find a spy costume?" Alana asked.

"Chico, help her look online."

The kids hovered over her tablet as Bea made dinner. Lonnie hated meatloaf, said his mother had made it too often for him as a child, but Bea had some ground beef and she was sick of making spaghetti. She'd throw a jar of gravy over it and pair it with some mashed potatoes and fresh string beans. The one vegetable that the whole house agreed on was string beans so dinner would be a partial hit.

"How's this?" Alana showed her a costume. Bea was just happy that she'd found something and whipped out her credit card and ordered it on the spot.

While they ate dinner, Bea mentioned her idea of having a dinner party for Sophia. She needed to put her eyes on her, inspect her movements the way she had with Alana to assure that she was all right. Be assured that her illness had not affected that precious baby.

"No kids"—she waved her fork—"except for Sophia."

"I want to come," whined Chico.

"Me too."

"Whatever you want," Lonnie added.

"No fair."

"Life's not fair," Chico said.

"Life is what you make it, son."

"It's been a long time since I've felt like being social. I'll start planning." The pills must have been working.

"Mama, why can't we come?"

"Because."

"Because what? We live here too."

"I know, sweetie."

"Make sure you hire the caterers. I don't want you slaving in the kitchen. I want you to enjoy yourself." He rubbed her hand.

Lonnie had not been home much in the past few weeks but when he was he turned all of his attention on Bea. It felt like he was trying to make up. Constantly going over the top to reassure her that their life together was good. For Bea, it was good to coast and not argue but things weren't fixed. There was a wedge there that flowers, gifts, and even the upcoming dinner parties couldn't fix.

Something inside of Bea had shifted after the birth of Sophia but she didn't know what to do with it. Some nights Bea lay awake wondering if this was all that marriage was for most people. Sloppily placed bandages over wounds that never healed, for the sake of sharing a name, the bleachers at kids' events, and eating dinner together. Was everyone's life like this or was theirs a special nuptial? No matter how much she thought about it she couldn't figure it out. Bea resolved to keep moving and not do anything, until something would push her down into the gaping hole and force her to look up. Like on Thursday morning, when she sat down to write her shopping list for the dinner party and heard the ding on her phone alerting her of a new e-mail. She touched the screen. It was from Connie. Every time her name appeared in her in-box it was like a stiletto through her heart.

The next payment for Alonzo's school is due on the 15th. Thanks so much for your agreement. He's received all As on his

progress report and seems to be adjusting to the new environ-
ment well.
Yours in parenting,
Connie

Bea hated that Connie always signed the e-mails *yours in parenting*. Bea had agreed to pay for the boy's schooling but could do without the updates. She never passed them on to Lonnie anyway. Never wanting him to get the idea of bringing that boy into their fold. She filed the e-mail into her e-mail folder called X and shut down her phone.

TWENTY

Adult Social

Preparing for Sophia's dinner party gave Bea something to focus on. She found herself humming to an old Whitney Houston song while pulling down the nice china to set the table. Bea had not exercised in ages and it felt good to move her hips to the beat. Two days prior she had decided to stop force-feeding herself the horse pills that Dr. Spellman had prescribed. Bea wasn't crazy and she wasn't going to find her happy in a pill. They'd served their purpose and helped her to get over the hump. She had not cried in more than a week and had not binged in three full days. She just needed to get to twenty-one days. Studies showed that it took twenty-one days to break a habit and Bea believed it. Twenty-one was her magic number.

Lonnie had left to drop the kids off at her mother's house when the caterer, Malcolm, arrived. Once Bea gave instructions on the layout, she dipped upstairs for a shower. She took extra care in combing her hair. At the last minute she decided to blow it out and wear it in a high bun, putting a silver butterfly clip on the side for pop. The lavender cotton dress fit well enough and she could hear her mother's voice in her ear telling her to wear her good bra and put on her Spanx, so she did.

The house smelled of love when Bea went back downstairs.

"Thank you so much." She smiled at Malcolm and his young assistant. They were both busy, chopping, sautéing, and moving around the kitchen. "You make the best Beef Wellington on the planet. I can't wait for dinner."

"It's always a pleasure to cook for you, Beatrice."

Bea flicked on the switch for her fireplace in the family room, thinking that baby Sophia might enjoy a little extra warmth. Then she lit a mix of taper and pillar candles on the dining table. She loved her dining table. It was handcrafted walnut and had been purchased from a specialty furniture shop she'd stumbled upon when they took the children to Baltimore for the weekend. The only reason she'd gone in there was because Alana needed to use the bathroom and she'd gagged at the price tags. But then she saw the table and couldn't stop running her hands over the wood. Lonnie bought it on the spot for her.

He came through the front door. "Everything looks beautiful. Especially you."

She blushed. "I hope Mena and Clark have a good time. I remember how hard it was to relax when Chico was born."

"We know how to throw a party, baby. Everything will be perfect."

He kissed her lips, long and loving. Bea found herself leaning against him, surprised at her sudden desire for him.

"I'm going to go shower, but I'm putting in a reservation for tonight, after the guests leave." He ran his hand across the curve of her backside.

"Go get dressed."

Bea watched him walk up the steps and then took a long exhale.

It amazed her that after twelve years of marriage, and all that they had been through, that man could still excite and confuse her. She turned her attention back to the planning. She wanted to document the evening so she went into the hall closet in search of her camera. It was fully charged. She couldn't remember the last time she'd actually printed pictures to make a photo book. That's what she planned to do. Make a book: one for her and one for Mena. The thought delighted her. Bea was snapping pictures of the table setting when the doorbell chimed.

"Hi, guys," she squealed. It was Mena, Clark, and Sophia.

"Bea, you look beautiful." Mena kissed her cheek. Clark carried the baby's car seat. A blanket was thrown over her. Bea kept snapping pictures as they walked through the door.

"Is it cold out there?"

"Temperature is definitely dropping for it to only be November."

"Come in here, I've got the fireplace already going for you."

Mena's eyes looked hollow. Even under the piped floral shift dress Bea could tell that she had lost weight.

Clark unraveled the baby from all of her layers and bundled her into Bea's arms.

"Hi, little miss precious," Bea said, taking a seat on the sofa and gesturing to Mena to join her. "You hot with all of these clothes on?" Bea teased.

Mena sat next to her and gave her the low-down on Sophia's sleep schedule. Bea pretended to be listening but she was really watching Sophia. Looking into her eyes, watching her take in her new surroundings. She squeezed her fingers and toes to see how she would react.

"How's she eating?"

"A lot. The child is always hungry. It's like she's starving all the time. She eats until she throws up so I have to monitor the bottle."

"What did the doctor say?"

"Right now they just want to make sure she's gaining weight. Last we checked she was seven pounds six ounces."

Bea tried to hide her concern as Awilda and Derrick walked in. It had been over a week since Bea had seen Awilda. She wore her hair straightened and her button-down blouse and jeans were simple. She looked more conservative than usual but her skin had an undeniable glow. Bea handed the baby over, picked up her camera, snapped their picture, and then they hugged.

"Hey, Beasely."

"Wilde, you look great. Did you get a facial?"

"No, I bought some new hair." She ran her fingers through her tresses and giggled. "Trying that Olivia Pope look. Whatcha think?"

"Love it." Bea leaned in and whispered while taking her coat, "Things better with you and Derrick?"

"Just a little." Awilda surveyed the room. "Anyone want a drink? The bartender is in the building."

"I'll take one." Clark lifted a finger.

Bea took Derrick's coat and then leaned in for a hug. "Just the man I wanted to see. How have you been?"

"Good."

"Keeping active?"

"Actually I have. All of a sudden I'm like the neighborhood handyman. My phone is ringing off the hook."

"That's wonderful, Derrick. I have a project in my garage that I've been putting off. We need some shelving and waiting on Lonnie to get to it is like expecting snow in July."

"I got you. Just tell me when."

Lonnie strolled down the stairs, commanding the attention of the room.

"Hey, now." He went around the room like a politician, shaking hands, kissing women, and then tickling the baby.

Joney walked in with a man Bea had never seen. He was squat and Asian, with long, dyed-brown hair and wood-framed glasses.

"This is my friend, Bill." Joney smiled.

"Welcome. Let me take your photo," Bea said. Joney and Bill leaned in and just that quickly Bea saw the halo over the two of them, the light between their oceans that joined them together. Clark and Mena had a similar energy between them.

Bebel Gilberto's album *Samba da Benção* was playing. Being a Brazilian artist, the album was in Portuguese. Bea didn't understand a word but she understood the feeling and loved the way the music made her float through the room like a beautiful quill. The baby was passed around and Mena followed everyone with hand sanitizer and a burp cloth, still sporting the new mom jitters. The appetizers were on display and drinks flowed. Bea didn't drink anything stronger than a ginger ale because she didn't want the alcohol to make her sleepy.

When it was time, they all fit comfortably at the dining room table and the conversation ping-ponged from heavy to light.

"Sophia's christening was so beautiful last week," Bea squealed.

"They did a great job," said Mena. "Your children looked adorable."

"Honey, Alana had that dress picked out for weeks."

"Yum. This soup is delicious." Awilda dabbed her mouth.

"It is, isn't it?" Bea snapped a picture of Awilda and she wagged her napkin at her. Bea needed to accost her alone and catch up.

"You know they still haven't caught the man who broke into that house around the corner," Joney said. "It's hard to understand why this is so hard for the local police. They had to get the state involved."

"I thought it would have been easy," Lonnie added. "They brought in two men but they didn't match the man on the nanny cam."

"I hate it when they act like any black man will do," Derrick said lightheartedly.

"It's not just black men," Bill added. "I was arrested in San Francisco for minding my own damn business. I was down at the wharf buying fresh shrimp when these two officers grabbed me from behind and threw me to the ground."

"Really?" Joney's eyes widened.

"This was before I knew you. They hauled me down to the station and roughed me up a bit before they realized that I was the wrong man. They were looking for a Chinese mobster and I'm Korean."

Everyone laughed.

"Mistaken identity."

"Did you sue?"

"I thought about it but then I just let it go. Decided to change my energy and focus on aligning with my future desires. A few weeks later, I met Joney."

She blushed. "When I practiced law, I saw those types of cases all of the time. Lucky for me, criminal wasn't my expertise. I don't think I could stomach it."

Bea leaned across the table. "Thanks for looking out for the kids, Joney, while I was having little Miss Sophia. You were a life-saver."

"Oh, please. That's what neighbors are for, darling." She winked.

Sophia dozed off in Bea's arms while dinner was served. Mena watched her, barely touching her food. When Sophia opened her mouth to yawn, Mena reached anxiously.

"She wants her mama." Bea handed the baby over. Sophia curled up in Mena's arms and was soon again fast asleep. Bea moved the food around on her plate.

"What's fatherhood been like for you so far?" Lonnie asked Clark.

"It's the best feeling in the world, to know that this person depends on me. On us. I just never want to let her down."

Mena shook her head. "I still can't believe she's here. I still can't believe that you did this for us, Bea."

"Wait until she gets bigger and starts talking back. See how thankful you'll be to Bea then," piped Awilda.

The crowd chuckled.

"The first word Amare learned was *no*. Drove me insane."

"Or when they become teenagers. I didn't think I'd survive it. I have two kids, two years apart, and I was going through a messy divorce when they were going through puberty," inserted Joney.

"Enjoy each moment, Mena. Sophia won't always be this easy to please." Bea rubbed her arm.

"Even though the journey twists and turns, it's joyous and fulfilling." Joney raised her glass of wine. "To the new family. May your life be filled with great health, love, and understanding."

Everyone raised their glasses and toasted.

As soon as the dinner dishes were cleared from the table, Mena stood and announced that they needed to go.

"Don't want to keep Sophia out too late. We're trying to get her on a schedule."

Bea snapped a few more pictures of them and then Lonnie walked them to the door. Dessert was on the table when he came back. Lonnie offered up more drinks.

"Me." Awilda raised her hand as Derrick's mobile rang. "Who is that?"

Derrick got up from the table and walked toward the kitchen. "Hey, Mom. What's up?"

Awilda looked at Bea and turned her lips up in a way that said, *see what I mean?*

Bea smiled back. "How's the blueberry pie?"

Awilda put a big bite between her red lips and beamed. "Amazing."

Lonnie placed her drink in front of her. "I'll have to have some of that pie too."

Derrick returned. "Babe. Mom locked herself out of the house. We need to head over and let her in."

"I just started my dessert."

Derrick looked like he didn't want to upset her. "Okay, I'll go and come back for you." He leaned down and kissed her on the forehead.

Joney and Bill were cuddled together, eating pie from the same fork. The music was jazzy and soft. Lighting dimmed. Bea couldn't remember feeling such bliss. It was like a high that she wished she could hang on to forever. Everything had turned out right. The camera was on the table in front of her and she clicked back through the photos she had taken, half-listening to the conversation about the recent oil spill and the effect it was having on wildlife. It was amazing how many photos she had taken in such a short space of time and as she flicked through them, the folks around the table seemed to grow louder until they were too much and she tuned them out.

Bea had reached to scratch a mosquito bite on her ankle when she noticed something in one of the frames. It sent a sensation through her chest that made it hard for her to form words. A halo. It was an active energy that she had not detected before. Moving her face closer to the camera she went from photo to photo, studying what all of a sudden she knew with all of her heart to be true. She clenched her knees together under the table to stop her stomach from swaying and shooting up her food. How could she have missed it before? Her nose was so close to the frame that she bumped it before pulling away.

"You should see Lonnie swim." Awilda cackled. "The water barely moves. What was your record in high school?"

"I went to the state finals," Lonnie bragged.

"So you two went to the same high school?" Joney asked.

"Yeah. Bea and Lonnie met through me. Our mothers worked together at the same school. That's how we became besties."

Joney said something in return but Bea couldn't hear her. It seemed like Joney was speaking bubble language under water. Bea closed her eyes to regain her composure. The colors behind her eyelids began to spin like saucers and spun her from the table out to the garage. It was not until she stepped onto the cold slab of dusty concrete that she remembered that she was barefoot.

The force piloted her. Then the outrage pulsed through the tips of her fingers as she swept the top ledge for her key to the safe box. Inside that box was the key to the gun storage. From a distance, she could hear Joney calling to her that she was going to walk Bill out. Bea mumbled, knowing that Joney couldn't hear her but that she would continue on her way anyhow. All night it'd felt like the two of them couldn't wait to be alone.

It was funny, the hand that life dealt, Bea thought with the weight of the .22 in her hand. Bea knew how to load a gun. Lonnie had taught her. They used to go to the gun range very early on when they lived in D.C. It was before they'd gotten married but after his cheating the first time. That was how Bea kept time. Children born. Lonnie's affairs. She hadn't been shooting in years but that didn't stop the memory of how to do it from climbing to the top of her thoughts.

Bea pointed the barrel in a safe direction and then ejected the magazine. She knew to check that the gun was completely empty before inserting one round at a time. It had been a while so she had to push hard with her thumb on the center of the round and slide it back until it was below the retaining lip. Once full, she reinserted the magazine and pushed firmly until she heard the familiar click. Bea walked soundlessly back into the house. Chico always got mad when Bea startled him because she was that good at creeping through the house. It was part of her Carmen Santiago detective persona that she put on when she had to find things out. She moved as quietly as a mouse undetected.

Lonnie and Awilda were sitting where she had left them, drinks refilled. The music had gone from soft to old-school rap and the two were singing along with the track.

"Peter Piper picked peppers, but Run rapped rhymes . . ."

Awilda threw her hands in the air while Lonnie picked up a spoon and used it as a microphone. As she watched them from the kitchen door, she realized that she had not been sure of a lot in her life. Often she made decisions that were wrong but this wasn't one of them. The gun was hidden behind her hip.

"Where have you been?" Lonnie flashed his magic. "I paid the caterers. They wrapped the leftovers and put them in the fridge."

Bea raised the gun from her hip and pointed it at him.

"Bea, what the . . ."

"Sit, dear." Her voice didn't sound like her own. It had a glacial layer of ice and Bea felt as cool as the crisper section of the refrigerator. She used the remote control to turn down the music with her free hand and then swung the gun at Awilda.

"Girl, stop playing before someone gets hurt. What's wrong with you?" Awilda's voice was steady but her eyes were big. She was afraid. Awilda was never afraid. That's how Bea knew that she had trapped the right pussycat against the tree.

"Wilde, I'm going to ask you a question. Please remember that I know you very well. So answer truthfully. It's only one question. Ready?"

Awilda's chest heaved up and down. She managed a nod.

"I'm going to need you to use your mouth, dear. You know how to use that big mouth really well. Are you ready?"

"Bea, what is this about?" She sat on her hands.

"No, no, hands where I can see them."

Awilda put her hands on the table. Her nails were painted Pepto pink.

"Are you fucking my husband?"

Lonnie spoke up. "Honey, that's ridiculous."

She swung the gun. "I'm not talking to you, Lonnie, I'm talking to Awilda. Are you?"

"Sweetie, you know I've never been attracted to Awilda."

Awilda whipped her hair. "Why you got to say it like that?"

"Like what?"

"Like I'm some ugly duckling or something."

"Let me deal with Bea. Please just stay out of this."

"You want to get like that now?"

He stuck out his chin. "Bea is my wife."

"Oh, now you want to pull the 'I'm married' shit? Really, dude? You wasn't saying that last . . ."

"Shut up!"

"Unbelievable." Awilda cast a wounded look at him. "You been trying to seduce me since high school 'cause I was the one girl that never got swept up in your shit, the one who wouldn't drop her panties."

"She's lying, Bea." He threw a nasty look at Awilda. "I've never seduced you."

"Coming to the gym when you knew I would be there. Taking

me to dinner, saying shit. And now it's 'Bea, you know I've never been attracted to Awilda,'" she mimicked his voice with attitude.

"Bea, don't believe a word she's saying." Lonnie moved to stand. "Baby . . ."

At that moment, the room shook beneath the three of them. The sound echoed off of every surface and piece of furniture in the house. Time didn't move as their eardrums smashed into the middle of their ears and then recovered.

The kickback made Bea stumble through the space. When she opened her eyes, Lonnie was falling to the ground.

TWENTY–ONE

Undercover

"What the fuck!" Lonnie grabbed his thigh and slumped down against the legs of the dining room table.

"Bea, you shot him," said Awilda.

Bea looked at the gun. She didn't even remember pulling the trigger. How in the world did she shoot him? Her finger must have slipped. The gun was only supposed to scare a confession out of them. Show them who was boss. Take back her power. Not hurt anyone. The gun dangled in her hand. How easy it would be to put it to her temple and just blow herself away. The world would be a better place without her. Lonnie and Awilda could ride off into the sunset together and live happily ever after. Her children could . . . her children. She was such a terrible mother. They would probably be better off without her too. Lonnie would probably move Connie and little Alonzo in if she died. Make room for his new family. That's probably what he wanted. She was light-skinned, thin, with free-flowing hair. The type of woman that other men admired at dinner parties. Bea moved the gun toward her stomach.

Lonnie pressed both of his hands into the wound, trying to stop the blood with his fingers.

"Call an ambulance," he croaked. The blood seeped through his crème pants and onto the Persian garden area rug that he'd insisted on buying because it made a statement. Now it was wet and ruined. Bea was deep in thought, wondering if a bullet through her stomach would do the trick. She would really hate to blow her own brains out. That sounded shockingly painful. No one would want to clean up blasted brain pieces from the wall and floor and furniture. On one of those shoot 'em up movies that Lonnie liked to watch, Bea had seen what brains looked like splattered and it was enough to make anyone hurl from the sight of it. She had such vivid images playing in her head that she had not noticed that Awilda was standing right in front of her.

"Give me the gun, Bea."

"No."

"Honey, before anyone else gets hurt, please let me have the gun." She spoke in that soothing voice that made people do what she wanted.

"Come on, sweetie. Let me help."

The tone worked. Bea moved the gun from her stomach and let Awilda take it.

As soon as it was in her hands, Awilda spat. "What is wrong with you? Did you go off your Paxil?"

Bea shrank like a thirsty violet.

"I need you to get a towel and then stop his leg from bleeding." Awilda dusted Bea's prints from the gun with a dinner napkin.

"Here." She handed the gun to Lonnie.

"Why are you giving this to me? I don't want it." He tried to give it back.

"Can't you lock it or something?"

Lonnie put the safety in place and handed it back to Awilda. She took it with the napkin and then placed it inside the buffet.

Bea heard her voice but was unable to send the signal from her brain to move her feet. Lonnie moaned. Awilda kneeled by his side. Then she looked up at Bea and yelled, "Come put that damn nursing degree to use before your husband dies on your dining room floor."

"I'm dying?" asked Lonnie. "Oh, God!"

"No, fool. You'll live. Bea, go."

Bea roused herself enough to go into the bathroom to get her first-aid kit from the closet. It wasn't the Johnson & Johnson kit that came from CVS. It was the one she had used in nursing school and it was stocked with all of the very best equipment. With her hands around the handle, her brain received the picture. A nurse was needed to help out at the scene. She switched gears, surveyed the wound, and went into action.

Joney walked through the unlocked front door. "Bea, I didn't get my pie . . ." She took in the scene. "What in the world happened here? I thought I heard a gun go off but I convinced myself that it was just a firecracker."

Blood was everywhere. Bea was wrapping a strip of cloth around Lonnie's thigh. Derrick walked in and almost bumped into Joney.

"Hey, I could use . . ." He stopped in his tracks.

Bea looked at Awilda, who got to her feet and rubbed her hands on her jeans, streaking them with blood.

"It's nothing, guys. Bea went to show Lonnie the gun. They've had it for a while but forgot where it was." Awilda swallowed. "As she handed it to him it went off and he accidentally shot himself in the thigh. It all happened so fast. I'm glad you guys are here."

"We should get him to the hospital," Derrick injected.

"Do you want me to call an ambulance or should we drive him? Overlook isn't far," asked Joney, running her fingers through her hair.

Bea pushed away from Lonnie and leaned her back against the wall. The gun. Why had she given it to Awilda? She should have fired it into her stomach when she'd had the chance. The pain in her heart wouldn't go away and her ears were ringing with so much noise it was giving her a headache. Lonnie and Awilda. Awilda and Lonnie. Images of them touching and kissing kept running through her head. She needed some air but her body was so heavy she couldn't move.

Then the doorbell rang. Everyone in the room jumped. Joney went to answer it. Bea could hear her talking at the door but couldn't make out what she was saying, then in walked two police officers.

"What's going on here? A neighbor reported a disturbance."

"Guys, this is Officer Burkes and Officer Cage. Officer Cage went to high school with my son. I know him as Mikey. Glad you two came."

"Sir, are you okay?" Officer Burkes said, moving toward Lonnie, putting his hand on his wrist and taking his pulse.

"Yeah."

"What happened here?"

Bea kept her eyes on the ground. She could tell the officers that she'd tried to kill her husband and best friend so that they would arrest her. But jail was so stinky; it didn't appeal to her like her bed. She wished she could just get up and go upstairs and get in her bed.

"It was an accident," said Awilda.

"He shot himself in the thigh, showing off his new gun. Such a stupid thing to do but as you know it happens every day. I just read about that football player losing a finger playing with fireworks on the Fourth of July. Mikey, call for an ambulance, would you honey?" coaxed Joney.

"Who's this guy?" Officer Burke put his hand on his weapon as he turned his attention to Derrick, who at that moment walked in from the kitchen carrying Bea's good towels.

"He's my husband," said Awilda.

"Has he been here all night?"

Derrick looked both terrified and annoyed.

"He's fine, Officer Burke. These people are neighbors. Would you please just figure out how to get this man to a doctor before he bleeds to death?"

"The ambulance is two minutes away," said Officer Cage.

"Thanks, Mikey."

Awilda and Derrick followed Lonnie's ambulance to the hospital. Joney promised to look after Bea.

"Come with me, dear, and let me fix you a cup of tea."

Bea got up off the floor. What she really wanted was a bowl of her mother's soup. The air was chilly as she walked across the grass. As soon as she entered through Joney's back door into her kitchen, it became easier to breathe. The smell of Joney's house was reminiscent of the rented cottage in Wildwood, where she and her mom spent the second week of August on vacation each year. It was a combination of citrus and cilantro and in both cases might have been a good mix of potpourri and lunch.

The kitchen was painted a cheeky mint green, with simple and timeless furniture and corky wall decals that read: THE UNIVERSE IS ALWAYS WORKING ON BEHALF OF MY HIGHEST AND BEST GOOD.

Bea took a seat at the kitchenette.

"Just push the mail aside," Joney told her as she put on the kettle. It was shaped like a black-and-white kitten, the tail was the handle.

"Where's Bill?"

"Gone. He doesn't live too far."

"Sorry to intrude on your night."

"Don't apologize for anything, dear."

Bea was so exhausted her bones hurt. "Do you have any pain medicine?"

Joney reached into her top cabinet and put a bottle on the table. She poured two cups of hot water over tea bags.

"How do you take yours?"

"Doesn't matter."

When Joney put the hot mug in front of her, it read: ALL IS WELL AND I AM SAFE.

"Do you have affirmations everywhere?"

"Yes, plastered in every room. If they made it in wallpaper I'd have that too."

"Why so many?"

"I find that I need constant reminders to stay the course." Joney blew on her cup, then proceeded slowly. "I was just like you, Bea. In my marriage to Sonny. I put up with more than I care to recall. I was broken, damaged, abused. Lucky for me he left before I had a chance to hurt him. I did think about burning the bed before with him in it."

"What stopped you?"

"I love this house. It's where my children were born. I still have Penelope's growth chart written on that wall." She pointed to a spot near the broom closet. "And in the living room, there is still a spot where Ethan decided to draw a Mother's Day card on the floor."

"I shot him." Bea felt herself tear up. "It was an accident. I was just trying to scare him into telling me the truth."

"Which is?"

"That . . . he and Awilda have been . . . messing around. I could just tell. I saw an energy between them. What? Do they think I'm stupid? Why would they do something like that to me? I don't deserve it. I'm good to everyone. I'll help anyone out and this is what I get back?"

"Some people can only give you what they know, Bea. It's unfortunate."

"He has a son." She had lost control of her secrets. Those four words loosened the weight tied to Bea's chest. "Lonnie. He has a son in Miami. Same age as Alana."

"You've been keeping this?"

Bea nodded. "No one knows. He's been so careless with my feelings. But I'm the fool. I've stayed through it all."

"Why?"

"Because I don't know how to leave."

Joney looked deeply into her eyes and then patted her hand. "I know you feel like your identity is tied to him."

"I've been with him my whole adult life."

"You know what helped me through my separation and then divorce?"

Bea sipped her tea, starting to feel the effects of the painkiller easing the tension in her breastbone.

"I had to admit to the part that I played."

"I didn't play a part. I'm the victim."

"There are no victims. Life is a dance, Bea. Lonnie can't dance if you aren't moving your hips to his beat."

Bea's face reddened. "Are you suggesting that I brought this on myself?"

Joney rested her pointer finger on her forehead and took three deep breaths before answering. "I'm saying, dear heart, that it takes two. That's what years of therapy, yoga, energy work, acupuncture, and holistic healing have taught me. You name it, I've tried it, and I've learned that on this beautiful journey called life, we must realize the part that we play so that we can stop playing it. We have to change the energy and stop beating the drum of what we don't want."

Bea looked down at her fingers.

"We have to forgive and love and forgive and love. It's not your job to hate him for the rest of your life. That's toxic for you."

Bea went from pissed off, to soothed, to deeply listening. Joney had a woo-woo quality that Bea had always been attracted to. Watching her move in her body always put Bea at ease. It made something inside of her unravel.

"I'm bulimic," seemed to be stuck to her ribs like a membrane, but when she got the words out she had to put her hands on the table in front of her to steady herself. When she looked into Joney's face, it made her drowsy.

"Feels good to let this stuff out, doesn't it?"

Bea dropped her head down to her chest.

"Why don't you sleep in my guest room tonight? I'm sure you'd benefit from a change of scenery."

"Thank you."

As Bea walked through the hall and up the steps, her feet felt like lead pipes. Joney's house held a calm that was so tranquil, she was sure she was asleep before her head even hit the memory-foam pillow. She slept for twelve hours.

TWENTY-TWO

Spreading like Wildfire

Bea left Dr. Spellman's office with a referral to see a psychiatrist.

"I'm worried about you, Bea," she told her before she left. "You're still very hormonal from having the baby. You have to stay on your pills until I tell you to stop."

Bea had agreed to stay on the pills but she had no desire to engage in talk therapy. She remembered going to the school therapist after her father died and feeling like she didn't want to talk about it. After various breakdowns in her relationship with Lonnie, she went to a therapist in Adams Morgan and it worked for a while but then Bea lost interest. Now she didn't feel like talking. What she wanted was to keep Lonnie out of her bed, Awilda out of her house, and to go through the pile of papers and forms that had accumulated since the start of school. But Bea had never been lucky.

When she pulled into her driveway, Awilda was sitting on her front steps, dressed in a red one-piece pants jumper. Her hair was pulled back into a ponytail. If Bea was still her best friend she would have kissed and hugged her and commented on how cute she looked.

Cooed over where she'd purchased the jumper and then invited her in for whatever leftovers were in the refrigerator. But they weren't friends.

"Why're you here?" She slammed her car door, fresh anger spilling down her spine like water.

"You're not going to speak to me ever again?"

"There's nothing to say."

"Come on, Bea," Awilda whined. "I'm sorry, okay? It was the stupidest thing I've ever done."

"Sorry? Sorry doesn't cut it when you've been fucking my husband." Bea looked around to see if any of her neighbors were out. Last thing she wanted was to be the brown family on the block causing a scene. The police had already showed up at her house and Bea was sure that news had spread like whooping cough.

"Can I come in?"

"No."

Awilda followed Bea up the steps. When they got to the side door, Bea tried to close the door behind her but Awilda pushed her way into the kitchen. "Bease, I shouldn't have done it. I take full responsibility for being weak."

"And desperate."

"What's that supposed to mean?"

"Desperate. Want me to look it up in the dictionary for you? So desperate for love that you would try and take my husband. After everything that I've done for you. My mother has done for you."

"Bea, Lonnie's been cheating long before we had our tryst."

"So that makes it right? I trusted you with my life. You don't get that, do you? You betrayed me." Bea's hands shook as she repinned her bun. "But why should I be surprised? You've been a hoe since I met you. You even sure Derrick is Amare's father?"

They stood glaring at each other with only the kitchen island between them.

"Little girl, if you had taken the time to put on some lipstick and high heels once in a while instead of running around here in those damn yoga pants, maybe you could have kept your man in your bed. Don't blame the holes in your marriage on me," Awilda growled.

Bea could hog spit in her face. She had shared her mother with this girl and now she had gotten into bed with her husband.

"Get out."

"No. We need to work this out," Awilda said flatly.

Bea had not fought anyone since she was eleven. The rolling pin was in the sink and she reached for it. "Get out of my house, now."

Awilda looked at her incredulously. "You going to hit me with that? Seriously, Bea. I'm embarrassed and sorry. Didn't we vow not to let men come between us?"

"Are you listening to yourself? That man is my husband." Bea banged the pin against her palm. "Are you in love with him, chili101?"

Bea watched as the recognition of her screen name washed over her face. "Were you with him when I was giving birth to Sophia?"

Awilda crossed her arms over her big bosom and Bea couldn't stop picturing Lonnie unsnapping her bra and taking a huge mouthful. He had always been a breast man.

"Answer me, damn it, you owe me that much."

"Yes."

"How could you?"

"We're in love with each other."

Bea's hand dropped down to her side.

"Don't you get it? It was always me and Lonnie. I was always the girl he wanted but never got. Thought I'd save him for later. I had no idea that when the two of you met it would turn into all of this." She gestured at their grand kitchen with her hand.

"So why did you set us up in the first place?"

"When you went away to college, your mom was worried about you like you were moving to Afghanistan, Beasley. I just thought he'd keep an eye on you. Not marry you."

Bea clutched her belly as if she had been punched. "You are just another hoe to him."

"It's different between us. We have history."

Bea laughed out her pity. "You sound like all of the floozies I've caught him with, stupid."

Awilda cut with her eyes.

"Go. Don't make me do something we will both regret."

"Fine. At least I was honest. That's more than Lonnie can say." Awilda trudged out the back door and left it wide open. Most people would slam the door but when Awilda made an exit, she always left the door open. Like: *you want me gone, then close the door behind me.* She was so petty.

Bea locked the door behind her. When she turned around the dark horse was right there, making her skin itch. Bea opened up her refrigerator, searching for peace and control. She piled the food on the counter. Ate with blatant fervor, then flushed five days of abstinence down the toilet, along with her friendship and her marriage.

"Dad's been shot?" Chico slung his backpack onto the floor of Bea's van.

"Huh?"

"Everyone is talking about it in school. Saying that Dad was shot and the police came to our house. Did they?"

Bea was glad that it was Wednesday and that Alana was still at school for after-school enrichment.

"Is that why Dad hasn't been home?"

"Son." Bea looked through the rearview mirror, gaging how much he knew and what she should say. She should have been prepared for this but she wasn't. "Who told you this?"

"Carter's uncle is a police officer and now everyone is talking about me. Saying I'm related to the man who broke into a woman's house around the corner and beat her up in front of her kids."

"That's ridiculous." To them, all people with a little color looked alike.

"I'm not going back to school."

"Chico."

"My name is Alonzo." He sucked his teeth. "Where's Daddy? Tell me the truth, Mommy."

Bea hadn't bothered to check on Lonnie since he had been taken to the hospital but she knew he was there. Her mother had called that morning chastising her for not being involved in his recovery.

Irma said, "*Mija,* what's gotten in to you? Lonnie said you haven't been to visit him once since Saturday. I caught two buses and had to walk up the hill to see him. What's wrong? He wouldn't tell me much more."

"Not over the phone, Mami."

"Is it bad?"

Bea struggled with whether or not to tell her mother. She would be devastated if she knew it was Awilda because she felt like she'd practically raised the girl, with all the weekends and taking her in after Amare was born.

"Sweetie, he's a good man."

She didn't feel like hearing her opinion so she made an excuse and got off the phone.

Now Chico peered at her from the backseat with those same dark, demanding eyes as her mother. "Answer me, Mama."

"Put your seat belt on. Hurry up, I have five minutes before I need to pick up Alana."

"Did he get shot? Just tell me!"

She sighed. "Yes."

"What happened?"

"He was cleaning his gun and didn't realize it had a bullet in it and accidentally shot himself in the leg."

"Dad has a gun?"

"For recreational use only."

"What does that mean?"

"It means he only uses it at the gun range. Not on people. It was an accident." Bea flipped the radio station until she found a song that she thought he would like.

"You want to wait here while I grab Alana?"

He nodded.

Bea got out of the car, took a deep breath, and walked toward the schoolyard. It was only a few feet to where Alana stood on line but in the thirty seconds it took to reach her, it felt like every parent and caretaker glanced at her with a look that asked: Is that the woman whose husband got shot? Bea pushed up her sunglasses and waved to Alana.

"Hey, baby." She kissed her daughter on the ear. "How was your day?"

"Good. I got a hundred on my word sort."

"Wonderful, sweetie."

"Got any snacks? I'm so hungry."

"Yup."

When they were buckled back into the car, Bea tossed her a bag of pretzels from her tote bag.

"Me too."

She tossed a bag to Chico, who didn't even look up to say thank you. His fingers moved over the bike-racing game on his mobile phone.

As soon as they walked through the door, Chico picked up the cordless. "Alana, want to call Dad with me?"

"Where is he?"

"In the hospital."

"What's wrong with him?"

"Dad—"

"Hurt himself, sweetie. He's fine." Bea gave Chico a look that communicated that Alana didn't need to know all of that. "Call him on his cell phone and take the phone into the family room so that I can concentrate on making dinner."

Bea tied her apron around her waist and then looked into the refrigerator. What to serve for dinner had been on her mind all day, though she hadn't come up with anything. All of the choices in front of her made her feel lethargic. Bea removed the half-gallon of lemonade and sat down at the island, drinking it straight from the container.

"I thought you told me not to drink from the bottle?" Chico smiled. "Dad wants you."

"What's for dinner?" Alana bounced in behind her brother. "I have homework on the computer tonight."

"Really?" Bea hoped this time Alana's password worked. Last school year the system had been buggy. The teacher had said it was because Alana was new.

"Here, Mom." Chico stretched the phone.

"Start your homework, please. And no fighting."

"Can I have some lemonade?"

"Get a cup."

Bea left the lemonade and took the phone out onto the back patio. She closed the sliding door behind her before she opened her mouth.

"What?"

"Hey, babe."

"Lonnie."

"I can't get a 'hey, babe,' back?"

She stayed quiet, waiting for him to state his business. When he didn't, she asked, "What do you want?"

"You."

She blew air through her teeth.

"They got the bullet out safely. It didn't hit anything important, just damaged some tissue. I'm getting out tomorrow and I need you to come and get me."

"Take a taxi. Or ask Awilda."

"Come on, Bea. They will only release me to the next of kin."

"Whatever, Lonnie."

"Seriously, my nurse told me that a few minutes ago. Please be here around nine. I need you."

Bea didn't know if it was a lie or the truth but she agreed.

"Mom, can I watch TV?"

"Do what you want."

"Can I watch *Austin & Ally*?"

"I don't care."

Alana did her happy dance. Bea abhorred most of those silly shows but talking to Lonnie had made her too pooped to parent.

"Chico, I'm going to take a nap. Keep an eye on Alana."

He looked up from his phone. "Are you sick?"

Yes, she thought. *I am sick. In the head and in the heart.* "Just please don't bother me." Bea climbed the stairs. Her body was completely out of whack from taking the pills, then skipping a few days, and now taking them again. A familiar fatigue settled on her shoulders. Her life was a mess. She'd lost her husband and the closest thing she had to a sister in the same minute.

The crazy part was that Lonnie and Awilda acted as if they were owed her swift forgiveness in the name of their triangular friendship. Their attitudes didn't account for her feelings and she was the one done wrong. *It was more like we accidentally slept together, sorry. Forgive us.* They reminded her of two wayward children.

Bea pulled back the covers on her bed and got in, knowing that there came a time when sorry didn't cut it. She was done being the doormat that Lonnie wiped his feet on as he walked into another woman's house. Especially now that it was Awilda's house. Out of the billions of people in the world, how could they do it? She didn't care how they'd felt about each other in high school. Now was now, and wrong was absolutely wrong. Joney was right. Lonnie did what she had allowed and it was up to her to stop it.

Bea closed her eyes thinking about Derrick. Imagining what he would do to Lonnie if he found out. A scene of them fist fighting played out colorfully in her mind. It seemed like a quick dream but when Chico shook her awake, darkness draped.

"Mom. It's eight o'clock. It's time for Alana to go to bed. I made her a peanut butter and jelly sandwich and gave her a cookie for dessert. She wouldn't eat the carrots but I ate mine. What's wrong with you?"

"I'm fine, sweetie. Just . . ." Bea sat up in her bed and pushed her hair over her shoulders. She felt like a terrible parent for sleeping through the evening rush. It was certainly a first.

"Tell me what's wrong, Mommy."

Bea pulled Chico to her chest. How do you explain to an

adolescent boy the ugly side of marriage? The side that no one tells you about before you say *I do*? Bea had put her belief in marriage. When things went wrong, she nursed her wounds and went back with the full belief that things could get better. That if Lonnie would just keep his attention on her, they could overcome the odds and attain the miracle of a happy and successful marriage. Do what her mother couldn't do legally with her father. Be more than just her happy holiday card. But this, with Awilda, was different. It had shoved her headfirst through the hole in the wall.

"Did she shower?"

"No, she wouldn't listen to me."

"Tell her I said to put on her pajamas and I'll come tuck her in."

Bea's temples throbbed. In her bathroom sink she cupped her hands under the faucet and drank greedily from the tap. It tasted disgusting but she was too thirsty to care.

"Mom, do you have a migraine?" Alana jumped up from her reading corner.

"Where did you get that word from?"

"Chico said it."

"I'm fine, butterbean."

"Why didn't you wake up?"

"Just tired."

"We didn't do my computer homework."

"Can we do it in the morning?"

"My Scholastic book order is due, Mommy, and you promised I could order this time since you forgot to give me the check last time."

"In the morning."

Alana got out of the chair. "Can I sleep in your bed since Daddy's not home?"

"Not tonight. Maybe over the weekend."

"But I'm scared."

"Scared of what?"

"I think there is something under my bed."

Bea knelt down on the floor and checked. The movement pulled on her incision from the C-section. "Just shoes, baby." She got up and closed the curtains, then she handed Alana two stuffed bears.

"Good night."

"Can you leave the hallway light on?"

"Okay."

Bea made her way down to Chico's room. He was bent over his notebook and it made her proud that he was doing the right thing without her having to nag him. She watched her son from the doorway, wondering what type of husband he would be.

"Don't stay up too late, son."

" 'K."

Bea shut his door.

As she moved down the hall she could feel the dark horse breathing, coaxing, urging. She turned toward the stairs and then caught herself on the top step. She turned away from the steps and went down the hallway to her bedroom. Sleep felt like the lesser of the two evils.

TWENTY-THREE

Foxtrot

Bea dressed carefully the next morning. She dug out her best pair of jeans, the ones that hadn't fit since before she got pregnant with Sophia, and paired them with a tangerine shirt and bronze jewelry. Her hair was loose and hung below her shoulders.

"Where're you going?" asked Alana.

"I have to run some errands this morning." She left off the part about picking up Lonnie.

"You look like the mommies on TV who go to work."

Bea smiled. In the back of her mind, she had visions of going back to work. Had even skimmed the career sites for a few job postings. With all that was going on, she was afraid of what her being committed to a job outside of the home would mean for her children. She was already sleeping through the evening; what would a full-time job do to her?

"Come on, don't want to be late," she called, while tucking an apple and banana into her tote bag.

After dropping the kids off, she popped her pill, turned the radio dial to *Morning Edition,* and munched on her fruit breakfast. Control, she had to eat with control. The back roads were clear and it didn't take her long to arrive at Overlook hospital.

Lonnie sat on the edge of the hospital bed, still in his gown. Begrudgingly, Bea had put on her wife cape that morning and packed him a change of clothes: dark jeans and a sweater. She handed him the overnight bag.

"Thanks, baby."

She took a seat in front of the bed.

"How are the kids?"

"Fine. You ready? I have someplace to be," she lied.

"And I thought you dressed up for me. You look so pretty. I've missed you."

Bea looked out the window. Lonnie hopped up on his good leg and tucked his crutches under his arms. "Can you open the bathroom door for me?"

Bea rolled her eyes as she walked to the tiny bathroom and opened the door. As Lonnie passed her, she could feel the heat from his body and turned her face just at the moment he leaned in to kiss her.

"Just hurry up." She pushed him off.

The nurse entered. "Mrs. Colon?"

Bea searched the pale woman's face, wondering if she had caught their exchange.

"Here are his discharge papers. His prescription has already been called in to the pharmacy closest to your house and should be ready soon. Bandages should be changed daily and the wound cleaned. No baths or direct showers on the leg for a week. His follow-up appointment is November sixteenth."

Bea took the paperwork and thanked the nurse. Lonnie came out of the bathroom. She had purposely picked clothes that weren't his best and he still managed to look good.

"Do you want a wheelchair, Mr. Colon?"

"No, my wife and I will take it from here."

As soon as the nurse closed the door, Bea looked at him and said, "I don't want to be near you."

"I never meant to hurt you."

"You slept with Awilda. How could that not hurt?"

"I know what I've done was wrong. I can see how much pain I've caused."

"You don't know anything, Lonnie."

"I didn't mean for it to happen." He sat back down. "It was like she was pursuing me. Since high school, really, but you know she's not my type. That's why we were always goofing off together—because there was nothing there."

Bea tapped her foot. He said, she said.

"That night in the car, when you told me to take her home after the barbeque. She *did* mean she wanted to have sex with me. I left that part out because you were pregnant with Mena's baby and I didn't want to upset you."

"Out of all of the women willing to get in bed with you, it had to be Awilda?"

"She started coming to the gym at the same time as me. We'd eat together. Drink some beers and watch a little baseball."

"You two were going out?"

"She kept flirting with me. One day I was driving her back to her car and she reached into my pants. It had been a while, maybe even weeks since you and I had been together. I just lost control."

Bea stood up. "You're sick. How dare you put this one on me? I was pregnant with your cousin's baby, you asshole."

"I know, Bea. I'm just saying Awilda caught me in a vulnerable situation. Hell, she was vulnerable too, with Derrick's illness and job situation."

"Now I'm supposed to feel sorry for her too?"

"Listen, Bea, I didn't mean—"

"Lonnie, I'm done listening."

The nurse knocked and walked back in.

"Sign here, Mr. Colon, and you'll be free to go." She handed him the clipboard. He didn't bother to read the document, he just scribbled his name at the bottom.

Bea was in her head on the walk to the car. As soon as Lonnie slid in next to her, she asked, "Where can I take you?"

"Home."

"You don't seem to be understanding what's going on here. I don't want you there."

"Bea, think about the kids."

"You should have been thinking about the kids when you rammed your dick into the woman they call auntie."

Lonnie looked out the window. He was quiet for a long time and then he turned to Bea with moist eyes. They were at a red light.

"I know I really fucked up this time. If I could take it back, I would."

"But you can't. So where are you going?"

He sighed. "Just let me come home. I'll sleep on the couch."

Bea wished to God that she didn't have to deal with this. If she let him come home then she would be uncomfortable, tiptoeing around the house trying not to breathe the same air as him. Lonnie would do his best to slip back into their lives, which made her skin swirl with itchiness. But the kids. She had to consider their feelings and what was best for them. She tightened her grip on the steering wheel as the light changed. She wanted to dump him at a hotel but motherhood trumped all. The children needed to see their father so she drove him to the house they all shared.

As she predicted, the kids were ecstatic to have Lonnie home. Alana played nurse, bringing him juice and crackers. Chico seemed to follow Lonnie foot to foot, room to room. Bea made a quick pasta dinner and did the laundry while the three of them ate together. After she got the kids into bed, she brought down two pillows and a comforter and made up the sofa.

"Bea." He said her name softly, in the same tone he used when he was sorry. It tugged at her, sending conflicting chills up her spine. But how could she rightfully entertain anything he had to say?

"No," she responded and went upstairs.

Bea slept a dreamless sleep. When she woke up, Lonnie had his foot draped over hers. She was disoriented for a moment. The clock read seven. It was a school day. She had not set her alarm clock and now she was late. And he was not supposed to be in her bed. She threw the covers back.

"What are you doing in here?" Her cheeks reddened.

"I couldn't sleep on the couch so I came up in the middle of the night. I didn't mean to touch you."

His face was beautifully etched with sleep and she caught him in between a smile and a yawn. For a split second she had caught sight of the Lonnie that she had loved. But then she remembered him and Awilda and it was gone.

"Bea."

"This isn't going to work."

"Bea." He grabbed her arm.

"I can't go back to the way it used to be. Don't you get that? You crossed the fucking line." She slapped him hard against his face. "You destroyed our family."

Bea moved out of the bedroom and into the hallway. Her emotions were seeping out of her pores and it was giving her a dizzying headache. She had to get it together.

"Honey, it's time for school." She shook Chico awake.

"Ma. Why were you and Daddy yelling?"

"We weren't yelling."

Chico rolled toward her. "I heard you."

"Get up. We're running late."

Normally Bea coaxed her children out of bed. Rubbing their backs, touching their hair, but today she flicked on the light and then headed down the hall to wake Alana. Bea moved through the house barking orders, packing lunches, laying out bagels for breakfast, not caring whether the kids preferred cream cheese or butter. She argued with Chico for trying to wear that stupid Miami Heat shirt that was too small and hollered at Alana, "Would you just eat the damn apple slices and stop complaining all of the time?"

"Mommy, you said a bad word."

"Eat. So we can go."

"Why are you being so mean?" Alana began to sob.

"I'm not."

"You are, Mommy," said Chico.

"Grab your things for school and let's go."

The kids followed her out to the driveway. It was chilly but she was burning up from within. They drove in silence with the windows cracked. Once she dropped them off, she regretted her morning attitude. All she needed was for the teachers to ask why they were upset and for them to mutter some version of what was going on in their home. Bea's foot was heavy on the gas as she made her way back home. Lonnie was in the gray robe she'd bought him two Christmases ago, sipping on a cup of coffee, checking his e-mail.

"Want a bagel or something?" he said casually, as if she hadn't shot him in the leg six days ago, as if their lives were normal and fine. Lonnie never wanted to deal with an issue. He preferred to pile the dirt under a carpet. But that pile of dirt now included Awilda. The hump was huge and Bea would not allow herself to trip over it. She wouldn't step over it and she wasn't going around it. She wanted it removed.

"I want you to go. I'll drive you to a hotel."

"I'm getting sick of you asking me to leave my house, Bea." His brows knitted.

"It's you or me. And if I go, you'll have the responsibility of the kids."

"I can't even drive."

"Not my problem."

"Why are you being so unreasonable?"

"I need some space to think, Lonnie, and I can't do that with you here." She sighed. "Please, I'm asking you for the sake of the children to go."

"I've given you a good life. Women wish they had a life as cushy as yours. You don't work. You buy what you want and I don't say nothing. You have free time to do whatever the hell you please and all you do is whine." He snapped his laptop shut.

"How dare you?"

"I'm tired of begging. You want me gone? Fine. I'll leave. See how you make it in this house without me." He grabbed his crutches, tucked his computer under his arm, and went toward the stairs.

Bea balled her fists. She wanted to make him hurt and feel her pain. She walked around the kitchen in circles. Then a scream escaped her throat and she hurried out the back door. The keys to her van were on the counter and she didn't trust herself to go back for them. She remembered the twenty-dollar bill she'd tucked into her front pants pocket that morning and decided to walk to Main Street, grab some breakfast, and get her head right. Walking always helped but her legs shook beneath her. By the time she got to the corner, she had to hunch over to keep from falling.

How is this her life? Bea sat down on the curb. She needed some relief. Something to make herself feel better. She thought about all of the Saturday afternoons she spent alone with the Happy Meals her father brought in. The food was meant to placate her, to make up for the fact that he was only there to see her mother, to quiet her loneliness. The high-calorie, cheaply priced food had been her pacifier and in that moment she longed for a suck.

Luckily, the closest McDonald's was farther then she felt like driving. She didn't need to eat that food anyway. Bea wanted to stop letting the people around her keep her sick. This was her life and she needed to gain control. Bea got up and made her way to the town park. Trees, grass, fresh air: a path to sanity. Bea had only been to this park a few times since they moved to Evergreen. Alana had enjoyed a few playdates in the playground area and Chico liked to go to the other end and shoot hoops. The basketball court only had one working hoop. Lonnie told Bea that the other one had probably been taken down to discourage teens from other neighborhoods from coming in and taking over the park. No doubt it was meant to deter the black and brown kids. Bea huffed. The sandbox was tucked away in the corner near the gate. There was an abandoned plastic beach shovel next to it. The earth called to her and she moved toward it. Then she was standing in it. Without hesitating, Bea picked up the shovel and started digging.

She tunneled until there was a hole big enough to put her foot in. Then she continued to plow until she could slide her leg in up to her kneecap. Bea dug until she could get both feet in, until she could get both legs in.

"The old Bea is gone. I bury her in this sandbox."

Bea didn't know where the words or ideas were coming from but she followed them. She stayed there, squishing it between her fingers until a calm came over her. She felt a healing from the sand. A connection. At first Bea pretended not to see the three mothers with strollers, gawking at her with unabashed stares. But then she did something she had never done in this town. She stared back at them with her hands on her hips, doing her best to silently convey: *What the hell are you looking at?* They got it, because in a matter of seconds, all three women dropped their gaze and returned to their frivolous conversation.

PART 3

What happens when people open their hearts?
They get better.

—HARUKI MURAKAMI

TWENTY-FOUR

Hotter than July

When Bea reached home, the house smelled of Lonnie but he was gone. No note on the counter, no abandoned socks on the floor, just his plate and fork in the sink. Bea went into the laundry room and took off her sandy clothes and then walked naked upstairs to her bathroom to shower. When she came out, the phone was ringing.

"Hello." She tightened her towel.

"Today is the day."

"Joney?"

"Put on some comfortable yoga clothes and meet me in the driveway in fifteen minutes."

"Huh . . ."

"Not taking no for an answer." She hung up the telephone.

Bea contemplated ignoring Joney but then did as she was told. This time when she went outside she wore her jacket.

"Come on, I'll drive," motioned Joney. Her hair was pinned in a sloppy bun.

Bea got into the passenger side of Joney's Mini Cooper hybrid. "Where are we going?"

"Yoga. It will help you release the toxins you're feeling in your body and lift that layer of depression I see around your eyes."

Bea nodded and then looked out the window as Joney drove a town over to where the class was being held.

"Here, put these quarters in the meter for me." Joney dropped the change into Bea's palm. The yoga studio was a storefront with four big glass windows. When Bea followed her in, the aroma of the lobby made the tension fade from the back of her neck. It smelled like a mix of lemongrass, rosemary, and sage. Bea slipped out of her shoes and frowned when she realized that her pink toe polish had chipped in three places. She worried if anyone in the class would notice and when she looked up, her pulse quickened.

"Hi, I'm Dakota. Is this your first class?" His generous lips opened wide to reveal snow-white teeth. His skin was buttered that rich color of ganache.

"Yes," she said, instantly calling to mind the song " 'Round Midnight" by Thelonious Monk. Bea wasn't big on jazz but she knew that song because her roommate in college had played it over and over. She'd said it helped her understand better what she was learning when she studied. The tune would always put Bea in a good mood and she smiled before dropping her gaze.

"Welcome." His long locks swayed gently. "Do you have a mat?"

"No."

Dakota reached to the rack behind the front desk and handed her one.

"Thanks." Bea held her yoga mat tightly to her chest as she crossed into the class and kneeled down beside Joney.

"Why is it so hot in here?" She fanned herself.

"Because it's hot yoga."

"Hot what?"

"I thought I told you." Joney sat crossed-legged on her mat with her eyes closed, perspiration already dripping down her face.

"You didn't." Joney breathed deeply, ignoring her. Now that Bea knew that it was hot, she felt like she was hyperventilating.

"How high does it get?"

"Only about ninety-five degrees or so."

Bea's mouth went dry. Joney must have lost her mind, dragging her to sweat. She had just gotten out of the shower. On all fours, she pushed herself to rise. She intended to leave but then when she turned around the door of the room was closed. Dakota walked past her and to the front of the classroom. He made eye contact with Bea and grinned encouragingly.

"Let's start in a seated position on our mats. If this is your first class, take breaks when you need to and drink plenty of water." Behind his head was a beautifully painted picture of a lotus.

"My name is Dakota. *Namaste.*"

Dakota. Did his mama name him Dakota or was that the hippy thing to do, change your name to something cool? He connected his iPod to the stereo and reggae music played.

"I know you weren't expecting to practice yoga to Maxi Priest but there is a strong connection between the two."

Dakota led them through what he referred to as a vinyasa. Bea looked at Joney and how her body moved through the air like a swimmer in the water. Bea decided to give it her all. Even though she felt clumsy and out of shape, it felt like she was supposed to be there. Dakota walked the room calling out instructions that Bea did her best to follow. She opened her arms wide, lifted them over her head and then pushed her heart forward. It made her want to cry, like something very painful was oozing out.

She did her best to emulate what she was seeing, peeking at Joney and watching Dakota move.

"Now flow through. Downward dog. Forward to plank. Chaturanga. Upward dog, or if you like, baby cobra, back to downward dog. Step the right foot forward, left hand next to your left foot and open your right hand to the sky. Twist your heart forward."

The tears ran freely down Bea's face. She was sweating so hard she didn't think anyone would notice as the water comingled.

"Back to downward dog."

Dakota placed his hands on either side of Bea's hips and pulled her hips higher into the air and then pressed down on her back, stretching the rest of her body forward. "That's the pose. Do you feel that?"

Her waist felt like it was exhaling from the spot where he touched her.

"Really concentrate on opening up your hips."

They went through a balancing series and then ended up on their backs. Bea was drenched and thirsty and when the class did a shoulder stand, she didn't even attempt it. All she could picture was her shirt sliding up and exposing the wiggly skin that hung around her belly after the baby. When the rest of the class came out of the pose, Dakota led them to what he called shavasana.

"Our final relaxation pose."

Quickly, Bea realized that of all of the poses this was definitely her favorite. Lie flat. Don't move. Breathe. Her eyes were closed and her mind drifted when she felt Dakota's fingers on her forehead massaging the spot between her eyes with oil that smelled like lavender.

"Slowly roll to your right side and bring your body into the fetal position. You have been reborn."

Bea liked the sound of that.

"Come up slowly."

After a final om, the class was over. Joney rolled off her mat.

"How was it for you?"

Bea admitted that the class had been wonderful. "I haven't felt so alive in my body in years."

"I'm proud of you, Bea. Thanks for trusting me."

The cool air in the lobby felt good. Dakota was behind the counter.

"Beatrice. How was it?"

Hearing her name on his lips made her stomach quake. She hadn't told him her name.

"It's here on the sign-in," he said, reading her mind.

"It was nice. Hot. But I feel good."

"We're running a promotion right now. Two weeks for fifty dollars but since you are new to our community, why don't you try out one week free? Here's the schedule." He slid the brochure across to Bea. "We have some wonderful teachers. I hope you'll give us a try." His mouth dipped and Bea was splashed with sunshine.

"See you next week." Joney waved to Dakota. Outside she rolled her neck. "That was amazing. He's one of my favorite teachers. He does bodywork too. You better not waste your free week."

Bea let herself into Joney's car.

"I do feel good, Joney, thanks."

"My pleasure." She pulled the car away from the curb. "How are things at home?"

Bea wished she hadn't asked because she wanted to hold on to the good feeling longer. "Lonnie left this morning. It was making my skin crawl, living with him. He left reluctantly, but whatever. He left."

"Kids know?"

"Not yet. They make this all so much more complicated."

"Children are resilient. You have to give them more credit."

"I can feel Chico watching me. He's always been like that."

"My son, Ethan, was too when I was going through hell with his father. The moment Sonny raised his fist at me, Ethan would be right there pushing his father, screaming at him, trying to protect me." Joney turned the corner. "Count your stars you didn't marry a fighting man."

Bea didn't want to think about being lucky.

"I have a few books that I want you to read that will help. Trust me, Bea, you are on your way. It's about acknowledging where you are and knowing that you are okay. The universe has your back and so do I." She gave Bea a hug, even though they were sticky, smelly, and wet.

TWENTY-FIVE

The Last Supper

Bea didn't make it back to yoga for her free trial week but she managed to keep her food down for the next seven days. It hadn't been easy but she'd gone back to her basic coping mechanisms: mini meals on a small plate, her notebook, and walking when she felt stressed. She made it a point to stroll past the sandbox as a reminder. The faith bracelet that she'd purchased from QVC also became part of her change. She wore it every day and just feeling it hug her wrist prompted her to stay the course.

Chico demanded to know why Lonnie hadn't been home and Bea had lied, blaming it on work. It was wrong but the best she had in the moment. Then Alana wanted to know why Auntie Awilda hadn't been over for dinner.

"I miss her so much, Mommy. Can I call her?"

"Not right now, sweetie," was Bea's answer to her daughter's daily question.

Irma bugged her every morning, pulling out all of her motherly tricks from her bag of guilt. But still Bea knew what she had to do.

Lonnie called to speak with the children every night and on the last call had asked her to breakfast. Bea agreed to meet him on Friday. She drove the ten minutes to the diner on Route 22 after she dropped the kids off at school. Bea sat in her car for a few minutes with the radio off, not wanting to go in and face him but knowing it was the only way.

Lonnie looked better than anything on the menu when she spotted him at the table. He wore a crisp, grape button-down shirt opened at the collar. His hair was neat, his face clean-shaven, and his eyes shone like two copper pennies.

"Hey, baby," he said, leaning over the table for a kiss on her mouth but she pulled back so all he touched was her air.

"Okay," he said, like she'd hurt his feelings.

"Coffee?" the waitress asked.

"Two, please. And give her a spinach and feta omelet with home fries. I'll have the corned beef hash with rye toast." He was trying to be cute and Bea didn't say anything when he ordered for her. Under the table she slid her bracelet around between her fingers.

"So, how have you been? I've missed you."

"Lonnie, I'm going to ask you a question. I want you to answer me honestly. No games. No lies. No charades. I haven't asked for much in this marriage. You owe me at least this one thing."

He looked at her. "Okay."

"How long were you sleeping with Awilda?"

"Why does that matter?"

"It matters to me."

"I don't remember. Why do you keep bringing this up? All I want is to come back home to you."

"Lonnie."

"Seriously, Bea. This has gone on long enough."

She looked him in the eye. "I want a divorce."

"Bea, come on."

Keeping eye contact she replied, "I'm serious."

"Because of Awilda?"

"No. Because of me."

"What the hell is that supposed to mean?"

"It means let's be cordial about this for the kids' sake and be good co-parents. Here's what I want." She slid a piece of paper across the table. Joney had come over two nights ago with her lawyer hat on to help iron out the details.

"You're serious? You've hired an attorney?"

"It's been coming to this for a long time."

The waitress put the food down. Lonnie thanked her and told her they were fine. Bea didn't touch her food but Lonnie spent the next several minutes forking big chunks into his mouth. He always ate when he was nervous. She had never acknowledged it before but it was something they had in common.

"Take a look at the list, please, and get back to me. It's simple. I just want weekday custody of the kids and for you to live close enough to either take them to school every morning or if that's too much, just commit to weekends. The kids and I will stay in the house and you will continue to pay the bills as always. It states how much I'll need for child support. I've tried to make the number as manageable as possible. This isn't about trying to hurt you. I want an amicable split. As neat at possible."

"You're fucking crazy." He balled up the piece of paper and threw it in her plate. "Have you lost your mind?"

"I've e-mailed you a copy."

Lonnie knocked over his coffee cup, causing the hot liquid to spill into her plate of food.

"Well then."

She got up from the table and walked out of the restaurant,

knowing that Lonnie wouldn't run after her. He would never make a scene in a public place. Bea's legs felt like iron as she moved across the parking lot. Inside her car, she rested her head against the steering wheel and let her emotions flow.

TWENTY–SIX

Fresh Air

Bea had been living without Lonnie for two weeks. It was the longest they had been apart in the twelve years that they were married. The bed felt massive without him and she often woke up cold with the covers tossed to the floor. The Paxil helped—a life jacket that kept her feet from sinking into depression. She craved food less and she had not binged or purged in over twenty-one days. Instead she'd organized the cabinets in the kitchen and carried nonperishable items to the food bank in Hillside, and cleaned out dresser drawers in the children's rooms and taken what was too small to the Goodwill in Springfield. At night, after she put her children to bed and checked that all of the doors were locked, she read.

Joney had given her a book called *Ask and It Is Given: Learning to Manifest Your Desires* by Esther and Jerry Hicks. Esther Hicks had channeled a collective of higher nonphysical entities called Abraham, and their teachings were all about the Law of Attraction. The conversation was totally over Bea's head but she'd taken the tattered paperback anyway. Joney was so full of vitality and positive energy that Bea would try whatever she suggested. She hadn't gotten past the introduction but she was determined to read a page or two a night before picking up a time-travel romance novel by Diana Gabaldon that would take her breath and body away.

Keeping a schedule was important for finding and maintaining this new lifestyle, so on Wednesday she went to the open-air market as she always had, but without Awilda. Bea hated to admit it but she missed the hell out of her sister-friend. It was hard to walk through the grounds without remembering snatches of their conversations. It was here by the fresh herbs stand that Awilda told her that Amare had lost his virginity. Awilda knew this because she had picked up the telephone while he was talking to the girl and listened. The mother-in-law run-ins had been the best and would often have Bea holding onto her sides with laughter. No one in the world could make Bea laugh as hard as Awilda. She knew where Bea's funny bone sat and would press it until Bea chuckled out of control.

The leafy greens made her think of how Awilda complained about having to wash and dry lettuce and then Derrick only took a few bites and reached for the meat, the main event on his plate. Derrick. Bea wondered if he knew. Awilda had called her almost daily but Bea sent the call to voice mail and then pressed delete without listening to what she said. Every year Awilda took the children to New York City for the annual Rockefeller Center tree lightning. When she was straightening Alana's bedroom she noticed it marked on her calendar. Bea would have to figure out how to break the news to her because this year they weren't going.

"Beatrice."

She looked up. It was Dakota, the yoga instructor, holding a basket with one hand and waving with the other.

"Hello." She smiled and they both walked, shortening the space between them.

"You didn't utilize your free week. Now when you come I'll have to charge you." He poked her in the arm. What was it about him? Every cell in her body felt alive.

"I know. My life has been so busy, with the kids and getting ready for the holidays."

"How many children?"

"Two. Boy and a girl."

"What are you making?" He gestured to her basket.

"Pasta, it's the one thing my kids can agree on. I'm going to chop up some asparagus tips and hope they don't notice."

"Sounds good. Have you tried the lemonade here?"

"I have. It's really delicious."

"Want to grab one with me? I'm dying of thirst."

Bea nodded, switched her basket to the other arm, and followed him the few steps to the stand. He ordered two lemonades and when she reached for her wallet, he waved her money away. They sat on the same bench that she and Awilda did. The one where she'd told her that she thought Lonnie was sleeping with someone. Now Bea wondered if that someone had been Awilda.

"Penny for your thoughts." He looked her way.

"Nothing. I just love coming here. The sight of fresh fruit and veggies and the smell of flowers and home-baked bread makes me happy."

"It's why I come too. What's the plan for Thanksgiving?"

Bea sighed. "It'll be my first without the kids."

Dakota looked at her with a kind expression.

"My husband and I just separated so things are a bit messy. They're spending the holiday with him. I think I'm spending it with my mother."

"Sorry to hear it."

"Don't be. It's for the best. Trust me."

"How long have you been married?"

"Twelve years."

Dakota raised his Styrofoam cup to her. "May the next twelve bring you more happiness than you've ever known."

Bea smiled so brightly her cheeks hurt. "Thank you, same to you."

"So, when are you coming back to yoga?"

"It's hard because I have the kids by myself in the evening."

"What about Friday at noon? The day after Thanksgiving."

"Yeah, I should be able to do that."

"Good. If you promise to come, I'll give you another free trial week."

"You don't have to do that."

"I know, but I want to." He stood. "So, I'll see you Friday?"

"Okay." Bea smiled, sorry to see him go. The only people she talked to lately were her kids, her mother, and Joney. It was nice hearing a man's voice. Her list was in her jeans pocket. She reviewed it one more time and then finished her shopping.

The kids had a half day. When she picked them up, she decided to take them to a movie.

"What's the occasion?" Alana wanted to know.

"Just simply because I love you."

The kids coaxed her into buying M&M's, popcorn, and slushy drinks. Bea sat in the middle with her arm around each of them. The movie was surprisingly enjoyable. When they got home, they played a few rounds of Connect Four and then she sent them to bed.

"Can we sleep together in your room?" Alana wanted to know.

"Okay."

"Can we fall asleep with the TV on?"

"Okay."

"Yes." Alana pumped her fist, like today had been her lucky day.

Bea went into the kitchen more out of habit than really needing anything. Her telephone rang. She checked the caller ID and picked it up.

"Hi, Mami."

"Listen. Tia Marie said that you didn't have to bring anything to Thanksgiving dinner but I want you to make something. If we walk in empty-handed, she'll talk about us for days. The coconut drink is in the fridge and I've been marinating the *pernil* all day. Gonna put it in the oven first thing in the morning. It will have this whole building smelling like love."

Tia Marie was Irma's first cousin and her mother's only living relative in this country. They were best friends but talked about each other with reckless abandon. The competition between their families came up in every conversation as they bragged about this one or that one. Irma felt that she had the upper hand because Bea had married Lonnie and lived in Evergreen. Tia Marie had more grandchildren, but Irma said they were all hooligans and there were just too many baby daddies to keep track.

"Unless you've changed your mind and decided to go with your family?"

"Ma, don't start. What time do you want me to pick you up tomorrow?"

"Honestly *mija,* I think you are making a mistake."

"Ma."

"Two is fine. She said to be there at two but you know she won't be ready. We'll probably walk in and have to help her set the table. I hope this year she has enough forks. Last year we had to make do with plastic spoons."

"Okay, tomorrow at two. I'm looking forward to it," Bea lied. The truth was she'd rather stay home and eat a TV dinner. She was only going because she didn't want to seem pathetic at home alone on a national holiday. Besides, being around so many people would keep the dark horse at bay.

"If you change your mind I can get a ride; don't worry about me."

"Bye, Ma."

Bea had finally dipped into the money that Mena had given her. Joney had connected her with a high-end divorce lawyer who was very expensive and well-respected. Because Bea had come through Joney (who said he'd had a crush on her for years), he only charged her one-third of what he charged most clients. The second splurge was a yoga mat and two pairs of colorful yoga pants with matching tops from lululemon athletica. She had drooled over the clothing line when other mothers wore their pieces to the school. Ten minutes before Lonnie was scheduled to arrive, she slipped on one of the outfits and pulled her hair into a nice ponytail. When she got downstairs, he had let himself in again even though she had asked him not to. She would have to really make a point to call the locksmith to have the locks changed. Alana was in his arms.

"Hey."

"Hey." She could feel his eyes on her, sizing her up the way a man would a woman for sex. It was weird but it made her feel good. Like she still had it. The first time he came to pick the kids up, she had offered him some breakfast out of habit. Then she resisted the urge to put him to work. There was a laundry list of things in the house that needed his attention: the ink in the printer, the water filter in the fridge. The mechanic had called and said it was time for her tires to be rotated. But Bea wouldn't ask.

"Kids ready?"

Bea nodded. "Put your shoes on, Alana. Did you brush your teeth and wash your face?"

"Yes."

"Chico, deodorant? I know you didn't make your bed so please go do it."

Bea leaned against the island.

"You look good."

"Thanks."

"What are you doing for dinner tomorrow?"

"Mom."

"You can always pop in on us, everyone would be happy to see you."

Bea smiled politely and then busied herself with wiping down the countertops even though they were shiny and clean.

"You probably should start looking for a job because I can't pay your way and mine too."

She stopped and darted her eyes at him. "Your children live here."

"We could all live here but that's not what you want. I can pay the mortgage but that's it."

"Not a problem."

He stumbled back on his left foot. Bea could tell that she had caught him off guard. Lonnie had expected her to beg. Bea went back to polishing the countertop. Thanks to Mena she wouldn't have to. She had already cut the cable down to basic, her cell phone to a cheaper plan, and put the heating system on a timer while the kids were at school, and when the temperature in the house dropped, she'd bundle up in a heavy sweater. Bea shoved Alana's stuffed bear into her backpack. The mortgage would wipe her out quickly but as long as he covered that she could handle the few incidentals for several months. Her résumé was posted on careerbuilders.com and she had started applying for positions at the neighboring hospitals. She had even sent her résumé in for a school-nurse position at an elementary school about thirty minutes away.

"Have fun." She kissed both kids. Lonnie didn't look back at her as the kids scooted into the back of the hired car. He wasn't using his crutches anymore but Chico had told her that he couldn't drive for another week.

Alana turned and waved and Bea blew her a big kiss, trying very hard not to feel anything.

Bea had made it through Thanksgiving at Tia Marie's, enjoying her loud family and all the homemade dishes on the table. She ate more than she'd intended and drank so much with her cousin Mercedes that she had to gulp down two cups of strong coffee before she felt ready to drive her mother home. It was nice to sleep in the next morning, with no one calling her name. When she finally got out of bed, she ran herself a hot bath with Epsom salt and mint to wake her body up. She had phoned Joney to see if she was going to yoga but found out she wasn't; her daughter was in town and they were going into Manhattan to sightsee. Bea was on her own. She toweled off and skipped the lotion, knowing the heat from the yoga class would only make her sweat it off anyway.

The class started at noon but she arrived ten minutes early with the intention of just sitting and breathing. Dakota was at the front desk chatting with an older woman when she walked in. He stopped when he saw her.

"Beatrice."

"Please, everyone calls me Bea."

"Beatrice makes me think of the character in Shakespeare's *Much Ado About Nothing*."

She smiled. Beatrice was by far one of the most delightful characters in all of the Shakespeare that Bea had read. She was witty, clever, talkative, and assertive in a way that Bea longed to be. She liked that Dakota had connected the fictional character to her.

"I'm glad you came. Today we are going to concentrate on opening up the heart and letting the light in."

"I like the sound of that."

Bea went inside and set up her new yoga mat, feeling like having her own meant that she was on the path. The room was warm but this time the heat didn't feel suffocating. The studio filled quickly. Looking around there were men and women of all ages, colors, and creeds. She liked that. It made her feel like she was up on some sort of revolutionary way of life. The music began.

"We are going to start today's class with the sun salutation. The breath is very important during this sequence. To begin, bring yourself to the edge of your mat in mountain pose. That's it, Beatrice."

She tried not to smile at the tingle his uttering her name caused. Sweat began to drip down her face as her body heated up with the sequence of moves. Then they moved into balancing poses: tree, dancer, and then half moon, which seemed more manageable than the warm-up. When Dakota told the class to give a final stretch and then rest in shavasana, Bea felt like she had done well enough. On the inside she felt clean and free. When she rolled over on her mat to the right and sat up, Dakota was saying to the class, "You have been reborn. You are free. Go out in the world and love with an open heart. Be present in your body and follow your bliss."

They all said "*Namaste*" together and then it was over.

Bea felt amazingly light. It was almost as if she had lost ten pounds. She sprayed her mat down with the vinegar solution that was being passed around.

"How do you feel?" Dakota asked from behind the desk. The lobby felt cool compared to the classroom.

"Good. Actually, amazing."

"Awesome. That's what I like to hear. Hang on a minute, would you?"

Bea nodded and walked to the left where the bookshelves were full of books. She picked up one and read the inside flap. Then she saw the book that Joney had given her, *Ask and It Is Given*. On the window ledge, she sat and reread the intro while she waited for him.

"Ah, the bible of the Law of Attraction."

"You've read this book?"

"Several times."

"I can't get past one or two pages at a time."

"That's how it's supposed to be read. Sipped like a soothing cup of tea."

"That makes me feel better. It was feeling so heavy."

"It's simple really. Just think of it as taking the power of positive thinking to the next level."

Bea tilted her head.

"I wake up every morning thinking: 'How can I change my life by aligning with the vibration of my desires?' And it usually works."

"How do you know?"

"You're standing here." His eye contact was so intense that Bea felt her cheeks blush.

"Stop it."

"Running into you at the market wasn't an accident, Bea. We all have energy and when our energy aligns with what we are intending, we receive it."

"You intended to see me?"

"For sure. I've been dying to have a meal with you. Do you have to rush to get your kids?"

"I need to take a shower. The kids aren't back until tomorrow."

"How about we meet for a late lunch?"

"Okay."

"Three-thirty, okay? Do you mind vegetarian food?"

"All fine."

"I know the perfect spot."

Bea didn't want him to come to her house and she was glad that he had offered to meet her at the studio.

She went home, showered, brushed her hair, and put it into a side bun. She didn't want to look too fancy, like she thought it was a date, but she didn't want to wear her drab mommy clothes either. She went through a few different outfits before settling on a pair of royal blue jeans that she had hardly worn, a white cotton sweater, just a little gloss on her lips, and a pair of ballerina flats. When she looked in the mirror the first thought that occurred to her was that Awilda would tell her to put some mascara on, so she did.

The yoga studio was only fifteen minutes from her house and she arrived ten minutes early. Dakota was there.

"Hey."

"I'm glad you're early. I'm so hungry I could eat my wrist. The place is about a ten-minute walk, you up for it?"

"Yeah."

He held the door open for her and as she walked past him he smelled of coconut oil and a hint of almond. She wondered if it was a cologne or coming from his hair.

"Do you live in town?"

"Evergreen."

"I hear they have a good school district."

"Yeah. It wasn't my first choice but it works."

"Where would you have picked?"

"South Mountain. It's more diverse and has that arsty-fartsy feel that I'm drawn to."

"Yeah, I can feel that too."

They talked and the walk seemed to take two minutes instead of ten. They found a seat in the window near the fireplace. The waitress brought them menus.

"What's good?" Bea asked. Dakota pointed out a few of his favorite dishes and they decided to order the barbeque tempeh, a chickpea salad, and a vegan panini. The conversation was easy and the time together breezed by.

"Wow, this is delicious. I never knew vegetarian food could have so much flavor."

"It's actually vegan."

"You eat like this all of the time?"

"I've been vegetarian for almost twenty years. I've dabbled into being vegan, but it gets hard sometimes because I love cheese. I can go long breaks without it but yesterday I had to have my sister's famous mac and cheese."

"Mac and cheese would get me every time."

"I even brought a small container home with me." He laughed. "I don't know what she puts in it but it's like crack."

Bea told him about her Thanksgiving and then they talked about his day job as a CFO for a nonprofit. Bea confessed that she had applied for a few positions and was nervous about going back to work after so many years home with the kids.

"I always admire involved moms. It's a thankless job but the planet is better off because of mothers like you."

"Thanks." Bea smiled.

They walked down the street to the coffee bar and had coffee and more wonderful conversation before walking back to her car.

"I enjoyed hanging out with you."

"Me too." Bea leaned in and gave him a hug, they touched hands, and then she turned to go.

"See you around."

"Is it okay if I take your number down off the yoga log?"

"Sure." She smiled and then waved.

Inside her car, her pulse raced. That was the most exciting time that she'd had in years. She put the key in the ignition and then eased out of her parking space.

TWENTY–SEVEN

The Only Way to Get Ahead

A week later, Bea took a job as a school nurse at a charter school in Newark on Central Avenue. It was an easy commute, with the school being right off of I-280, but the day was full. Two weeks in and she was already whipped trying to keep track of all the schoolchildren's problems as well as her own. Her body was not used to the constant movement and it was never quiet. The students appeared in her office for every little thing. Honestly, she couldn't understand why the teachers sent them down for some of the things she had to deal with: small scratches with no blood, banged elbows, a loose tooth, wanting a Band-Aid or a throat lozenge. It was nonstop, non-emergency traffic in her tiny office. But Bea was grateful. There was no better feeling than bringing in your own income. Her first paycheck dropping into her personal checking account was a satisfying accomplishment.

Lonnie was giving her a hard time with proceeding with the paperwork for the divorce and Christmas was in a little over a week. It would be their first holiday without Awilda, Derrick, and Amare coming for Christmas brunch. Alana threw a fit when she realized that Awilda wasn't taking her to see the tree lighting. Then the other night, Chico asked if he could go to Amare's season opener basketball game and Bea had to tell him no.

"Why? I'm old enough to go without you. Amare invited me."

"Not this time, sweetie."

"Why can't Auntie Awilda pick me up on the way?"

"She just can't, all right?"

"I'll call and ask her." He picked up his cell phone. Bea snatched it out of his hand.

"Go upstairs. You have to learn to listen. You're not grown."

"Can I have my phone back?" He pouted.

"No. Now go."

He moped about it for two days and it added to Bea's daily angst.

Dakota called her every night at 9 P.M. It was after the kids were in bed and she looked forward to the call like a second helping of dessert. His voice settled in her chest and loosened the phlegm from her day. From their conversations, she was learning not to worry so much about the future but to live and breathe in the present moment. On most days that was easier to hear than to practice but he lightened her mood and made her try.

Irma was at the house more with Bea working and Lonnie gone. She was a godsend really, cooking two to three meals for them and doing a good portion of the laundry. On the evenings Irma stayed over, Bea would put the children to bed and after her conversation with Dakota, she and her mother would watch television together. One night Bea had not noticed her standing in the doorway of her bedroom while she was on the phone with Dakota.

When she hung up, her mother looked her up and down and

sucked her teeth. "I guess you need one man to take the taste of another man out of your mouth."

"Huh?"

"I don't approve."

"It's not like that, Mami."

"Better not be."

It was Thursday: her mother's must-see TV night. Irma had just pulled a throw up to her waist and slipped the straw to her Coke into her mouth when Bea walked into the family room clutching a bowl of air popcorn.

"*Mija,* you look terrible."

Bea didn't really need her mother to tell her that. She hadn't been sleeping well.

"Want some?"

Her mother reached for the wooden bowl. "You need to talk to Lonnie. Why throw away a good thing, baby? You're killing yourself for no reason."

The fatigue from work did not compare to the bone tiredness she felt every time her mother tried to push her back into Lonnie's arms.

"Mami, give it a rest."

"Honey, you can't keep this up. You don't have to. If you ask, he'll come back. I can see it in his eyes when he picks up the children. You're being plain foolish. And Tia Marie agrees with me."

"Tia Marie? What?"

"Just call the man."

Bea reached for the belt of her robe and tightened it. "Did you ever consider that I don't want him back?"

"Nonsense. You are just playing hard to get."

"Do you hear yourself?"

"Do you see yourself? Dragging around here, trying to do it all when you don't have to. You have a husband."

"Whatever."

"I wasn't lucky enough to have a husband. And if I did, I certainly wouldn't treat him like you are treating Lonnie."

Bea tried to bite back her tongue but it wiggled in her mouth. "I'm not going to accept a piece of a man, Mommy, even if it makes my life easier."

"Silly girl." Her mother scooped up some popcorn. "Women have worked with less."

"That was your way. It's not mine. Not anymore."

"How dare you?"

Bea raised her voice. "How dare *you*? Do you realize that you've pushed me to be a floor mat for that man? You have taught me to eat his shit no matter what—"

"Watch your mouth." Irma sat straighter in her seat.

"He's cheated more times than you know."

"All men do."

"With Awilda."

Her mother looked as if she had seen her father's ghost.

"That's not true." She made the sign of the cross.

"Why do you think she hasn't been around? When's the last time you've spoken to her?"

"I don't know."

Bea let that thought breathe and then hit her mother again. "Lonnie has a son in Miami."

Her mother patted her chest with an open palm.

"Same age as Alana. Same name as Alonzo. I'm not putting up with him anymore just because he can provide, Mommy. Yes, this is hard but I'd rather work five days a week and struggle than live my whole fucking life miserable."

"I keep telling you to watch your mouth. What's come over you?"

"You! And all of your Roman Catholic ways! You should be telling me that the marriage vows need to be honored before God. But what should I expect from someone who spent fifteen years as a chick on the side?"

"I was never a chick on the side. Your father loved me."

"But he was married. Had a whole family across town. Why did you even stay with him? You should have demanded more."

Bea didn't even realize that her mother could move so fast until her palm crashed across her face.

"Ungrateful little girl. The sacrifices I have made for you."

It was the second time that a woman had called Bea a little girl.

"Sitting there on your throne judging me, like the women on our block. Calling me *puta* behind my back but smiling up in my face. You don't know anything about trying to survive in a country that's not your own. That's what I've been sheltering you against your entire life. Maybe that's where I've failed you. You were too sheltered. I should have let you see more of the world's flaws."

Bea rubbed her cheek, unable to believe her mother had slapped her. Like she was a naughty teenage girl caught out after curfew. This was her house.

"Yes, your father was married. He told me he was going to leave his wife and I believed him. I never planned to be his mistress; it just happened." Irma's eyes were wild with indignation. "And he was a good provider. You know how much I got paid as a school secretary? Thirteen thousand dollars a year. Just a smidge above the poverty line. I didn't qualify for help from the government so I had to do what I needed to do to take care of you. Dance lessons, art, recitals, and costumes. None of that was cheap. None of it. So I needed your father just like you need your husband. Now if you want to throw him away because he was unfaithful, as all men are, then do it. I did what I did to survive and I have long stopped feeling guilty about it."

Bea looked at her feet. "I can't."

"Fine. But know that women have had to put up with more for less."

"Not me. And not Alana. I will not pass this on to her. I'll struggle alone and I will survive."

"Call me a cab."

Bea stood. "You don't have to go."

Her mother walked to the back office behind the family room where she kept her stuff. Bea didn't pick up the telephone to call the cab but she didn't stop her mother from waiting for the one she had dialed—on the front steps—either.

TWENTY–EIGHT

Crush

Christmas was only days away, traffic everywhere had been impossible, and Bea hadn't shopped the way she had in the past for the kids because she'd been too busy with work. The school wasn't near any stores or malls so when she had a free moment she ordered a few things online and had them sent to her mother's house. Irma still wasn't over their fight but she did sign for the packages and texted Bea when they arrived.

Alana still believed in Santa Claus and Chico was a good sport at letting her believe. Bea had bought the Elf on the Shelf and Chico made it his business to hide it each night for Alana's glee. Whenever Bea thought about all the work she had to do to prepare for Christmas, she wanted to eat the entire gingerbread house and then throw it all up. But she wouldn't. She had long passed her twenty-one days of binge freedom and between that and the hot yoga she'd committed to twice a week, she had the gusto that she needed to keep going. The class had become like the vitamins she needed to feel good.

When her mother stopped coming over, Joney offered to stay with the kids and feed them dinner so Bea could make it to yoga.

"I know what you're going through, kiddo." Joney would smile and then push her mat into her arms.

On Saturday mornings, she and Joney would go to class together after Lonnie usually came to pick up the kids. This week Dakota was teaching the class and she had woken up excited to see him. Then Lonnie phoned and canceled because of a last-minute work engagement.

"On a Saturday?" Bea argued.

"It's last minute."

"Sounds like a chick to me."

"Don't do that."

"Same dude, different day."

"What does that mean?"

"It means I don't believe you. Why don't you come for them later?"

"Why are you stressing me? You have a date?"

"Because I'm the one who will have to pick up the broken kid pieces." She slammed down the phone.

When she went into the playroom, Chico was on the Xbox and Alana was in the middle of a tea party. Bea told them the news.

"Why isn't Daddy coming?" Alana pouted. "He doesn't want to be with me?"

"It's not that."

"But he promised."

"I know he did."

"Can I call him?"

"He texted me that he'll call you guys later, see?" Bea held up her phone. She needed to think of something to save the moment. "I have an idea. Get dressed and be downstairs in five minutes. I'll set the timer."

"Where are we going?"

"If I tell you it won't be a surprise. Put on jeans and a sweatshirt."

The kids ran to their rooms. Bea found the farm that they had gone to last year to pick pumpkins and even though it was too late in the season for that, they could go on hay rides or something. She typed the address into the GPS system on her phone.

"Ready? Time's up," she called to the kids.

Alana walked in wearing purple jeans and a bright yellow and red sweatshirt.

"Honey, that doesn't match."

"But I want to wear it."

"Okay." Not in the mood to argue about fashion. "Make sure you grab your hat and gloves. Chico, we are getting in the car."

Once everyone was strapped in, Bea backed out of the driveway, then she stopped to text Joney that she wasn't going to class. When they got to Route 78, Chico ran his finger down Bea's ponytail.

"Ma, where are we going?"

"To the farm."

"Yes," said Alana.

Chico sucked his teeth. "I thought we were going someplace fun."

Bea ignored him. She turned up the music, cracked her window, and drove. There was still a tiny bit of foliage, but the trees were moving toward brown or bare. By the time she pulled into the lot, Chico had come around. The kids ran in the fresh open air, feeding the farm animals, and jumping in the bouncy house. As Bea watched the kids, happy to have distracted them, she paused when she recognized that she missed Lonnie. Not him, per se, but what he represented. She missed them as a whole unit. Not only was it the first weekend that he hadn't come since they separated, this was the farm that they'd brought the kids to last October, shortly after moving to New Jersey.

When she sat on the bench with the kids for hot apple cider and donuts, Bea couldn't help noticing the other families huddled together. Dads. Husbands. Boyfriends. She was alone. Bea repinned her hair into a tighter bun and watched a bird soar up into the clouds. Alone but not lonesome, she thought, pondering her nightly conversations with Dakota and remembering their plans to meet for a movie. But even with that, she couldn't imagine painting him into this picture. Her family portrait. Was she really prepared to go through life single? Was her mother right? Had Bea behaved like a foolish little girl?

"Can we get an apple pie to take home?"

Apple pie was Lonnie's favorite. The one they bought last year didn't even make it out of the car before he gobbled a slice.

"Of course. We can have it with ice cream for dessert." Bea kissed Alana's nose.

"I want Daddy."

"I know you do, sweetie." Bea gave her a hug.

"Let's go check out the corn maze. Bet you can't make it through."

"I can make it through." Chico crushed his plastic cup in his hand and tossed it up in the air like a mini basketball. Then he pretended to do a spin move around Bea's back.

"Can we go together, Chico?" Alana tugged.

He grabbed her hand.

"I'll wait for you guys here."

As she waited for the kids, she remembered the family meeting two weekends ago, where Bea and Lonnie explained that he'd be officially living in the city for a while. Chico wanted to know why, of course.

"Because sometimes mommies and daddies don't get along. Just like you and Alana don't get along."

"Yeah, but I can't just move out. Why don't you just go to your room?"

"It's not that simple, son," Lonnie explained, while cutting his eyes at Bea like this conversation was all her fault.

"Michael's parents are getting a divorce." His fingers moved over his phone. "Are you two getting a divorce?"

Bea remembered looking at Lonnie and then answering. "We are taking it one day at a time." Alana didn't say much in the meeting. She sat curled up in her daddy's lap. Bea didn't know if she just wasn't listening or if it wasn't registering—the magnitude of everything. But when she woke up in the middle of the night and Bea ran to her, she cried for Lonnie.

Bea could set her watch by her mother's Sunday schedule, ten o'clock mass and then a walk to the *panaderia* for a pastry and a coffee over the *El Nacional*. Irma was putting a sticky bun to her lips when Bea and the kids walked in.

"Nona!" Chico shouted, followed by Alana.

Her face lit up at the sight of her grandchildren.

"*Hola, mis hijos,*" and she slathered them in Spanish.

Chico surprised the hell out of Bea by responding to her mother in Spanish.

"He always speaks Spanish with me. Have to preserve our heritage." Her mother chuckled in a way that let Bea know she was okay. Her gold crown was visible in the side of her mouth. Bea took a seat across from her mother and then reached into her purse for a ten-dollar bill.

"Chico, take Alana to the counter. Make sure you count your change."

The place was warm and packed with families. Mostly Catholics who congregated here before or after service.

"So what brings you here? Were you at the service?"

"No."

"Should have come. Your children need to know Jesus."

Bea hadn't been to church other than for Christmas and Easter in over five years.

"I know. Maybe next Sunday."

"So why the visit?"

"I've missed you, Mami."

Bea's mother reached across the table and squeezed Bea's hand. Then she brought it to her lips. "*Eres el amor de mi vida.*" *You are the love of my life.*

"Want to come back with us for dinner?"

"What are you cooking?"

"I put ribs in the Crock-Pot this morning."

"You are so American with that slow cooker. Pork, I hope?"

"Yup." Bea leaned over and kissed her mother's cheek.

TWENTY-NINE

It's Getting Late

On the first day of winter, Bea forced herself to decorate the inside of the house. Lonnie usually decorated outside but this year she had paid one of those 1–800 companies to come and do the work for her. It had cost her a small fortune but she wanted to create as much normalcy as possible for the kids. They'd always had a big Christmas with all of the family over for dinner but this year it was just the three of them.

"Is Daddy coming home?" Alana still said "home." And to Bea it felt like she asked the question every single day. Even her mother, who had been over her house most nights, wasn't going to be there for Christmas.

"*Mija,* I've been telling you for months that I'm going on a cruise with Tia Marie to the Bahamas."

"Oh, I guess I didn't realize it was over Christmas break. For some reason I thought you said New Year's."

"You're going to miss your mami," Irma teased. Bea didn't find it funny. She actually found it oppressive to be so alone.

. . .

On Christmas Eve, she struggled with the urge to binge. The dark horse had been breathing down her neck since she had opened her eyes that morning. Dakota had gone to Mississippi to visit with his grandparents and she felt alone. When the doorbell rang she thought it could be that last package she was expecting from her online shopping. When she peeked out the window, she saw Santa Claus.

"Ho, ho, ho. Merry Christmas." It was Lonnie. He had to ring the bell because Bea had finally gotten around to changing the locks.

Chico ran to the door. "Who is it?"

"Ho, ho, ho," Lonnie said again, swinging a big red bag over his shoulder.

"Alana, come quick. It's Santa." Chico reached past Bea for the latch on the screen door and let Santa in. Alana stood in the foyer with her mouth wide open. "Santa! You came! I've been praying for you and you came. I need to sit on your lap. I need to ask you for something." Alana grabbed Santa and pulled him into the living room and sat him down on the overstuffed chair.

"What can Santa do for you, my dear?"

"Can I have some privacy?" Alana turned to Chico and Bea.

"Jeez," said Chico, walking into the kitchen. Bea followed him. "Mom, doesn't she know that's Dad?"

"Apparently not."

"I'm glad he came. I was thinking Christmas would be a bust without Dad. You didn't even make gumbo this year."

It was true. Bea and Lonnie's tradition was to make gumbo and chocolate-chip cookies from scratch on Christmas Eve. The seafood gumbo was more his project than hers so she'd decided to skip it this year. Bea cocked her head toward the living room so that she could hear Alana, who was a terrible whisperer.

"Santa, I only want one thing. I wrote you in the letter. Did you get it?"

"Um. Ho, ho, ho. Refresh my memory," Lonnie said, making his voice deeper.

"Okay. My dad doesn't live here anymore. Mom said they needed a time-out. But when she gives me a time-out, it's for five minutes or one hour. This is a very long time-out. I want my dad to come back home."

Bea watched as Santa's shoulders dipped.

"I don't know what Dad did to have to live somewhere else but I need you to bring him back. Can you do that, Santa? Can you put my family back together?"

"Um . . ." Santa shifted Alana on his lap. "Santa will see what he can do. Santa doesn't make those kinds of promises." He stole a glance at Bea. "Santa usually brings toys. Are there any toys you want?"

"Nope. Just my family again. Santa, promise me you will do the best you can."

Santa hugged her back.

"Ho, ho, ho," he said, standing. "Merry Christmas." He waved a white-gloved hand in the air and then left through the front door.

Bea didn't know what to say to Alana. It was a holiday and she knew that her daughter was hurting. They were all hurting. Bea hadn't even sent out Christmas cards this year. Every year they took a family portrait and sent cards. This year she had considered just sending a card of the kids, but with work and the kids' schedules she never got around to it. The doorbell rang again.

"Chico, look out the window and tell me who it is."

Bea had a bowl of popcorn on the counter. She had planned to let the kids string it around the tree. What she wanted was to dip the bowl to her face and swallow it all down. She fingered her bracelet.

"Daddy!" Chico shouted.

Alana almost fell off the kitchen stool running. "Daddy!" she shrieked.

Lonnie came through the door. Bea stood by the stove. She didn't know what to do. Didn't know what to feel. Hated to admit that was she was breathing a sigh of relief, for the kids' sakes anyway.

Lonnie went into the living room and sat in the same seat that he'd sat in as Santa. The kids buzzed around him. Alana was telling him about Santa's visit when Chico started in about school.

"I was talking," she demanded.

"Chico, let her finish," Bea called from the spot she seemed rooted to in the kitchen.

Alana wanted to show him what she was learning in hip-hop class but Chico wouldn't give her his tablet so that she could play the music.

"See, Daddy? That's why I need my own tablet. Dang it. I should have told Santa when he was here." She thought a moment. "Do you think it's too late to send him a letter?"

"It's Christmas Eve, honey."

"Do you have his e-mail address?"

Lonnie thought for a minute. "Maybe Santa is telepathic."

"What does that mean?"

"It means that he can receive your message with his mind. If you sit real quiet and concentrate on sending Santa the message with your mind, it might work."

"Oh, that happened on *Spy Kids*. On it." She dashed away.

Chico was next to Lonnie. Bea watched them, pretending to wipe a spot on the kitchen counter. Chico spoke softly and the two giggled. The next thing she knew they were playing Connect Four. First Lonnie played with Chico. Then he played with Alana. When Lonnie walked into the kitchen, she pictured what she looked like: sweatpants and an oversized T-shirt. Her ponytail was more like a knot at the nape of her neck. Right away she thought of Awilda's comment. *You can't even be bothered to put on lipstick and heels.*

"You look beautiful," Lonnie said.

"That's inappropriate."

"Sorry, I couldn't help it."

"What are you doing here?"

"I know I should have called but I didn't want to ruin the surprise."

"I could have had company." What would Lonnie have done if he walked in and Dakota was here?

"The more the merrier."

She turned her back to him and started soaping the few dishes in the sink.

"Let me help."

"Really, dude?"

He took the sponge and fork from her hand. "It's Christmas. Relax, will you?"

Bea didn't know how to relax. She leaned against the island counter watching him. Lonnie turned his face toward her. She hated that he looked so together. Freshly shaven. Crisp button-down shirt and loose blue jeans. He had taken off his boots at the front door and she saw the oxford socks she had given him for his birthday.

"I'm going to take a shower." Bea left the room. Why was she letting him stay? She shouldn't let him stay. The holiday season had been hard enough to get through without him showing up playing Santa/Daddy. She could hear the kids downstairs with him, riding their happy wave. It wasn't fair. She turned the water as hot as she could stand it. She washed her hair and soaped up her body. When she got out, she couldn't decide what to wear. She didn't want to look like she cared about him but she also didn't want to look raggedy. A smock top and some leggings were a nice middle ground. She combed out the knotty hair and made a proper pony-tail. She looked better than she had in days, she thought, pinching her cheeks.

"Can I help you make the cookies?" Alana met her in the kitchen.

"Sure." She tied on her apron. "Ask Chico if he wants to help too."

Alana yelled to Chico, who yelled back, "no."

Bea pulled out the premade cookie dough and showed Alana how to roll it out with the pin and then cut the dough with the shapers. With oven mitts on, Bea guided Alana to place the cookies in the oven.

"Come back in ten minutes to check on them."

"How will I know when ten minutes are up?"

"Let's set the timer."

"Good idea."

When the cookies had finished cooling on the rack, they ate them in the kitchen. Bea sat at the counter and the three of them sat at the table. Lonnie and Bea talked to the kids but not to each other. The night ticked on; it was time for bed. They both tucked the kids into Chico's bed and kissed them good night.

"Daddy, please be here in the morning when we wake up. I want you to see if Santa got my tel-e-pat message on the tablet."

"Telepathic," Chico corrected her.

"Yeah, that."

Lonnie kissed her cheek. "We'll see, baby."

Bea followed Lonnie down the steps and whispered, "How could you say you may be here? You are not sleeping under this roof."

"I'll stay out of your way. I'm not expecting anything from you. Let's just have Christmas together and deal with the rest later. For the kids' sakes."

"If you were worried about the kids' sakes then you . . ."

"I come in peace, Bea, not war. I know this is just for the moment. Let's just wrap presents."

Bea dropped it. She could make it until tomorrow morning. But he couldn't stay for Christmas dinner.

They were in the den. Bea was on a stool reaching into the back of the closet for presents.

"Can I fix you a drink?"

"No."

"I won't make it strong. It's the holidays." Lonnie left the den. He was trying to disarm her. Lonnie was good at that. Spinning a web and trapping his prey, that's why he was great at cheating. He knew the soft landscape of women. He returned with two glasses.

"I put mostly cranberry juice in yours."

"Lock the door." The den was small and warm. Lonnie questioned her with his eyes.

"So that the kids don't wander in here and see me doing Santa's work." She rolled her eyes.

"Wait, I'll be right back."

Bea sipped her drink. It was fruity and easy to get down. It only took a few minutes for her edges to soften. Lonnie returned with three big bags. He locked the door.

"You brought all of that?"

He pulled out a tablet for Alana. "I got Santa's tel-e-pat message." He laughed.

"Good, because I didn't." Bea was actually happy that Lonnie was going to mix his gifts with hers under the tree because she had not bought a lot this year. It didn't fit into her budget and she'd refused to ask him for anything.

"Did you bring wrapping paper?"

"Don't you have the big box of paper you bought last year on clearance in the garage?"

Bea nodded and took another sip. Delicious.

"I'll get it." Lonnie went out and returned with the paper. "We need Christmas music. We can't wrap gifts without Christmas music." He turned on the stereo.

"Baby It's Cold Outside" came on. It was one of Bea's favorite Christmas songs. She sang softly as she worked. They shared the tape but had two pairs of scissors. Lonnie had never helped her wrap Christmas gifts before. This was a first. He had a few messy edges but for the most part he did a decent job.

"How's your thigh?" she asked, surprising herself.

"Still gets a little tender but mostly it's fine. I've been doing a little light lifting at the gym."

Bea had two more drinks with Lonnie and her mood drifted from somber to gay. "This Christmas" by Donny Hathaway came on and she turned up the music a notch.

"This is my all-time favorite Christmas song." Bea rocked.

"I know. You play it enough over the holiday season."

"It makes me think of my father. I don't know why but it does."

"Wanna dance?"

"Get a life."

"Damn, Bea."

"Seriously, Lonnie. I can't go back to the way things were."

"What if we start something new?"

Bea stood with gifts in her arms. "I'll throw you down a pillow and blanket. Can you put the rest of the gifts under the tree?"

"Sure."

"And Lonnie, if you come upstairs again, I will shoot you. This time, it won't be an accident." Bea walked upstairs without looking back.

THIRTY

A Lifetime of Lifelines

Every December twenty-sixth, it was Bea and Awilda's tradition to get up early and run out to the stores for the after-Christmas sales. Chico didn't want to go. Lately Bea had been giving him a little leeway, leaving him for an hour or two while she ran an errand. After giving him her usual "home alone" spiel, she grabbed Alana and drove to the mall.

Bea was in Macy's when she spied a shapely woman with big hair and immediately thought it was Awilda. When the woman turned, she realized it wasn't her. Bea stopped in the middle of the girls' department between the wool coats and hats and cried. The tears ran down her face before she could catch them.

"Mommy, what's wrong?" Alana had climbed out from beneath a clothes rack and looked up from the floor.

"Nothing, baby. I just got some dust in my eyes."

"Is that like when you cut onions and cry?"

"Yes."

"Oh." She went back to playing her made-up game.

Bea blew her nose with the used tissue she found in her pocket. Not having Awilda in her life had been like nursing a constant tooth-ache and the pain wasn't getting any easier to deal with. Most days she would just put her feelings on ice until she felt numb. But it was the little things that reminded her of Awilda. Two women buying bread at the open-air market, hearing the wind at her back door and believing it to be Awilda walking through unannounced for dinner. They had that kindred spirit between them that sometimes Bea just had to think of Awilda and her phone would ring.

As she was putting the packages in the back of her van, her cell phone vibrated in her pocket. She knew without looking that it was her. Bea hesitated and then answered the phone.

"Hello."

"Bea?"

"Yes."

"Derrick's in the hospital. He's had a seizure."

Bea gripped the phone. "Are you kidding me?"

"No."

"I have to run home and grab Chico and then I'll be on my way."

"Overlook. Hurry."

"Where're we going?" Chico stumbled out to the car in a hoody and a hat.

"Why didn't you put a coat on?"

"I don't know. Where are we going?"

"To the hospital."

"Why?"

"Uncle Derrick isn't feeling well."

"Are we going to the one that has the children's play area?" Alana asked.

"Yes. I don't know. Listen, I need quiet so that Mommy can think. Hold your questions."

"Can we talk to each other?"

"Softly."

Bea turned the music up because she didn't know what else to do to ease her nerves rattling in that space between her heart and chest. Then she thought of her mother and Bea knew what she would do. She said a prayer with her eyes on the road. She prayed to St. Juliana, the patron saint of chronic illnesses. She was her mother's favorite saint and so Bea asked her to help Derrick and to heal him.

When she arrived at the hospital, the kids ran to Awilda, who sat alone in the waiting area flipping through a magazine. She looked shocked. Her hair was frizzy; her sweatpants were the ones Bea could picture her wearing around the house on cleaning day.

"Hey guys," she said weakly with her arms around both kids. "I've missed you two."

"Why haven't you been over?" Chico stepped back, like too much public affection would ruin his reputation.

Awilda glanced at Bea. "Things have been busy but I've thought of you."

"I wanted to go to Amare's basketball game but Mom said no. Can you just pick me up next time?" Chico asked.

Awilda looked at Bea and told him of course. Alana sat in Awilda's lap sniffing her scent and rubbing her hair. Bea sat across from them. Watching the reunion scene.

"You look nice," Awilda commented.

Bea liked the compliment but tried her best not to show it. "How's Derrick?"

"He's stable."

"Can I see him?"

"Yeah. I'll stay with the kids."

Awilda gave her Derrick's room number and Bea walked down the hall and rapped lightly on the door.

"Hey there." She walked in.

"Bea."

"How are you feeling?"

"Like I've had the wind knocked out of me. Where've you been?"

"I got a job."

"You what?"

"Yup, working as a school nurse in Newark."

"Do I say congratulations? Is everything okay at home?"

Bea looked down at her fingers. "Lonnie moved out."

"Man."

"It's tough on some days but it really is for the best. We've gone as far as we can."

"Are you sure?"

Bea nodded, searching his eyes to gauge how much he knew. Derrick coughed and Bea poured him some ice water from the plastic pitcher, then pushed his tray closer.

"Thanks."

"How have you two been?" She rolled her eyes toward the door.

"Getting along pretty well. Awilda's been more agreeable lately. She said you two had a fight?"

Bea thought for a moment. Derrick was one of the good guys and Bea decided in that moment that she would not introduce him to her pain.

"Yeah, you know Wilde. Always doing something."

"She really misses you. You should see how she's been sulking around the house. Whatever it is, you two have been friends for too long not to work it out."

Bea smiled at him. "You get yourself better."

"I'm serious, Bea."

"I know, Derrick, I know." She squeezed his hands. "I better go check on my kids. How long are you supposed to be here?"

"I'm hoping they'll let me go tomorrow. When I get home, I could sure use some of your lasagna and a bowl of your mother's soup."

"Consider it done."

Awilda was standing up when Bea returned to the lobby.

"Derrick is awake."

"Kids, why don't you go down and see Uncle Derrick? He's in room 411." Alana led the way down the hall.

"It's on the left," Bea called. "No running."

The waiting room was traditionally decorated with four brown chairs sitting in a row. Two end tables piled with magazines and a coffee table.

"Sit a minute?" Awilda asked her. Bea moved to the chair.

"I didn't tell Derrick if that's what you want to know."

Awilda breathed a visible sigh of relief. "Thank you."

"I thought you didn't want him anymore."

"I thought that I didn't either."

"I'm getting a divorce from Lonnie. I've started filing the papers, hired a lawyer and everything."

"Bea. Are you sure this is what you want?"

"Most days." Bea couldn't believe how easy it was for her to be honest with Awilda. She wanted to punch her in the face until her eyeballs bled but she also wanted a hug.

"I've started going to yoga. Hot yoga."

"You?"

"My next-door neighbor, Joney, convinced me. It's been helping me a lot actually."

Somehow, without Bea's permission, they slipped back into friendship and they talked about what had been going on in their lives recently. Awilda couldn't believe that Bea had gotten a job.

"And so far away from home? I can't believe you drive all the way down there every day. Would have pegged you for picking something in the suburbs."

"It's actually good to be in the city. The kids are hypochondriacs but they keep me entertained with their stories and I think it offers me balance."

"How's Irma?"

"I told her."

Awilda looked at the ground. "I know, she called me and told me off on my answering machine. Luckily it was my cell so Derrick didn't hear it. She blames me for you throwing Lonnie out of the house and asked me to fix it."

"Fix it how?"

"I don't know. Get you two back together."

"That woman. She just doesn't get it."

"She means well."

Awilda looked Bea in the eyes. "I know now that Lonnie wasn't for me. I think the fantasy of us being together all of these years made me do it. But I'm over it. He's out of my system. I promise you that."

Alana walked back in. "Uncle Derrick wants you, Auntie."

"Guess that's my cue. Wanna do lunch or something?"

Bea shook her head. "Not really."

"Well, when I call, will you at least pick up the telephone?" Awilda walked over and gave Bea a quick kiss on the cheek, then disappeared through the doors.

THIRTY-ONE

Can't Help Who You Love

Bea knew from the beginning of her marriage with Lonnie that she was not marrying her best friend. She was marrying a man who would provide for her, love her to the best of his ability, and who she hoped would be a good father.

But we all need something more, and what Bea needed, Awilda gave. Gave her the extra nourishment. From the moment thirteen-year-old Awilda walked through Bea's front door like she'd been there before, they were destined to make memories. They could lay on her bed for hours doing nothing but listening to music and talking, sharing secrets, and planning their futures, which always had each other in it. Always had them as maid of honor, godmother, and ultimate best friend. Awilda knew everything about Bea, down to her first crush, first kiss, and the boy she lost her virginity to with the time, date, and place stamped in her memory. She knew how devastated Bea was when she lost her father and the hole in her heart from never knowing her sisters. Awilda showed Bea how to kiss and what it would feel like when a boy touched you here or there. Awilda was in the room when Chico was born and the only reason why she missed Alana's birth was because she had been at a doctor's appointment with Derrick, as he was undergoing the test for his MS. Awilda introduced Bea to her first joint and taught her how to talk the latest slang. She was Bea's right to her left.

Bea was a lot of things to Awilda too—the voice of reason, the one who could talk Awilda off the ledge and put her to bed until her sense returned. She kept Awilda and Derrick together and was there when Awilda couldn't go to her own mother. They were two halves of the same whole. They had managed to hold onto a twenty-year relationship with ups and down and spins and turns. Awilda had hurt Bea to her core, but where would her life be if she went on not forgiving her? Joney had once told her that, "Until you forgive, you cannot move forward." And Bea wanted nothing more than to move forward. She had come so far in such a short amount of time, and she knew in order to be who she wanted to be, she had to try.

The phone stood on the wall, the same phone on which she had listened to both good news and bad. Bea put it to her ear and dialed the number she knew by heart.